Beating Heart

Laura Pavlov is the *USA Today* bestselling author of sweet and sexy contemporary romances that will make you both laugh and cry. She is happily married to her college sweetheart, mom to two amazing kids who are now adulting, and dog-whisperer to one temperamental yorkie and one wild bernedoodle. Laura resides in Las Vegas where she is living her own happily ever after.

Also by Laura Pavlov and Published by HQ

The Magnolia Falls Series

Loving Romeo
Wild River
Forbidden King
Beating Heart
Finding Hayes

Beating Heart

LAURA PAVLOV
INTERNATIONAL BESTSELLING AUTHOR

ONE PLACE. MANY STORIES

HQ
An imprint of HarperCollins*Publishers* Ltd
1 London Bridge Street
London SE1 9GF

www.harpercollins.co.uk

HarperCollins*Publishers*
Macken House, 39/40 Mayor Street Upper,
Dublin 1, D01 C9W8, Ireland

This edition 2024

1
First published in Great Britain by
HQ, an imprint of HarperCollins*Publishers* Ltd 2024

Copyright © Laura Pavlov 2024

ISBN: 9780008719630

This book contains FSC™ certified paper and other controlled sources to ensure responsible forest management.

For more information visit: www.harpercollins.co.uk/green

Typeset in Sabon Lt Pro by HarperCollins*Publishers* India

Printed and bound in the UK using 100%
Renewable Electricity at CPI Group (UK) Ltd

To all the women who have had their hearts
broken . . . don't give up.
Sometimes heartache leads to happiness.
Sometimes love shows up when you least expect it.
Sometimes everything you ever wanted is right
there in your grasp.

Xo Laura

'His words were a balm on my tattered heart.'

1

Nash

"I feel fine, Pops. I don't know why we have to go back to see Doc Dolby," Cutler said, as I pulled my truck into the parking space in front of his pediatrician's office.

"It's just a follow-up, buddy. And then I'll drop you at camp. I want to make sure your breathing is back to normal this morning."

My son had been rushed to the hospital after his baseball game this past weekend when he'd had the worst asthma attack he'd had to date. It had scared the shit out of me, and I was trying hard to keep it together so I didn't scare him.

"But I am back to normal. And that was the best game ever, wasn't it?"

I put the truck in park and came around to help him out of his booster seat. "Yeah. You killed it. That was an amazing hit."

"And I still can't believe the Ducks won the championship." I took his hand in mine and led him to the entrance.

I had zero excitement about the Ducks winning the fucking championship because I'd watched my boy struggle for air, unable to speak after the game.

I'd never get that image out of my head.

I hadn't slept much the last two nights because we'd spent the first night in the hospital as a safety precaution. Last night we'd come home, but I'd decided to sleep on the chair in Cutler's bedroom to make sure nothing happened while he slept.

"It was a great game. You should be very proud of yourself. You worked hard this season, and you hit a home run in your final game. That's something special," I said, as I pulled the door open, and we stepped inside.

I'd been coming to Doc Dolby's office since I was a kid, and not much had changed, aside from the few updates his wife, Rose, had made to the front office. There was a fresh coat of paint on the walls, and over the years she'd traded out the toys that were here for patients to play with while they waited.

"Hey there, Cutler. How are you feeling?" Lana asked as she smiled at my son.

"Hi, Miss Lana. I'm feeling all better. I told Pops I don't know why we're bugging Doc Dolby today."

She chuckled and turned to look at me, and she had all the empathy in the world when her gaze met mine. "Hey, Nash."

I nodded as I signed Cutler in on the clipboard. "Morning."

"I'm sure your daddy is just wanting to be safe. You gave us all a big scare this weekend. But I heard you hit a home run," she said, as she handed the file to Petra, the nurse.

"I did. I hit it out of the park." Cutler waved his hands around, proud as hell.

My chest puffed up with pride because my boy was a rock star. But right now, none of that really mattered. We needed to figure out his breathing issues so that it didn't happen again.

Last night, I'd thought about all the scenarios that could have happened while I sat in that chair, dozing in and out of consciousness.

What if I hadn't been there when it happened?

What if he'd been at camp and they hadn't reacted quick enough?

These are the thoughts that haunt me now.

"Come on, Superstar. Let's get you in the back. Dr. Chadwick is almost ready to see you," Petra said, and my shoulders stiffened because I didn't recognize the name she'd used.

"Dr. Chadwick? What are you talking about? We're here for Doc Dolby." My words had a lot more bite than I'd intended.

"Oh. Oh, my. I'm sorry. I thought Doc had already spoken to you because I knew he'd come to see you this weekend. Um, he'll be right in to explain." She fumbled over her words.

My gaze narrowed when I took the seat beside Cutler, and Petra looked away from me.

I scrubbed a hand over my face. I was exhausted and knew I was being a dick. I had a full day of work ahead of me, and acting like an asshole wasn't going to help things.

"Pops, you're being real grumpy today." Cutler raised a brow, and Petra chuckled. I took in my boy, who was wearing a light blue tee that read: *Call the vet because these puppies are sick*. There was a cartoon photo of a muscled little dude flexing his biceps with a smirk on his face.

"Your dad's just worried about you. I get it. Doc Dolby will be in shortly." She clapped me on the shoulder before she stepped out of the room.

"You know I'm not big on surprises," I said to Cutler as I cleared my throat.

"Doc probably has a friend in town he wants us to meet. And I love surprises." He shrugged as he moved to the chair with wheels on the bottom and started sliding in each direction.

The door opened, and in walked Doc Dolby, a man I'd known my entire life. He was more gray now, and I teased him constantly about the fact that he appeared to be getting shorter every time I saw him. There was a woman right on his heels who I'd never seen before. She was probably in her late twenties, around my age. She was much younger than any doctor I'd ever met. All the doctors I knew were old. She was petite and lean, with brown hair pulled into a knot at the nape of her neck. She wore a white lab coat over what looked to be a skirt and blouse, and her gaze focused on my son.

"Nash, Cutler, good to see you both," Doc said as he dropped the file he was carrying onto the counter, and my son rushed to hug him. They'd shared a bond for as long as I could remember. But Cutler had a way of attaching himself to the people in this town. The kid was all heart.

Cutler Heart.

"I feel fine, Doc. I don't know why Pops brought me here. I should be at camp right now. But maybe it's 'cause you've got a new friend you want us to meet."

Doc smiled and then patted the examination bed, motioning for Cutler to jump up and sit. "I asked him to bring you down here. And you're right, I wanted to introduce you both to someone."

"Your friend is real pretty," Cutler said as he waggled his brows, and the woman chuckled but then quickly straightened her features when she looked up to see me watching her.

"Cutler, this is Dr. Chadwick. She's just moved to town and hasn't even settled into her new place yet, but she wanted to get started today and was looking forward to meeting you both."

"Hi, Cutler. I've heard lots about you from Doc Dolby. It's nice to meet you," she said.

"I just gave her a quick breakdown about what happened this past weekend. We haven't had time to catch up yet because we had a sick baby over at the hospital early this morning, so I apologize that I didn't get in here first to speak to you." Doc was looking at me now.

I narrowed my gaze. "I hope the baby's all right."

"Yes. Everything is fine now," he said, crossing his arms over his chest, as if he were preparing for my wrath.

4

"So what is this? You're taking on a partner?"

Dr. Chadwick raised a brow at my question, her plump lips forming a straight line. There was a little spackle of freckles over her nose, and it was the first time my gaze had locked with hers, finding her jade-green eyes watching me now.

"This is a conversation that I'd planned to have privately with you, but with Cutler going to the hospital this weekend, there just hasn't been time to sit down and do that." He cleared his throat. "I'm stepping back from the practice, and Emerson here—er, I'm sorry, Dr. Chadwick is going to be taking over things for me here. Magnolia Falls is really lucky to have her. She's just completed her residency at one of the top children's hospitals in the country."

"Not sure how lucky I feel with you springing this on me when we need to get this sh—stuff figured out with Cutler." I made no attempt to hide my irritation.

My boy could have died.

We didn't have a plan, and now we were changing doctors.

Someone who didn't know him, didn't know us, was going to be deciding what to do moving forward.

"Nash, I'm not abandoning anyone. I'll still be around for Dr. Chadwick to lean on any time she needs me. I hadn't found a match to take over my practice, so I was holding out, which is why I hadn't said anything. And then her application came through, and I jumped on it. She has trained under some of the best doctors in the world during her residency. She's far more equipped and educated on new cutting-edge medications and procedures than I am. This isn't something that you need to be worried about. Cutler will be in great hands, and she knows how important he is to me, so she's agreed to keep me abreast of everything."

"Pops is being a big grumpleton today. Sorry about that," Cutler said, smiling up at Dr. Chadwick before glancing at me with this look that told me to stop being a dick.

The kid was six years old.

He didn't have a fucking clue what was happening.

He saw a pretty lady and wanted to focus on that.

I need a fucking doctor to make sure my boy is okay.

And how good could this woman be when she was just out of residency? Barely old enough to even be here.

"Cutler," I said, my tone even, but I shot him a warning look that let him know it wasn't the time or place to try to be funny.

"How about this," Doc Dolby said. "What if Cutler comes with me, and we go run a few tests down the hall to check his oxygen levels, and I let him pick out a few stickers from the treasure box while you two chat for a bit? Would that be okay?"

"I'll pick out a sticker for my new doctor, too," Cutler said as he hopped off the table.

How was he so cool about this? He'd known Doc his whole life. He didn't know this woman.

I sucked in a long breath, giving Doc a curt nod before he walked out the door with Cutler's hand in his and shut the door behind him.

Dr. Chadwick stood with her ass pressed against the examination table that Cutler had just been sitting on, her feet crossed at the ankles as she stared at me.

"I understand your concern. What happened this weekend must have been terrifying. I'd like to come up with a plan that we can put into action moving forward. But I'd prefer to meet with both you and Cutler's mother so we can all be on the same page. Is your wife available to meet as well, or can we get her on the phone while we chat?"

This was why I didn't like change. I didn't feel like explaining my situation, nor was it anyone's business.

"I raise Cutler on my own," I said, my words coming out harsher than I'd planned once again.

Her cheeks pinked the slightest bit, and she nodded. "Okay, no problem. We can move forward with just the two of us then."

"Obviously. Not sure why we'd invite anyone else to the conversation about my son."

She reached for the folder and read over a few things before looking back up at me.

"Listen, Mr. Heart, I'm not the enemy. I understand that being caught off guard about your doctor leaving is upsetting."

"You aren't from here, so I wouldn't expect you to understand why this is a big deal."

"Well, he's retiring. He's worked far longer than most; you can't be that surprised."

Who the fuck is she to tell me how to feel about it?

"And you know this how? You've been here for all of five minutes."

"I'm just saying, doctors retire all the time. It's part of life. And I am more than qualified to treat your son, so I'm just asking you to hear me out."

"It doesn't seem like I have much of a choice, does it?" I said, knowing I was being a dick but unable to stop myself because I was just not up for much at the moment.

"You always have a choice. If you want to take him somewhere else, and you think someone is better suited than I am, that is your choice."

"Well, we live here, so it's kind of important for Cutler to have a doctor in town. Especially with all that's going on." I leaned forward, resting my elbows on my knees.

"Fine. So we agree on something."

"We agree that I need a doctor and you happen to be one."

"Great. Looks like we're off to a fabulous start," she said, oozing sarcasm as she forced a smile.

This was not the way I saw this morning going.

And I was not happy about it.

2

Emerson

I'd experienced pushback from parents during residency.

Being a woman.

Being young.

If I had a nickel for every time I was asked if I was a *real doctor*, I'd be a very wealthy woman.

But this guy—he was a close-minded prick.

He'd judged me before I even spoke.

I understood being worried about his son, but he didn't need to be an asshole to me. I was here to help.

I'd come here to Magnolia Falls—the last place on the planet I'd expected to be.

But you know what they say . . . when life gives you lemons, pack up your shit and get the hell out of town.

Maybe I'll make that the new saying.

I let out a long breath and stared down at Cutler's file. "I suggest that we start by putting together an asthma action plan. I'm assuming you had one of sorts with Doc Dolby because you knew what to do when Cutler had that asthma attack after his baseball game. But this would be far more specific."

"All right. What would that entail?"

It's progress. At least he isn't growling at me anymore.

"I'd like to get you a peak flow meter, which will let us know how well the lungs are working. This is a handheld device that you can use before you notice symptoms. It's a helpful tool to know when to adjust the treatment, or it can give us a heads-up if a flare-up might be coming."

He nodded. And his lips twitched, which I guessed was the closest I'd get to a smile from this grump of a man. "I can do that. We'd use it daily?"

"Yes. I think it will help with peace of mind, as well, because you'll know how his lungs are doing each day."

He cleared his throat and started to speak but stopped himself.

"What is it?" I pressed.

He shrugged. "I'm fucking nervous that this is going to happen when I'm not there. That it'll happen at summer camp or at school, and the teachers and counselors won't know what to do."

"I get it. You have every reason to feel that way. So, we come up with an asthma action plan, and everyone in Cutler's life will be aware of what that entails. Everyone needs to know what to do if this happens again."

"Okay. I can get on board with that."

It was the first time I'd noticed his steely gray eyes. His chiseled jaw was peppered in day-old scruff, and his dark hair was shorter on the sides and longer on top. The man looked like he'd just stepped off the set of a magazine photo shoot with his effortless good looks and broody demeanor.

I'm sure women drooled over his presence, but lucky for me, men were not on my radar. I'd officially sworn off all men two months ago—and even the hottest man on the planet wouldn't get a reaction from me right now.

"We have a lot of different options for medications. I know you have an inhaler now, but Doc Dolby and I discussed running a few tests and then deciding where to go from there.

There are other meds that we could try, and I'd be happy to go over those with you now."

He let out a long breath and sighed. "All right."

"I want to make sure you know that I will do everything in my power to provide the best care for your son. I may not be from Magnolia Falls, but I promise you, I'm here to help."

At least for the next six months, which is the contract that I've accepted.

I'd needed to get away to somewhere I could think and figure out what I wanted to do with my life moving forward.

After all that had happened, I'd never been more lost.

And somehow, I ended up here.

We spent the next thirty minutes discussing different options such as the inhaled corticosteroids he'd already been using and combination inhalers that would offer two types of medications at the same time, as well as filling him in about biologics, which are shots that target certain parts of the immune system.

He listened, and we agreed the best plan would be to start slowly and change the inhaler Cutler was currently using with a stronger medication before we try a different option. He agreed, and I saw the fear and exhaustion there, and I actually felt bad for the guy.

At least for the moment.

Doc Dolby walked back into the room with Cutler, who happened to be one of the cutest kids I'd ever met.

"How's it going in here?" Doc asked. He was a nice man, and when I'd met him over Zoom after I'd applied for the position, I'd warmed to him immediately.

"I got a breathing treatment, Pops," Cutler said, walking over to stand by his father.

Nash rumpled his hair, and it was endearing.

But most endearing was the way that Nash Heart looked at his son.

You could see the love, the concern, the fierce need to protect his little boy, all in that gray gaze of his.

So, I'd give him a pass for being a bit of a dick to me, because it was coming from a place of concern.

"Great. We're going to try a few new things, too," Nash said.

"I wrote out the prescription for a new inhaler with a stronger medication, and you can pick up the peak flow meter at the pharmacy, as well. So we can start with these right away." I handed him two pieces of paper.

"Well, if you have any problems with the new meds, you're in luck. Dr. Chadwick is renting the house from Winston and Mary Hall right next door to you. She moves in this weekend. They had a holdup with getting the utilities turned on, so she's been stuck at the Magnolia Falls Inn for now," Doc Dolby said.

What are the chances that this guy who already didn't like me was my new neighbor? And why the hell was Doc telling him where I was going to be living? That was none of his business. I'd shared the fiasco about my move with him this morning because I'd had to have the movers hold off on delivering all my furniture while I was holed up at the hotel in town over the weekend. But I certainly didn't need him telling patients about it, even if he'd eventually figure out that I was his new neighbor.

"She's moving next door to us?" The man sounded like he'd just been told a serial killer was moving in next door to him. My new neighbor clearly didn't care for me. "That house has been empty for years, aside from a few summers when the Halls used to come down for the weekend."

"Yeah, I spoke to them when she accepted the position, and they agreed to rent it out to her for the six months that she's staying."

Nash's face hardened. "Six months? Seems tough to provide

11

this phenomenal care you keep promising when you'll just be passing him off to the next person in a few months."

Who the hell does this guy think he is?

I squared my shoulders. "It's a six-month contract. I will provide the best care I can during my time here."

Nash pushed to his feet, surprising me, as he had to be at least six foot two inches with the way he towered over me. "You couldn't find someone more permanent, Doc? I don't like the idea of switching doctors every six months."

Doc clapped him on the shoulder, and it was clear they had a close relationship. "You worry too much, Nash. Plus, I think she's going to fall in love with Magnolia Falls and extend that contract of hers."

Wishful thinking.

This was temporary.

I just needed some time to figure out how to rebound from the dumpster fire that was currently my life.

I cleared my throat and bent down to meet Cutler's gaze. "It was nice to meet you, Cutler. I'd like to have you come back in a few weeks so we can see how the new inhaler is working. Would that be okay?"

"Yes. And now that we're friends, you can call me Beefcake. That's what all my friends call me. And if we're going to be neighbors, we should be friends for sure. You can even be my girl."

I chuckled at the unusual nickname and the fact that a six-year-old appeared to be hitting on me.

Hey, my self-esteem is in the shitter, so I'm not going to look a gift horse in the mouth.

"Cool name, Beefcake. And we can definitely be friends. How about you call me Dr. Emerson instead of Dr. Chadwick? Since we're friends and all." I winked before pushing back up to stand as I turned to his father and raised a brow. "And do you have a nickname that I should be calling you?"

Nash's lips twitched in the corners before his eyes hardened again. "I don't think you're sticking around long enough to be using nicknames, Dr. Chadwick."

He took his son's hand in his and led him out the door as Cutler turned around and waved at me.

The little guy had his dark hair slicked back with a ton of gel, and his cherub cheeks were pink and adorable.

"Well, that went well," I said, not hiding the sarcasm as I reached for the file once they made their way down the hall.

"He's just a protective dad, but he's one of the best men I know. I can promise you that. Nash has never cared for surprises, and I should have spoken to him first. I assumed his friends had filled him in because I'd talked to them at the hospital. But with everything that's been going on with Cutler, I'm guessing it just didn't come up."

"Nothing like being neighbors with a guy who clearly can't stand you," I said, shaking my head as I followed him out of the room.

"He'll be a great neighbor once he gets over the shock of me leaving." He reached for his water bottle and took a sip. "He's a contractor, so that'll come in handy if you have any problems at the house once you move in. And I like the idea of you being next door if Cutler has any issues."

I gaped at him. I certainly wouldn't be going next door to ask the man to change my lightbulbs, and I wouldn't expect him to knock on my door every time his son got the sniffles. He clearly noticed my surprise at the way I'd reacted to what he'd said.

"I thought you told me you grew up in Rosewood River. Aren't you a small-town girl at heart?" he asked me.

I shrugged. "I did, and I am. But I've been living in San Francisco for the last decade while I attended school there and did my residency at UCSF."

"But you know small towns, Emerson. Everyone knows everyone, and we look out for one another."

I didn't want anyone looking out for me. I wanted to be alone. I came here to get away. To start fresh.

"Yeah, but I don't live here, and I'm not from here. I'm very capable of doing my own handiwork around the house." I glanced down at my phone when it vibrated to see a text from my brother.

"I'm not surprised. You mentioned that you have a large family, right?"

"Yep. I've got four brothers, one being my twin, and two cousins who grew up next door to us, also boys. Let's just say that I know my way around a toolbox and a car engine."

"Impressive. Not only a doctor but a woman of all trades, huh?" he asked, as Petra called out to him that he had a phone call. "You can take a break while I take this call."

"You got it." I made my way down to my new office and sat at my desk as I pulled out my phone.

EASTON

What's up, girl? How's the first day as a small-town doctor?

Well, the first kid I saw was adorable, but his father was not pleased to have a newbie on staff. So that was fun. 😵

EASTON

You know how small towns are. They need time to warm up to new people. That's why I told you that you should have just come back home instead of picking some random town to go to.

Oh, sure, I could come home and have everyone in town talking about poor Emerson Chadwick. Being a jilted bride sucks as it is. I certainly don't need everyone gossiping about it. At least no one knows my story here.

EASTON

Need I remind you that we're Chadwicks? We don't give a shit what anyone thinks of us. And if anyone so much as looks at you wrong, you know you've got backup.

I needed to go somewhere new for a while, you know? Take some time to figure out what I want to do with my life. I've been so set on how my whole life would play out for so long, and now it's just—a mess.

EASTON

You've never been a mess, Em. You are rock fucking solid. Always have been. You just picked an asshole of a man who never fucking deserved you. And if that piece of shit shows his face in this town anytime soon, I promise, he won't live to see another day.

That's a bit dramatic.

I chewed on my thumbnail, fighting back the lump in my throat as I thought about all that had happened over the last two months.

EASTON

What Collin fucking did to you requires all the dramatics I can muster. He better stay the fuck away. And we all feel that way, so if he knows what's good for him, he won't show his face for a while.

Gee. I wonder why I wanted to go somewhere new. 🤭

EASTON

Just know we've got your back. Always. And if you change your mind and want to get the hell out of Magnolia Falls, just say the word. We'll get you moved back home in no time.

I signed a six-month contract, so I'm locked in for at least that long.

EASTON

Hey, I know a good lawyer who's great at getting people out of contracts. 😉

I chuckled. My brother was an attorney, and a ruthless one at that. He may have chosen to open his practice in the small town we grew up in, but he was highly sought after and often commuted to the city for trial cases.

Love you, E.

EASTON

Love you, Em. Remember, we can activate these twin powers of ours anytime, so if you need me, I'm there. You know that, right?

Yes. But I'm good. I promise. Get back to world domination and stop worrying.

EASTON

I sighed and tried to push away all the thoughts that were flooding my mind when my phone vibrated again.

UNKNOWN NUMBER

Hey, it's Collin. Please unblock me, Em. It's been so long, and I miss you. I want to explain things.

I blocked this latest phone number, just like I'd done to all the numbers he'd tried to reach me from since our relationship imploded.

There was nothing to explain.

But his arrogant ass thought he could talk his way out of this.

He was definitely giving himself way too much credit.

3

Nash

Why does one think it's okay to move into a home on a Saturday morning when the sun is barely even up yet?

ROMEO

Early bird gets the worm?

KING

Hey, I'm a morning guy. I like to start the day out right. I always like to please my lady before the sun comes up.

HAYES

Are you fucking kidding me right now, you dicksausage? I will beat your ass if you talk about pleasing your lady on this group text.

I barked out a laugh. Kingston was dating and now living with Hayes's sister, Saylor. They had hit some bumps in the road when it initially happened, but everyone was happy about it now. But Kingston loved to push the envelope with his comments, and Hayes wasn't having it.

KING

Relax, you overbearing grump. I made her pancakes in bed. 😵

Well, after I pleased her, of course. 😉

ROMEO

Do you have a death wish, King? 🤭

RIVER

It's the new doctor moving in next door, right? It might be nice having her there if anything comes up.

Yeah. The doctor who is staying for six months and then we'll get another doctor. It's bullshit. I cannot believe Doc is okay with this.

RIVER

Maybe the next one will stay long term. Or who knows, maybe this one will change her mind.

She's a big-city doctor. She probably gets some sort of extra credit for doing some time in a small town. It pisses me off.

KING

I don't think they do extra credit once you're out of school. She's a goddamn doctor. She clearly just wanted to come here for a while.

Why? Who moves for six months?

RIVER

Someone running from the law.

ROMEO

Maybe she murdered someone and needs to lie low for a few months. 🤭

KING

Oh, like secret witness protection type of shit. Or maybe her family is in the mob and she's hiding from them. You know, she woke up with a horse head in the bed and ran to Magnolia Falls.

HAYES

Are you eating more gummies, King? You get crazier every day.

KING

It's called being in love and happy, brother.

Well, this has been zero help. I came on here to bitch, and you all took it to crazy town. So, fuck you very much.

RIVER

Maybe go offer to help her with the move. It might be a good thing to be friendly with the doctor. For Beefcake's sake.

Not looking for new friends. If Cutler has an issue, I can go to Doc Dolby's. Retired or not, he's our doctor.

KING

Very mature.

ROMEO

Demi said the new doctor came into the coffee shop yesterday, and she likes her, so maybe don't be a dick and give her a chance.

That means nothing. Beans likes everyone.

Beans was the nickname that we called Romeo's wife, Demi.

There was a knock on my door, and I startled before setting my phone down and climbing out of bed. It was a miracle that Cutler was still sleeping with the loud moving truck out front, and I was pissed that I wasn't doing the same.

I pulled on a pair of joggers and made my way to the front door, ready to rip someone a new one for knocking on a man's door this early in the morning on a Saturday.

But standing before me was Emerson Chadwick, wearing a pair of jean cut-off shorts and a white tank top. Her long brown waves fell down her back and over her shoulders, and she held her hands up in apology.

"I'm so sorry. I know it's early," she said, as her eyes raked down my bare chest before they snapped back up to meet my gaze. "We have a little situation."

"And that requires you knocking on my door this early in the morning?"

"Ummm, yes. When that someone has their truck parked in the street in front of my house, so the moving truck can't get close enough."

"Fuck," I said under my breath, remembering that I'd left the truck on the street because I was planning to stain the concrete on the driveway today. "I'm guessing that's why the asshole honked his horn a few times. Let me get my keys."

As I turned to move to the kitchen, a giant ball of fur sprinted right past my new neighbor and into my house. It was large, with black, white, and brown fur.

"Oh, my God! No. Winnie, get back here," she whisper-hissed.

"What the fuck is that?"

"That's my dog, Winnie." Emerson was now chasing after the dog, who was currently running down the hallway.

Happy fucking Saturday to me.

My eyes trailed over her perfect ass and long, tan legs as she jogged down my hallway like she owned the place.

"Winiford Chadwick!" Emerson was still whisper-shouting, but Cutler was all laughter now, because apparently, the big horse-dog had gone right to his bedroom and jumped in bed with him.

Only my kid would have no issue with a strange dog jumping into his bed and waking him up.

I stood in the doorway as Emerson frantically tried to pull her beast off his bed, and Cutler was hugging and loving on the large dog.

I crossed my arms over my chest. "Welcome to the neighborhood, Dr. Chadwick."

The dog fought her off as it continued to climb all over my son, who was enjoying every minute, and Emerson covered her face with her hands. "I'm so sorry. I did not want to start off this way. I just needed you to move the truck. I thought I'd secured her in the fenced area on the side of the yard."

"How about this? You stay here for a minute with Cutler and your horse dog, and let me go move my truck."

She nodded. "Yeah. Of course. Thank you. And just so you know, Winnie is hypoallergenic."

I chuckled, because that was the least of my concerns at the moment. "Good to know."

I walked back to the kitchen and grabbed my keys before slipping on my flip-flops and jogging out to my truck. There were two guys with their backs to me, standing there, obviously waiting for me to move out of the way so they could get their truck closer to the house.

"She's hot as hell, man. Did you see those legs and that ass? I'd like to tap that, if you know what I mean," one of the dipshits said.

I'd noticed her legs and her ass, but I wouldn't be standing out here talking about her that way. And it pissed me the hell off at hearing them act like a bunch of assholes.

"Yeah. But she's got an edge. She glared at me when she

23

caught me staring," the other dickhead said. "Like she could read my mind about how badly I'd like to bang her. But I get the vibe she'll cut my balls off if I stare too much more."

Good girl.

She shouldn't take that shit for one second.

They barked out a laugh, and I cleared my throat before they both whipped around and startled when they realized I was standing there.

"Do you think it's appropriate to be sitting out here talking that way about a woman who hired you? I doubt the owner of your company would be okay with that." I crossed my arms over my chest and shot them a warning look.

"And who the fuck are you?" Dipshit number one said.

I moved closer, towering over the little shit. "I'm your worst fucking nightmare. So I'll be watching you closely, and you better keep your eyes and hands to yourself. Do you hear me? And if you speak one more fucking word about her, you're going to find my fist in your throat."

They both straightened, and the other guy held up a hand nervously. "We didn't realize you were with her, dude. No disrespect intended."

This was the kind of shit that pissed me off. "Listen, asshole, she doesn't need to have a boyfriend for you not to stand out here like two fucking horny assholes talking like that. Show some fucking respect. She's glaring at you because she can tell you're looking at her like a bunch of fucking pariahs. But unless you want to eat your teeth for breakfast, you best put your heads down and get the job done without another word."

They nodded. Dipshit number one looked more irritated than remorseful, but the other guy looked mortified by what had happened.

I still didn't trust them, so my Saturday had definitely just gone from bad to worse.

Because there was no way I was letting her go back into that house with these two scumbags.

I jumped into my truck and pulled into my driveway before jogging back into the house. There was laughter coming from down the hall, and I stopped in the laundry room and grabbed a tee and pulled it over my head.

I made my way down to Cutler's room, and my eyes widened at the sight of Emerson Chadwick lying on the floor beside Cutler, while her giant dog climbed all over both of them and licked their faces.

"I love Winnie," Cutler said over a fit of laughter.

I let out a loud breath, and Emerson shot up, sitting forward. "Oh, hey. Okay, let us get out of your hair. I'm really sorry about messing up your morning." She pushed to her feet and snapped her fingers, and her dog shockingly decided to listen this time. "Winnie, let's go."

"Cutler, get dressed. We're going to go fix Dr. Chadwick's fence."

Cutler was on his feet, excited, as he ran to the bathroom to brush his teeth.

"What? No. I don't need you to fix my fence," she said, as she tried to move past me in the doorway and paused when her chest bumped into mine.

I didn't step back. "Listen, I'd like to fix your fence. Consider it my *welcome to the neighborhood* gift."

Her gaze narrowed, and she shook her head in confusion. "You don't need to do that. I can fix it myself."

"You got us out of bed way too early on a Saturday morning, and your horse-dog came storming into my house. I'd like to make sure that doesn't happen again, and maybe I don't trust you to get the job done." I smirked, letting her know I was kind of kidding but wasn't taking no for an answer.

"Fine. Do you think you can move your hulk of a body out of the way so I can get back to my house to let the movers get things unloaded?" The corners of her lips turned up the slightest bit, and I took in that little spackle of freckles over her nose.

I nodded and stepped back. "Hey, Chadwick."

She turned around, Winnie on her heels. "Yeah?"

"Leave the front door and the back door open while they're unloading, all right?"

She stared for a long moment before nodding. "You do realize I came here from a big city, and I'm very capable of taking care of myself?"

"Can you just do this without questioning it?"

"Fine." She huffed. "All the doors will be left open, your majesty."

I laughed as she stormed out of my house.

"Let's go, Cutler!" I yelled down the hallway, and I had to cover my mouth with my hand not to laugh when he came walking out of his bedroom.

He wore a pair of jeans, a white tee, and the brown leather tool belt that I'd gotten him for Christmas strapped around his waist. He had on gold aviators, and his hair was slicked back with enough gel to make the top of his head look like a hard hat.

"I like Dr. Emerson, Pops. And Winnie is real funny."

"Well, they aren't staying long, so don't get too attached. She's just here for a little while." I handed him a banana and a granola bar. "You can eat this while I work."

"I'm going to help you because Dr. Emerson is my girl now."

I chuckled as we stopped at my truck so I could grab my toolbox before walking next door. I pulled out my handsaw and made eye contact with both of the dudes who were coming out of her house and heading back to the moving truck for another load. I used two fingers and pointed them at my eyes and then back at them, all while holding the saw up for them to take notice.

26

I'll be watching, assholes.

As we moved toward the backyard, I looked up to see Emerson Chadwick watching me while she stood on the side of the front porch and rolled her eyes. I'd been in this house dozens of times over the years, helping the Halls fix one thing after another.

"You're a bit of a Neanderthal, huh?" she said, keeping her voice low so only I could hear the comment. Cutler ran out to the yard with her dog.

"I've been called worse."

I moved past her and made my way to the fenced area and set my toolbox down, including the saw that wouldn't be necessary to fix this, but I'd known it would intimidate the dickhead movers. I chuckled as I took in the portion of the fence that Winnie had easily taken apart. None of these yards were fenced because they led down to the lake, and no one wanted to disrupt the view. But a few of the homes had dog runs on their side yards, which the Halls had put in years ago. It just hadn't been kept up.

"Thanks for doing this," she said as she followed behind me.

"It's the neighborly thing to do," I said, as I reached for my hammer.

"Well, thanks, neighbor." She chuckled. "Let me know if you need anything."

"We're fine. Just be sure to keep that door open, all right?"

I heard her grumble something about me being a caveman, before she said something sweet to Cutler as he made his way over to me.

Emerson disappeared into her house, and her wild dog decided to lie down in between me and the fence like the giant pain in the ass she was proving to be.

Cutler dropped to sit down beside her and eat his banana. "I like having someone live next door to us, don't you?"

27

"I prefer the quiet, so I was fine when this house was empty," I said, as I hammered in some support stakes that I had in my toolbox.

"Haters gonna hate," my smartass kid said.

"Who told you that?"

"Uncle King," he said over his laughter.

"Hey, just because I don't like being woken up first thing in the morning and having a dog barrel through our house, does not make me a hater."

"I think you're pretending to like it quiet. I think you like having a new neighbor just like I do, Pops."

I rolled my eyes and kept working.

But he was right. Maybe I liked it a little bit.

4

Emerson

"It's so fun having your pup here," Lana, the office manager, said. I'd liked her the minute I'd met her, but the nurse, Petra, was a different story.

"Yeah? Doc said it was fine to bring her. He thought the kids would love seeing her here. And with the yard out back, it's really nice that she can come to work with me." I rubbed the top of Winnie's head as she sat next to Lana's chair in the front office. Doc Dolby had apparently brought his chocolate lab, Sadie May, with him to work for years until she passed away a few months ago. He said the kids loved to go out back and play with her after their appointments.

"See? Small-town life isn't too bad, am I right? I bet you can't bring this big girl to work in the city."

"You're definitely right about that. She lived in an apartment with me in San Francisco."

"So, no backyard for her? How did you manage that?"

"Mabel, in apartment 3B in my building, was a dog walker, and she took her out a couple times a day for me." I laughed.

"Oh, wow. City life is so different. Do you miss it?" Lana asked. She was a few years older than me, married with a two-year-old little boy from what I'd learned over the last two weeks.

"I hate to break up this riveting conversation, but with Doc not coming in today, I'm going to need Dr. Chadwick to be on her game this morning." Petra crossed her arms over her chest as she scowled at us.

Lana gazed around the waiting area and then raised a brow. "Well, seeing as we have no patients here at the moment, I think she's doing just fine."

The office had been open for all of five minutes, and I'd actually arrived over an hour ago, long before Petra and Lana had gotten here. I was up to date on the charts for the patients I'd be seeing today, and I'd had a phone call with Doc Dolby last night when he'd called to say he wouldn't be coming in this week, and we'd gone over things then.

It was clear that Petra didn't care for me, and I didn't like how uncomfortable she made things every time she entered the room.

"Petra, how about you and I go grab a cup of coffee and chat for a minute," I said, before motioning for Winnie to follow me. "You're going outside for a bit, girl."

Petra sneered as I opened the back door and watched my pup run out and lay under the big tree. She loved it here. Loved being outside instead of being couped up in that apartment all day.

We both stopped in the break room at the end of the hallway. This office had originally been an old house that had been built over a hundred years ago, and it had been restored and made into a very charming pediatric office. The kitchen area had black-and-white-checked flooring and a little vintage refrigerator. The table had six chairs around it, and I waited for her to pour herself a cup of coffee, and then I did the same. We both took a seat at the farmhouse table across from one another.

"I feel like there's some tension between us, and I'd like to resolve it as quickly as possible." I took a sip of my coffee and looked back up at her. "It appears you have a problem with me."

"I don't have a problem with you, per se." She paused, and I waited for it, because there was clearly more coming. "I've just worked for Doc Dolby for a long time. Probably longer than you've been alive."

"So, you have a problem with him retiring?"

"I knew it was coming, but I didn't expect him to hire someone who was so . . ." She pursed her lips and stared at me.

"So . . . what?" I kept my tone even.

"Young. You're practically a child."

I chuckled. She was a woman who continued to work full-time, and she had to be pushing eighty years old, and she was discriminating against me based on my age?

"I'm twenty-nine years old, Petra. I've never asked your age or questioned if you were deserving of your position here. I graduated top of my class from medical school. I just completed a three-year residency program at one of the best children's hospitals in the country. So, this will be the one and only time I will have this conversation with you." I took another sip of my coffee while she gaped at me. Had she thought I'd roll into a ball and agree that I was too young to be a doctor? I'd been through a hell of a lot worse than being judged by a snarky woman, and I'd definitely developed a thicker skin over these last two months. "I am more than qualified for this position. And I'm here, so if my age is a problem for you, then I suggest you consider working somewhere else."

"Well, you're only here for six months," she snipped.

What is everyone's deal in this town with the timeline?

I either stayed forever or I shouldn't be here? It was ridiculous.

"Correct. I signed a six-month contract. So, you should be

31

pleased that I won't be staying long term. Maybe we can just agree to drop the sarcastic comments and show a little respect during the time we'll be working together?"

"Fine. I just thought maybe you'd want to prepare for the patients coming in today." She shrugged.

"That's very thoughtful of you, but I arrived over an hour ago. I've gone over each file already, and I spoke to Doc last night about the kids I'd be seeing today." I raised a brow.

She nodded. "I apologize for questioning you. I guess, well, I don't know, change is hard. I'm not happy that Doc is retiring. Maybe it makes me realize my days are numbered, as well."

"I get that. I just uprooted my entire life and moved here. It's scary. But if it's any consolation, I've noticed the way you are with the kids since I've been here, and I'm impressed. So I don't think your days are numbered just yet." I smiled, and her gaze met mine as I continued. "Charlotte Stratford had been so nervous about getting her shots yesterday, and you handled that so well. Talking her through the process and relaxing her the way you did. It was really sweet."

"Well, you might be the first person to ever call me sweet. My husband would probably argue with that." She chuckled. "But I do have a soft spot for kids."

"It shows. So, how about we do our best to provide great care and go easy on one another, huh?"

She nodded. "I can do that. And Doc thinks we're really lucky to have gotten you, so you can't be all bad."

Was there a compliment in there?

"Well, I hope he's right."

Lana appeared in the doorway and made a face before whispering. "Carrie Peters is here, and she's in a mood."

Petra pushed to her feet and then leaned down close to my ear. "Carrie is a bit of a pill. She pulled my hair a few months back when I tried to take her temperature, and she's also bitten Doc several times. She even broke skin once."

I shook my head in disbelief. "He did give me a heads-up. I'm ready for her."

He'd basically called her an eleven-year-old hellion with a mother who modeled similar behavior and defended her daughter at all times.

Petra left to go get her vitals and take her to room one, while I made my way to my office and gathered my files, leaving my coffee there before heading to meet my new patient.

Petra was coming out of the room as she pulled the door closed and hurried me a few feet away, her face flush. "I think she's probably got strep throat from the looks of it, but she's refusing to get swabbed. She already dug her nails into my arm, so I told her I'd come speak to you and see if there was another option." I glanced down to see the notable claw marks on Petra's wrist.

"She has to let us look at her throat and swab her in order to know if it's strep. Why don't we go in there together, and I'll talk to her and her mother."

"Her mother goes along with whatever she wants," Petra said, as if that made it okay.

"We've got this." I winked and walked back toward room one.

This was not my first rodeo with a difficult patient.

She followed me inside. The rooms were larger than I was used to in the city, and I appreciated it. There was cute wallpaper on the walls, each one a tribute to different animated animals, like a monkey, a pig, and a dog. There were two chairs in each room for the kids and the parents to sit on, and there was an examination table that had colorful paper with stripes and polka dots on it.

"Hey there. I'm Dr. Chadwick. It's nice to meet you both." I smiled, taking in Carrie and her mom. It was obvious Carrie wasn't feeling well, as her cheeks were bright red, and her lips were cracked from being dehydrated. I asked Petra to go grab us a Gatorade from the refrigerator, and she left quickly.

33

"I don't drink Gatorade," Carrie hissed, and I placed her file on the counter before bending down to get eye level with her.

Her mother glared at me. "Yes. It's pure sugar. I can't believe you keep that here."

"I'm certainly not suggesting you drink it daily, but your lips are cracked and you're clearly not feeling well. If you don't get hydrated, you'll end up in the hospital," I said, keeping my tone even and controlled as Petra came back into the room and handed me the blue drink. "So, how about you get a couple of sips in you while we discuss your options?"

Carrie narrowed her gaze, as if she were trying to figure me out, and then she nodded. She unscrewed the cap and tipped her head back, chugging the blue drink, and I pushed back up to standing. "I'd like to have you come sit up on this table so I can examine you."

"Doc usually examines her in this chair. She doesn't want to sit on the table. She's not a child," Mommy Dearest said.

"This is where I examine my patients." I met her mother's stare without wavering.

"Well, she's not getting that ridiculous Q-tip shoved down her throat," her mother grumbled. "She doesn't like it."

"I get that. I don't think anybody really likes it, if I'm being honest." I patted the examination table for Carrie, and she handed her mom the drink and wiped her mouth before standing. She walked over and hopped up to sit on the table.

I'd won a small battle, and I'd take it.

"So do something else," her mother said.

"If there were other options, I'd be happy to offer them. But everyone gets swabbed when we suspect strep throat. And I'm fairly certain not a single person enjoys it." I listened to Carrie's chest and asked her to take a few deep breaths.

"Did we get her temperature?" I asked Petra. I knew she'd had the altercation, but I wasn't certain if she'd gotten her temperature before she'd been assaulted.

"Nope. She refused it and dug her nails into my wrist." Petra glanced over at Carrie's mother before showing Carrie and me her arm that had open nail marks on it.

"So, we've got a few options here, and I'll let you choose." I looked at the young girl sitting in front of me. Her shoulders were tense, and it was clear that she was so used to fighting that most people probably just backed down because it wasn't worth the fight.

I wasn't going to do that.

"Okay," Carrie said, with a little less attitude than she'd had a few minutes ago.

"You came here for help, so I'm assuming you want it." My gaze locked with hers. "I can help you, and I can make you feel better pretty quickly, but you have to do your part."

"I don't like getting my temperature taken or getting that thing rubbed around on the back of my throat."

"Yes, we've established that. But it is what it is, Carrie. I'm not going to allow you to claw me or anyone in this office, nor will there be any biting." I raised a brow, because I wanted her to know that I knew what her normal behaviors were, and I wouldn't tolerate it. "You will not touch anyone in this office that way again, at least not while I'm here."

She startled a bit by my words and licked her lips, giving me the slightest nod.

"This is ridiculous. She's a child. She isn't hurting them," her mother said.

I turned to face her and reached for Petra's wrist. "Your daughter drew blood, and she's old enough to know better. She's not a toddler; she's a pre-teen. This—" I gave her one last look at Petra's arm before dropping it, "—is unacceptable."

"And what is it you're going to do to help her, now that you've established everything that my daughter won't be doing?" Carrie's mother glared at me.

I turned back around and faced Carrie. "I'd like to help

you. Getting your temperature taken is not painful. There's no reason to fight that." I motioned for Petra to hand me the thermometer, which I held up before quickly checking her for a fever. It took a few seconds as I grazed it along her forehead, and it was done.

"One hundred and two point seven is a fairly high fever. You must be feeling pretty terrible. So how about we make a deal?"

"What kind of deal?" Carrie asked.

"Well, I've got a whole bunch of brothers back home who happen to be grown men now, but they're all big babies when they're sick. So, we have this deal when it comes to swabbing their throats," I said with a chuckle.

"What is it?" she asked, not hiding her curiosity.

"I have them open their mouth, and I count to ten, and then I swab it as fast as I can. They always close their eyes, and they pretend that they are somewhere else. Like the beach or riding horses or whatever it is that they enjoy."

"Why do you count to ten?"

"Because you're tough, right? Anyone can do something that they don't like for ten seconds. And it works every time. So what do you say?"

"Are you giving her a choice?" her mother said from behind me.

"Of course, I am. She can say no, but untreated strep is no fun. Strep is a bacterial infection, and it needs to be treated. It can move to different parts of your body and make you even more uncomfortable."

"Why can't you just give her the medication and assume she has it?" her mom pressed.

I turned around to look at her. "Because I'm a doctor, and I wouldn't be a very good one if I didn't test her and just guessed what she had. If she doesn't have strep throat, she shouldn't be taking medication for it. So, no, I will not just assume anything. Your daughter's health is my priority."

"And you'll count to ten?" Carrie asked.

"I will. And I promise you I'll go as quickly as I can."

She nodded. "Okay. I'll do it."

Tears pricked her eyes, and I squeezed her hand as Petra moved to get the tray with the swabs for me, and she set them beside Carrie on the exam table.

"Hey, you've got this. I promise. Tell me where you're going to imagine yourself."

"Um . . . I love to go to the lake on the weekends. So I'm going to imagine myself in the water with my friends."

I pulled the long stick out of the protected seal and took her hand again in my free hand. Petra hovered beside us. "I think that's a great place to go. Open wide, and I'm going to count."

"Oh, my gosh, I can't believe you're making her do this," her mother grumped from behind me, but I ignored her.

"One, two, three . . ." I said calmly as I swabbed her throat as thoroughly and quickly as I could. "Four, five, six, seven . . ."

She gagged as I counted out the last three seconds, and I pulled it out of her mouth.

"You did it," I said. "How about we take a few sips of Gatorade, and you lie down here for a few minutes while we check this for you?"

She nodded, and her mother handed her the drink as I stepped out of the room.

Her results were instant, and she definitely had strep throat, so I was able to get her started right away on meds that would help her feel better quickly.

I was surprised when she hugged me goodbye, and her mother thanked me as well.

But we were slammed afterwards, and the day had gotten away from me. Lana stopped by my office and said goodbye as she was heading home, and Petra was standing in my doorway shortly after.

"Dr. Chadwick," Petra said, and Winnie lifted her head to look at her from where she lay beside my desk.

"Petra, you really don't need to call me that. You can call me Emerson." I stopped writing my notes and looked up at her.

"Okay. Well, Emerson," she said, her lips turning up in the corners just the slightest bit. "You were pretty amazing today. You have a gift for calming small humans. Especially the really challenging ones."

"Thank you. Like I said, I have a big family. I'm well trained with the challenging ones." I chuckled.

"I think Doc is right after all. We are lucky to have you." She gave me a quick nod before turning to leave. "Don't stay too late."

"Thank you. And don't worry, I'm heading out soon." I was happy that Petra and I were finding our way.

It had been a long day, and I was looking forward to a large glass of wine on my back porch as I watched the sun go down over the lake.

It had become my new favorite way to end the day.

5

Nash

Cutler and his best friend, J.T., were climbing on the jungle gym in our backyard while I flipped burgers and hot dogs on the grill. They'd been at summer camp all day, and I was hoping they'd be worn out because I sure as hell was. It had been a full day doing the build-out on a new restaurant downtown. Kingston and I were both working this job, since it was a large one. Installing a commercial kitchen was no joke, and we had our work cut out for us. We were adding on a large addition and dining area, along with renovating every square inch of the place.

"Almost time to eat, Pops? We're hungry!" Cutler shouted from where he sat on the swings.

"Yep. Go wash your hands. Let's go." I piled the food on a plate and set it on the outdoor table. I'd already poured the baked beans into a bowl and placed those beside the condiments.

They both sprinted past me and ran into the house. They clearly weren't tired just yet, so it was going to be a long night. J.T. was spending the night, as his parents had an event to go to, and I was always happy to have him here. Cutler was an only child, and he spent a lot of time with my friends, so anytime he wanted his buddy to stay over, I was good with that.

They took their seats beside one another, across from me.

"Pops," Cutler groaned. "Why do I have to have veggies every night?"

I'd put some carrots and cherry tomatoes on their plates. My boy wasn't a fan of salad, but he'd eat the veggies this way, so I always had them clean and ready for him.

"They're *vegetables*," I said, making sure to pronounce the word vegetables slowly. "And you want to grow big and strong, right?" I asked.

"But Uncle Ro says I am big and strong already," Cutler said.

"I don't know if I'm going to get big because I don't like carrots. But I do like this hot dog," J.T. said over a mouthful of food, and I laughed.

Out of my peripheral vision, there was movement, and I turned just as the horse-sized dog from next door came sprinting toward us.

"Winnie!" Cutler shouted, and the crazy-ass dog jumped right onto the wooden bench next to him and licked his face. Her paws were giant, and she rested one on his shoulder as he giggled.

"That's a big dog," J.T. said. "Where'd it come from?"

"Oh, no! I'm so sorry." Emerson came running toward us. I hadn't seen her since the day she'd moved in, and I'd fixed her fence. I'd left shortly after the movers had finished unloading her stuff. She'd left a plate of cookies on our front porch with a thank-you note the following day, and that was that. I'd seen her out on her porch a few times, but we hadn't done more than share a quick wave, and she'd always hurry inside like she didn't want to do more than that.

She approached our picnic table with her hands on her hips

as she glared at her dog. "What is going on with you, Winnie? This is so unlike her."

"What? Greeting people?" I teased. "She's not bothering anyone. She's just saying hello."

Unlike her owner, who appears to keep to herself.

She sighed. "I guess after living in an apartment in the city, she's enjoying this big open space."

"Yeah, it's tough for a dog to be confined all day. Let her run around and have some fun."

"Can she have a bite of my hot dog?" Cutler asked.

"Oh, that's okay, sweetie. That's for you. She just had dinner." Emerson snapped her fingers, and Winnie jumped down off the bench to sit on the ground.

"Can Dr. Emerson have dinner with us, Pops?"

This fucking kid.

He was always pushing, especially if a pretty lady was involved. That tinge of guilt, knowing Cutler didn't have a traditional upbringing, was always there. He didn't have two parents that were in his life. He had one dad who didn't know what he was doing most of the time. I prayed like hell that I wasn't messing this kid up.

"Sure. There are a few hot dogs and burgers left over if you're hungry." I reached for my beer.

"No, I'm fine. Thank you, though. We'll get out of your hair."

Cutler finished eating, and he and J.T. jumped up and started running around with Winnie, who sprang to life and started chasing them.

Emerson slapped her forehead in frustration and started calling out to her dog.

"Hey, how about you just relax for a minute, huh?" I asked, wiping my hands off with my napkin. "Chill out. Look at the water. The sun's going down."

She gaped at me. "Really? I'm quite aware of the gigantic

lake sitting in front of me. I swim in it every morning before I go to work. And I watch the sun go down every night from my back porch. I'm not oblivious." She huffed.

Thoughts of her wearing nothing but a swimsuit flooded my mind.

Pull your head out of your ass, dickhead.

She's Cutler's doctor, and she's only here for a few months.

"Are you always this uptight? Is it a big-city thing?" I asked, taking another pull from my beer.

"What? No. I'm not uptight. You're the one who had an attitude with me the first time we met. I just don't want to take advantage of living next door and letting my dog run in your yard. That's not a big-city thing; it's a considerate-human thing."

"I did not have an attitude the first time we met," I said, pushing to my feet and walking to the cooler to grab another beer. We were home for the night. I'd get the boys showered after they played for a while, and we'd call it a day. I held up a beer and shook it in invitation. "You want one? I mean, even considerate humans can have a beer with their neighbor."

"Fine. One beer. Winnie does seem to be having a lot of fun with the boys."

I popped the top off of each one and handed her the bottle, motioning for her to sit because having her stand there, all stiff and awkward, was making me uncomfortable. She sat down across from me, and my dick sprang to life when her lips wrapped around the bottle, and she tipped her head back. Damn. I'd never seen a woman drinking a beer look this sexy, but this woman oozed it in spades right now.

It had been a while since I'd been with a woman, as raising my son on my own and running a company with Kingston took most of my time. So reacting to a beautiful woman was perfectly normal, even if we seemed annoyed every time we saw one another.

"Wouldn't have taken you for a beer drinker," I said, chuckling when Cutler and J.T. helped Winnie climb the steps up to the slide and pushed her through. She ran around to do it again, so apparently, she liked it.

"You sure seem to have a lot of preconceived notions about me." She shrugged as she shook her head and smiled while she watched Cutler lead Winnie back down the slide.

"You don't seem all that hard to read."

She glanced back at me. "Really? That's quite the confident statement, ole wise one. So, tell me, then—since you think you can read me so easily—what do you see when you look at me?"

A hot-as-fuck woman. But I'd keep that to myself.

"All right." I set my bottle down as my gaze locked with hers. "You came from a big city. You probably went to some fancy Ivy League college and graduated top of your class. You're a rule follower. You've probably never broken a rule in your life."

"Wow. You make me sound so fun." She rolled her eyes and took another pull from her beer. "For the record, I did my residency in San Francisco because it has a fantastic children's hospital. But I actually grew up in a small town not too far from here called Rosewood River. So, you have me pegged as a city girl, but I'm actually a small-town girl at heart."

That surprised me. "Ahhhh . . . I wouldn't have guessed that."

"I guess I'm not as easy to read as you think I am."

"Okay. So, did you go to an Ivy League college? And are you going to claim you aren't a rule follower?" I smirked.

"I went to Stanford for undergrad, so that's not technically an Ivy League school."

"You went to fucking Stanford." I barked out a laugh. "Close enough. Let's give me that one, huh?"

"Fine. But you should know that I actually went there on

43

an athletic scholarship, not an academic scholarship, so I'm guessing you wouldn't have thought that," she said, and when she smiled at me, my fucking chest squeezed. The sun was setting behind her in the distance; the pink and orange sky looked more like a painted backdrop.

"What sport?"

"Volleyball. I played all four years." She shrugged.

"And where did rule breaking fall on your list of being a Division 1 athlete and going to medical school?"

Her lips turned up in the corners again, and she took another pull from her beer. "I think you'd be surprised. I have four brothers, but it was more like six brothers because two of my cousins lived in the same cul-de-sac as we did, so the seven of us were basically raised together. I can assure you that there were plenty of rules broken in my early days."

I chuckled. That was unexpected. She was a small-town girl with a slew of brothers and clearly a whole lot of secrets.

"You're full of surprises, Chadwick."

"So I'm not as easy to read as you originally suspected?" she laughed.

"I'll admit it. You're much cooler than I first thought." I glanced over at the boys, who were now trying to get the giant dog to sit on a swing, and I'd be dammed if she wasn't going right along with it.

"Well, you did fix my fence for me, so maybe you're not all bad either, even if you were a total jerk the first time we met, *Heart*."

I turned to look at her, my gaze holding hers for a few seconds before I spoke. "I was surprised Doc hadn't told me that he was leaving. I was caught off guard that day."

"I get why you're attached to him. I haven't known him all that long, but he seems like a really good man."

"He's the best. But I shouldn't have been a dick to you. It had been a stressful weekend after seeing Cutler struggle to breathe after his game. I hadn't slept much leading up to that day we met." I held up my beer before tipping my head back again. "Not an excuse, just the situation you walked into."

"How's that peak flow meter going?" she asked, her eyes filled with empathy.

This woman really was full of surprises.

"Nah. We're not doing the doctor thing right now. It's going well, and you aren't on the clock. We'll see you in your office this week. Right now, we're just two neighbors sharing a beer."

"While your son pushes my oversized Bernedoodle on a swing." She raised a brow and laughed.

"Something like that."

"And you raise Cutler all on your own?" she asked, catching me by surprise with the question.

"Oh, you're taking it there, huh? We're doing the neighbor thing now?"

"You don't have to answer. I just wondered if you had help."

"All right. You get one, then I get one."

"One what?" she asked.

"One personal question." I raised a brow. "Personal questions aren't my thing, but if there's a trade involved, I can tolerate it."

"Fine. I guess the rule-breaking childhood wasn't enough for you?"

I smirked before glancing out at the water. "I raise Cutler on my own. His mom and I weren't planning for a child. She wasn't from Magnolia Falls, and we spent a summer together, inseparable for those few months. But then she left to go back to her real life, before returning nine months later to let me know she was pregnant."

"Wow. That had to be a big surprise. Had you kept in touch before she returned to tell you she was pregnant?"

"We'd texted a few times. She'd never said a word before she showed up on my doorstep. So, I moved her into my place, and we gave it a shot. We quickly learned that we didn't have much in common when it came to the real world. Summer flings are fueled by booze and time on the lake, and the real world isn't quite as fun when you're paying a mortgage and preparing for a baby."

"Yeah, that's a lot all at once. So what happened?"

I studied her for a long moment, unsure why I was sharing so much with her. "She wasn't ready to be a mother. She stuck around for a few months, but she was miserable. We came to an understanding. We wanted different things. She shows up here maybe once or twice a year to see Cutler, sometimes less than that." I turned back to face her, surprised to see how intently she was listening. "It's all good. I got the best kid on the planet out of the deal."

"Wow. And you were just ready for fatherhood?"

I ran a hand over the back of my neck. "I wouldn't say that. I freaked out when she first told me. Suddenly I had a woman I didn't know all that well living with me, and a newborn on the way. But from the second that little boy entered the world, I knew that he was my purpose. I knew I was meant to be his father. Tara didn't have those feelings. It's better that she left."

Her gaze narrowed. "Not many men would be willing to step up like you did."

"I don't know about that. I've got four best friends who are godfathers to my boy, and every single one of them has stepped up for Cutler. Maybe you're just hanging out with the wrong men."

"You have no idea," she said, shaking her head and staring out at the water.

"Let me guess . . . you're dating a Stanford grad who also claims to be a rule breaker?" I asked, my voice all tease, but I was suddenly dying to know her story.

"My ex did graduate from Stanford, and he's definitely a rule breaker. But not the kind of rule breaker that's charming or fun. More like the devil pretending to be someone he's not and hiding behind a business suit." She pushed to her feet as if she were done with the conversation.

"Sounds like a real asshole. What did he do?" I asked, my hands fisting beneath the table at the thought of someone mistreating her.

Why did I care? We barely knew one another.

"That's a story for a different day, neighbor." Her smile was forced, and she held up her bottle. "Thanks for the beer. Have a good night."

"Yeah. You, too."

She yelled out for Winnie, and I called the boys over because it was getting dark.

"Can Winnie have a sleepover sometime?" Cutler asked her as he bent down and hugged her pup goodbye.

"Well, then I'd be all alone," she said, as she ruffled the top of his hair.

"Maybe you could sleep over sometime, too," Cutler said, and I barked out a laugh. "Right, Pops? Cause we're neighbors."

Emerson's gaze found mine.

"Sure. Our door is always open." I winked, and she shook her head with disbelief before walking briskly back to her house with her dog beside her.

"Thank you. Good night!" she shouted, and I was still laughing.

I enjoyed getting under her skin.

I enjoyed it a lot.

6

Emerson

"Hi, sweetheart. Did you kayak this morning?" my mother asked as Winnie and I walked to town.

"Yep. It's such a great way to start my day. I'm so happy I was able to find a house on the water. There aren't a lot of boats in there, especially in the morning."

"Did Winnie get in with you this time?"

"Nope. She dipped her big ole paws in and then ran and waited for me under the tree nearby." I chuckled.

"This is good for you, baby girl. You needed to get away from everything and everyone. Fresh start, right?"

"Yep. It's been very peaceful. I've been baking every night after work, swimming in the lake, watching the sun go down before bed. It's been just what I needed."

"I'm so glad. Everything works out for a reason," she said.

I hated that saying. Because I wouldn't necessarily say everything worked out, nor that there was a reason for the shit that happened most of the time. I'd lost two of the most important people in my life. And for what reason, exactly?

"Or sometimes, people are just assholes," I said, and she laughed.

My mom and I were very close, and I'd always been able to talk to her about anything.

"That's very true." She paused. "How's the job search going?"

"I started sending out my résumé to a few hospitals on the East Coast. Maybe I can get into a good program somewhere fresh. That's the goal." There hadn't been time when my life blew up with no notice a few months ago. I'd scrambled, because I'd needed to get out of the city, and I'd found an opening here in Magnolia Falls. I knew that it would buy me some time to figure out my new plan.

"Oh, I just hate the idea of you being that far away from me."

"I know, but I don't want to go back to a place where everyone knows my story, you know?"

"I get it. But let's just give it some time. Don't commit to anything yet. Is Collin still using other phone numbers to reach out to you?" Her tone turned serious. She knew I didn't want to talk about him.

"He is. But I just block him every time."

"He's got some nerve. I ran into Sylvie at the grocery store." Collin's mom, Sylvie Waterstone, was one of my favorite people, so it sucked that now we wouldn't be able to have a relationship. But when you give birth to the devil's spawn, you have to know it might bite you in the ass, right?

"How'd that go?" I asked, as I walked toward Magnolia Beans to get my daily boost of caffeine.

"She cried. I cried. You know, it's never going to be the same. She wants to reach out to you."

"Please tell her I'll reach out after some more time passes. I can't talk to her right now, Mom."

"I know, sweetheart. I just love you so much. Easton said he's going to come see you soon, and I tried to invite myself along with him, but he played the twin card. Said he needed some alone time with you."

LAURA PAVLOV

I chuckled. My brother knew me well. He knew I wanted to be alone. They all knew it, so they called and texted daily to check in, and we kept it casual. I didn't want to talk about it. I didn't want it to be the topic of conversation anymore. My mother had taken it as hard as I had, if not harder.

"Yeah, and I'll come home soon, I promise. I just need some time to settle into my routine here, okay?" I pulled the door open to Magnolia Beans, the cutest coffee shop in town, and stepped inside.

"You got it, sweetheart. And I can sneak away and come there any time you want."

"You'd love it here. It's so charming. I'll call you later. Love you." She said the same back, and I ended the call.

"There's my Winnie girl," Demi said as she came around the corner and bent down to greet my dog before hugging me.

I'd been shocked when she'd said I could bring her into the coffee shop the last time I'd been here, and I'd tied her leash to the pole out front. So now, this was our routine on my way to work.

It was slower here, more peaceful than anything I'd experienced in a long time.

Turns out, it was exactly what I'd needed.

Maybe my mom was right about things happening for a reason. Magnolia Falls was the first thing that actually made me think that staying might be right.

"Are you having the usual today?"

"Yes, please." I reached into my purse and pulled out the little bag with the cookies I'd baked last night. "I made you my latest. Shortbread with raspberry jam."

"Ahhhh . . . I swear, I'm going to have to come over so you can teach me some of these recipes," Demi said, as she started making my iced mocha latte, before wrapping up a blueberry muffin and handing it to me. We both shared an appreciation for tasty pastries. Baking had always been my outlet. Before

50

I'd gone to college, I'd been torn between pursuing a career in medicine or owning a bakery. My brothers used to find it hilarious that I was so conflicted between two very different careers. But in the end, I realized that medicine was my passion, and baking was my happy place.

"These should be illegal; they're so good," I said.

"I heard that, and I'm hoping that means you brought me a treat, too," Peyton said as she came hurrying out from the kitchen. "Am I getting praise for my blueberry muffins?"

I chuckled, and Demi gaped at her. "*Your* blueberry muffins?"

"What? I helped make those."

"You pulled them out of the oven," Demi said over her laughter.

"Hey, they would have burned if I hadn't been there, and then you'd be eating a burnt muffin, right?" Peyton smiled at me as I handed her the little white bag with a few shortbread cookies inside.

"Well, it's absolute perfection." I broke off another piece of the muffin and popped it into my mouth. They were both gushing about my cookies after they took the first bite and groaned, and we all laughed at how invested we were in our baked goods.

"And this is for Winnie," Demi said, coming around the counter. She'd had my dog try some pup treats this week, as she thought Winnie would be a perfect guinea pig.

"You won't get any argument there. This girl loves a treat." I watched as she gently took it from Demi and devoured it as we all laughed.

Demi made her way around the counter to wash her hands before turning around and handing me my iced coffee. "So, you're seeing Cutler today, right?"

I chuckled. I knew from what she'd shared that they were all really close, but they definitely seemed to be very involved

51

in Cutler's life. I was happy for him. He was a sweet kid, and I was thrilled to see how much love surrounded him.

"Yes. It's just a follow-up to see how the new inhaler is working and how he's feeling. He told you he was coming to see me?"

"Yes. We ride together on Saturdays. He loves it."

"Ride?"

"Oh, horses," she said with a laugh.

"My girl is a horse girl through and through. She's got a barn full of them." Peyton shrugged.

"I have two horses, not a barn full." Demi chuckled, and it was easy to see how close these two were. "How about you? Do you ride?"

I sighed. It had been a while since I'd been on a horse. "Yes. I grew up riding. We have a ranch back in Rosewood River, and I used to ride all the time when I was younger."

"You have to come ride with us next weekend. I've even got this one riding now," she said, flicking her thumb at Peyton.

"Yes. But that's only because I have major FOMO."

"FOMO?" I asked, my gaze moving between them.

"Fear of missing out," they said at the exact same time over a fit of laughter.

"Yes. I hate to miss a good time, and Demi, Ruby, and Saylor ride with Cutler on the weekends, so I had no choice but to join in. Demi's parents and grandparents have a bunch of horses, so there's plenty for everyone."

"That sounds like a lot of fun." I took a sip of my coffee.

"So, you'll ride with us next weekend?" Demi placed her hands together like she was praying, and I chuckled. I was only going to be here for a short time, and making friends was not the plan, but it was almost impossible not to be drawn to these two.

"Sure. It's been a while. But I'll give it a try."

"You'll have to come to Whiskey Falls with us, too," Peyton

said as she clapped her hands together. "We're going on Friday night. Come meet us for some beers and country music night."

I hadn't been out in so long. I wasn't sure I was up for that much socializing.

"I'm working late on Friday, so I'm not sure I'll be up for it. But I'll keep it in mind." I held up my coffee. "I need to get to work. I'll see you both tomorrow."

They both shouted their goodbyes, and I heard Peyton saying something about getting my phone number and Demi telling her to back off and stop being pushy.

I sucked in a long breath once Winnie and I were outside, and I made my way to work.

"You look nice today, not that you don't every day, but I don't know . . . something's a little different today," Lana said as she waggled her brows.

"What?" I said, looking down at my dark, dressy jeans and blouse, which weren't that out of the ordinary for me. I usually shifted between dresses and pants and skirts, but it didn't really matter once the lab coat was on. "I look the same as I always do."

"Nope. Your cheeks are kind of flushed, and your hair looks a little bouncier." She eyed my shoes. "Those have those red soles, don't they? You brought out the fancy shoes!"

I was laughing hard. "I just thought they'd be fun with this outfit."

So maybe I took a little more time getting ready today, knowing I'd be seeing Nash. Not for any particular reason. He was just a good-looking man, and I didn't mind the way his eyes raked over me that night I'd had a beer with him. So yeah, a girl needs a boost every now and then, and he had a way of making me feel . . . boosted.

When he wasn't growling or annoyed with me, that is.

"Your first patient is Cutler 'Beefcake' Heart. You know all the single women in town are obsessed with his father," Lana said, stretching out the Beefcake part and handing me Cutler's file. The kid was definitely going to be a heartbreaker when he grew up. He had all the women under his spell already.

"Really? Is he *that* good-looking? I hadn't noticed." I smirked, and her head fell back in laughter.

"Sure, you didn't. You haven't told me, even though I've tried like hell to pry it out of you . . . do you have a special someone back home?"

I shook my head. "Nope. I'm single. And the only relationship I want at the moment is one with myself."

She raised a brow. "Ohhhh . . . do tell. Those are words of a woman scorned."

"Nothing to tell. Just dated the wrong guy and am happy to be single and on my own right now."

"I get it. Before I met Carver, I dated this absolute jerk. I don't know what I was thinking back then. But once I kicked his ass to the curb, I met my sweet husband. It can happen when you aren't even looking for it."

"Well, then, it would have to bite me in the ass because not only am I not looking, I'm making a conscious effort to stay the hell away from all men for a while."

"I guess he really did a number on you." Her gaze softened, and all the humor was gone. I hated that. When I showed how hurt I was. It made me feel weak. I was already dealing with being blindsided, but I sure as hell was not weak.

My head was held high. My heart was still beating. And I'd proven I could survive just about anything.

"Well, I would say he surprised me with who he was. But I would be lying if I didn't admit that being on my own has been really nice, and I feel like I can breathe for the first time in a long time. So maybe I was settling all along, you know?"

"I get that."

"All right, I need to go reply to a few emails and get my

doctor coat on." I chuckled and knocked on the counter twice. "Let me know when they get here."

I called for Winnie to follow me as I opened the back door, and she ran out to the yard, dropping down to lie beneath her favorite tree.

I spent the next thirty minutes responding to emails and reading about some new asthma treatments that were working well for kids. I jotted down some notes just as Petra knocked on the door to let me know that Cutler and Nash were in room one.

"Nash said Cutler has been coughing a bit this morning, and he was glad they had an appointment already scheduled today so that you could listen to his chest."

I nodded. I was happy he hadn't thrown a fit that Doc wasn't here. He was here for a follow-up, and I was glad he wasn't fighting me about doing it. Doc wanted to retire, and he'd earned it. But he felt guilty completely walking away, so he was doing this the only way he felt comfortable, and he still popped in twice a week.

"Okay, I'll head in there now. Thank you, Petra."

"Don't tell anyone, but Cutler's my favorite. I think he's everyone's favorite. And for good reason." She winked and handed me his file, and I walked down to room one.

"Hey there," I said when I stepped into the room and closed the door behind me.

"Dr. Emerson! We just stopped by to see my girl Demi, and she told me you're going to ride horses with us on Saturday."

I chuckled. Clearly, there were no secrets in this town. I patted the examination table for him to hop up where I could take a look. "Yes. I said I'd give it a try. It's been a while."

Nash was standing against the wall, and he moved beside me. The smell of pine and mint filled the air around us, and I was making every effort not to be distracted by him.

I hate men. Well, at least the ones I'm not directly related to. *I have no interest in men romantically. Single men are the enemy.*

There. The world was better now.

Cutler coughed, and I could feel the large man beside me stiffen. I turned to look at him. "Seasonal allergies can cause someone to cough. All coughs are not bad."

He raised a brow, clearly surprised that I was picking up on his nervous energy, and he gave me the slightest nod.

"Pops worries a lot since what happened at my baseball game, so I try not to cough around him now."

"What?" Nash said, sounding completely offended. "You better not be holding in a cough on my account."

I tried to hide my smile and shook my head at him. "What if you take a seat over there so I can listen to Cutler's chest without you hovering?"

"Hovering? What is this? Two against one?" Nash said with a laugh, his tone lighter now. He appeared more relaxed as he stepped back and leaned against the wall a few feet away. "I'll move over here, but I'm not sitting."

"Spoken like a very mature person." I smirked before looking back at Cutler, who was laughing hysterically now.

"Sorry, Pops."

"He's fine," I said, and heard him bark out a laugh from behind me. "I need to listen to your chest, so no more laughing for a minute, okay?"

"Okay." Cutler straightened, and damn if this kid didn't melt my heart. His hair was gelled straight back, and he wore a white tee and a pair of basketball shorts. His gold aviators were in his hand, and it looked like he was heading to a meeting with the head of the mob from the neck up, and from the neck down, he looked like a six-year-old kid going to camp.

I put the stethoscope on his chest, and the room was silent now. "Take a deep breath in for me."

He did as I asked, and his chest was clear. I listened several more times and moved behind him and did the same, listening as he breathed, completely aware that his father was watching us intently.

"He's all clear. There's no wheeze or congestion in there. I'm guessing he has seasonal allergies that can often cause a little cough." I had him lie back so I could check his stomach, and everything looked good.

We spent the next few minutes with them telling me all about the peak flow meter and how it's part of their morning routine now, and adapting to the new medication had been a smooth transition.

"All of my uncles have done the meter thing with me. I taught them how to use it," Cutler said proudly.

"How many uncles do you have?" I asked as I looked at his vitals in his file that Petra had taken.

"I have four uncles. Uncle River, Uncle Ro, Uncle King, and Uncle Hayes."

"Wow. That's a lot of uncles." I set the file down.

"I don't have any brothers or sisters, so my uncles are my family. And now I've got my girls, Demi and Ruby and Saylor and Peyton. And now you're my girl, too." Cutler shrugged, and I glanced over to see the way Nash was smiling at his son before Cutler asked me a question. "Do you have any brothers and sisters, Dr. Emerson?"

"Ohhhh," I groaned dramatically, which made Nash laugh. "So many."

"What are their names?" Cutler asked. He was so curious in the way he listened intently to everything people said around him.

"Well, I have a twin brother named Easton. And then I've got Rafe and Clark and Bridger." I shook my head and laughed. "And my two cousins are more like brothers to me because they lived in the house next door when we were growing up. Their names are Axel and Archer."

"Wow. That's a lot of brothers. You're the only girl?"

"Yep. I'm the only girl in the family." I shrugged.

"Oh, man. Do you have a best friend, Dr. Emerson?"

My heart sank at his words.

I thought I did.

But I just stared blankly, as if I couldn't answer the question. Because the truth was too painful to say aloud.

7

Nash

There was clearly something about the question that had Emerson going completely silent. Even her skin had paled. Maybe she'd lost her best friend in an accident.

Cutler wasn't always the best at reading these things, and I didn't want him to push because she looked . . . wounded.

"Hey, as long as we have you here, can you check my heart? I told Cutler it only beats when he's in the room," I said, keeping my tone light as I attempted to change the subject.

"Pops always says his heart only started beating when I came into the world. My uncles say it's true, too. Can you check his heart and make sure it's working?"

She seemed to be pulled back into reality, and she chuckled. "Really? His heart doesn't beat when you're not around?"

"That's what he says. Tell me if it's beating right now." He jumped down from the table and walked over to where I was standing on the opposite wall. "Check him, Dr. Emerson."

She closed the small distance between us and stopped just in front of me. "I only listen to kids' hearts, so I'm not used to patients that are this big."

That had Cutler laughing harder. "That's why I eat my

veggies, so I can be big like my pops and my uncles. Can you hear his heart?"

She put the stethoscope to my chest and placed the two earpieces in her ears and listened intently before turning her attention to my son beside me. "What do you know? He's got a beating heart. It must be because you're in the room."

"Pops! What's going to happen when I'm not around?"

"I guess I'll have to keep you around, buddy," I said, and my eyes locked with her pretty jade gaze.

Something Cutler had said earlier had thrown her off-kilter, and she was trying hard not to show it.

"I think as long as your daddy knows you're happy and healthy, his heart will keep beating," she said.

"Can I listen to Pops's heart?"

"Sure." She motioned for me to sit in the chair, and she put the earpiece in Cutler's ears and pressed the stethoscope to my chest. He listened intently, but it was Emerson I was staring at. The way she watched him with such fascination as her lips turned up in the corners. "Do you hear it?"

"Yeah. He's got a good heart, doesn't he?"

I barked out a laugh, and Emerson chuckled. "He does."

"Can I listen to your heart, Dr. Emerson?"

Her eyes widened with surprise. "Um. Yeah. Sure."

She bent down and got level with him and adjusted the stethoscope so it was on her heart. "Wow! You've got the best heart, Dr. Emerson. It's a real good one."

She chuckled and pushed to stand, taking her stethoscope back. "You've got a way with words, Beefcake. You just won over my pediatric heart."

We spent the next few minutes with her telling me that Cutler was doing well with the asthma treatment plan and that I could try some over-the-counter allergy medication if needed, but hopefully, the cough wouldn't last long.

We were at the door when my son turned back around. "Can Winnie come over and play with me after camp tonight for a little bit?"

She looked torn by the question but straightened quickly. "Sure. I'm working late, but I'll take a look outside when I get home, and if you're out there, I'll let her come and say hello. She's here now if you want to stop in the yard and see her before you head to camp."

"Yes!" Cutler pumped his fist excitedly as we all walked out to the hallway. My son ran toward the backyard where he used to see Doc's dog, Sadie May. And I walked toward the front desk with Emerson beside me.

"Sorry about all the questions. And I'm sorry you were forced to examine my heart, too. I guess I got a two for one today," I said, my tone laced with humor.

"It's all right. He's sweet and inquisitive, and I love it." She sighed. "And it's good to know you've got a beating heart."

"Yeah. I'm not lying when I tell him it beats for him. Because there's been times that I wasn't sure it was working, but then I look at him, and I forget everything else, you know?"

She smiled. "I get that more than you know."

Cutler came running back inside. "Winnie said she for sure wants to play with me after camp."

"All right, you've made your point. Stop pushing," I said, reaching for his hand. "We'll see you around, Chadwick."

"We'll see you tonight after camp, Dr. Emerson."

I heard her chuckle as we walked out the door.

And for whatever reason, my mind was reeling from what she was hiding.

About whoever had hurt her and made her feel this way.

She wasn't here because she wanted to be.

She was here because she needed to be.

She was running from something or someone, and I was determined to find out who.

She was helping my boy, so the least I could do was try to help her while she was here.

When we got to summer camp, I talked to the director to make sure the counselors working with Cutler were aware of his asthma and that there was an inhaler in his backpack, as well as one that we kept with the nurse on staff. They assured me that everyone was aware, and I made it over to the restaurant to get moving on the renovation.

Our team was working hard, and the new addition was being framed now. Kingston was inside helping a few guys with the layout for the kitchen.

"How's it going in here?" I asked, as I glanced down at the blueprint the architect had drawn up.

"It's going. The appliances have been ordered, and I'm going to start building the large prep island today," Kingston said, pausing to take a sip of his coffee. "How'd it go with Cutler?"

"Good. The cough is just allergies, and the new inhaler seems to be doing the trick. I just dropped him off at camp."

He turned to face me while the guys got to work. He studied me for a long moment and then smirked. "You don't seem to hate the city doctor anymore."

"Nah. That was just me being an asshole. It's not her fault that Doc retired." I shoved my hands into my pockets.

"Saylor said she's stopped by the bookstore a few times, and she really likes her. I guess she's going to ride with them this weekend."

"Yeah. She mentioned that. Good for her." I shrugged, not sure where he was going with this.

"Just saying . . . she lives next door. She likes your kid. He talks about her incessantly. She's a doctor, which could come in handy. Don't rule it out."

"*Don't rule it out?*" I barked out a laugh. "What the fuck are you talking about?"

"You know . . . be a good neighbor. Maybe entice her with the goods." He waggled his brows, and I groaned.

"Get to work, asshole. No one is enticing anyone with their goods, although I do have an impressive package." I chuckled. "We're barely neighborly. And she's only here for a little while, so there's no point going there."

"See, that's what I'm talking about." He raised a brow. "You say you're barely neighborly, but in your next breath, you're listing the reasons why you can't go there. *She's only here for a little while.* So the fuck what? Have a fling. Get out there and have some fun. You've gotten too serious. You don't want to die alone."

"King," I said, giving him a knowing look.

"Nash."

"Dude, you're talking out of your ass. Now I'm dying alone? I think you do this to distract me from work. Let's get busy."

"I just know what it's like to wake up with a beautiful woman in my bed every day, and I think you might like it too."

I groaned and started walking backward toward the door. "I've got a little boy to raise and a company to run. I don't need anyone in my bed because I can't keep my eyes open when I finally lay my head down at night. But thanks for the therapy session, dicknugget."

"I'm here to help. I'll send you my bill."

I laughed and held my hand over my head and pointed in the direction I was moving. "I'll be working on the addition."

"I'll be here!" he yelled out. "I'm ordering sandwiches for lunch today. You want the usual?"

"Sounds good."

I spent the next few hours framing walls and cutting drywall. This was a large project, but it would be nice to have a steakhouse in Magnolia Falls, so I was glad to see more businesses going up in town.

I picked Cutler up from camp and took him home. He seemed a little off and didn't even ask to play outside with Winnie like I'd expected. He just lay on the couch while I made dinner.

"Did you get too much sun today?" I asked.

"No. I'm just tired, Pops."

"All right. Well, I'm making your favorite spaghetti," I said, as I plated the food and set it on the table inside. We ate outside most nights, but with him feeling like this, I figured he needed a quiet night.

He came to the table, and I noticed his face looked a little pale, and I placed the back of my hand on his forehead.

"You feel a little warm, buddy."

He shrugged and started shoveling food into his mouth before setting his fork down. "I think my tummy hurts."

"Yeah? Maybe you're eating too fast."

Before he could respond, his eyes widened, and he proceeded to projectile vomit across the table. I jumped to my feet as he burst into tears, and I hustled him into the bathroom. I got him down on his knees in front of the toilet and dropped down beside him, rubbing his back as he heaved over and over.

He'd had the stomach bug once or twice in the past, but nothing like this.

He was crying and puking, and I just did the best I could to comfort him.

I got a wet washcloth and placed it on the back of his neck, and he finally stopped heaving after a half hour of nonstop vomiting, before I sat back against the wall, pulling him with me as I did.

"You're all right, buddy," I said as he leaned against me, and I ran my hand over his head as his eyes fell closed.

"I'm never eating 'sketti again, Pops." His voice was barely a whisper.

"I know. It'll take some time. Do you think a bath would be good? We can get you cleaned up and in bed."

He nodded, and I propped him up against the wall and

64

pushed to my feet to run the water. I got him up and started undressing him, when round two hit hard, and he was back at it. Emptying everything in his belly into the toilet again. There was nothing left by the time he finished, aside from stomach bile. I knew from experience how miserable it was. He looked up at me with his tear-streaked face, and my chest squeezed.

There is nothing worse than seeing my boy suffer.

I'd give this kid the moon if I could.

I'd heard people talk about the way they loved their kids, and I used to laugh about it. But living it—hell, I understood it. This kid owned me. He was good to his core. Smart and kind and funny as hell.

All I wanted at this point was to give him the best life I could.

I'd already failed him when it came to giving him the perfect family.

I couldn't control what his mother did, but I sure as shit could control what I did. So I woke every day, determined to provide the best I could for him.

Most of the time, I didn't have a clue what I was doing, but I was trying.

I got him into the tub, and we washed him up quickly before drying him off and helping him slip into his pajamas. We had his teeth brushed and hair brushed in record time, and he didn't even fight me when I carried him to bed. He dozed off quickly, and I dropped to sit in the chair beside his bed as I sent a quick text to Doc Dolby asking what I should do. He said to keep an eye out for fever, but hopefully, it would pass. He told me to make sure Cutler stayed hydrated, and if he woke up during the night, to give him some Gatorade or ginger ale, which, of course, I didn't have on hand. I said I had apple juice, and he said that would be fine until I could get to the store.

I made my way out to the kitchen and started cleaning up the vomit before sending a text in the group chat.

Cutler just vomited exorcist-style.
We're talking liquid exploding from his
little body like aliens had invaded. I
won't be at work tomorrow, King.

ROMEO

Oh shit. That's the worst. Poor Beefcake.
Do you need anything?

RIVER

That sucks, dude. Let us know if you
need anything. I can drop it off.

HAYES

I'm at the firehouse tonight, but I'm off
tomorrow. I can swing by if you need me.

KING

You know that vomit freaks me out. I
have a very sensitive stomach. But for
Beefcake, I can deal with it.

RIVER

How are you ever going to have children
with all of your sensitivities?

KING

Are you kidding? I'm ready to put a
dozen babies in my girl.

HAYES

> Fuck you, King. What did I tell you about that shit on the group text?

I barked out a laugh. Kingston loved fucking with Hayes, and I had to admit, I found it very entertaining. There was a knock on the door, and I set my phone down and moved toward the door.

When I pulled it open, I was surprised to see my neighbor hurrying away from my porch. There was a six-pack of Gatorade and a box of Saltines sitting there.

"Hey, what are you doing?" I asked, and she turned around, eyes wide like she'd been caught with her hand in the cookie jar.

"Oh. Hey. I was just dropping these on your porch for you." She turned around to face me, but it wasn't the drinks that I was staring at now.

It was the white tank top she was wearing and the little pajama shorts.

The light from the moon was shining down on her, making a silhouette around her pretty face.

Her tongue swiped out and ran along her plump bottom lip, and my dick sprung to life with no warning.

I didn't miss the way her eyes traveled down my bare chest before snapping back up to meet my gaze.

"I heard you might need these."

That wasn't the only thing I needed.

8

Emerson

Small towns were complicated in the strangest way. There was an easiness when you lived in a place where everyone knew one another.

You felt safe.

Protected.

Everyone looked out for one another.

It was nothing like the city. The hustle and bustle. Bumping shoulders as you passed on a crowded street. Horns honking and noise surrounding you at all times.

But Doc Dolby calling me long after I'd taken my bath and settled on the couch with the new book I'd picked up from the cutest bookstore in town, Love Ever After, had caught me off guard. He'd asked me if I had Gatorade in case Cutler woke up during the night, and this was definitely a small-town thing.

No one in the city would request this.

They'd DoorDash or Uber Eats it. Or there was always Amazon Prime. You could have drinks, snacks, and over-the-counter medication at your door within an hour. You didn't rely on the kindness of your neighbors because you barely knew them.

But what was I going to say? No? Of course not. I was always prepared for what could happen.

Vomiting and puking—I had plenty of hydration liquids stocked in my pantry.

Headaches—I was well stocked with migraine meds and chocolate.

Periods—I always kept plenty of tampons and pads in my bathroom.

I had clothing for every kind of weather that could come my way. I'd always been this way. So, of course, I had Gatorade to spare.

It was my job, for God's sake.

But was I prepared to see Nash standing there with his muscled bare chest for a second time? To get a real up-close view of that deep V that led down to his happy trail?

Hells to the no.

I'd been engaged to a man who had been in fabulous shape, but he didn't look like this. Nash was masculine and manly.

And ridiculously sexy.

It should be illegal to look this good.

Collin worked out hard; his entire body was waxed and free of any hair. And he loved to flex as he looked at himself in the mirror. It was a different vibe. Not to mention the fact that our sex life had sucked for the past year, but it all made sense now.

How ravenous could he be with his fiancée when he was banging her maid of honor on the side?

All the puzzle pieces had fallen together.

"Are you all right?" he asked, with a light chuckle as he leaned against the doorframe. One arm up, abs on full display, and a wicked grin on his face.

My eyes snapped back up when I realized I'd been caught staring. "Am I all right? Of course, I'm all right. Why wouldn't I be all right? Are you all right? You're the one with a sick kid. I'm just the neighbor, relaxing at home. I'm good. No. I'm great."

Dear God. Please make it stop.

This was what I did when I was nervous. I rambled. It was something that always annoyed Collin. He said it made me seem young and unprofessional. Apparently, I'd embarrassed him at a corporate dinner once, and he'd reminded me every time we went out with his work friends after that. He'd always say the same damn thing.

"Less is more. If you don't have a sensible answer, just say nothing."

Maybe I should have come up with a saying for him.

"If you can't keep your dick in your pants, don't get engaged to your girlfriend."

Nash barked out a laugh. "Well, we've established that you're okay, then."

"Yes. I wasn't planning on chatting," I said, looking down at my attire, suddenly mortified that I wasn't wearing a bra. I sure as hell wasn't planning to see him. I was just going to set this on the porch and hurry back home. Was he standing next to the door when I'd knocked? How the hell did he get there so quickly, anyway?

"I think you look great." He smirked.

"Okay. I'm going to leave now." I started walking backward on his porch. "Is Cutler okay?"

"He's fine. He vomited more than I thought humanly possible. But he's sleeping now."

"Well, if he wakes up, you'll have everything you need."

His heated gaze was moving down my body, and the feel of his eyes on me was overwhelming. I needed to get out of here. I started to turn, just as my foot missed the step, and it all happened in slow motion.

I tried to right myself, but it was too late. My arms went out, hoping to break my fall, as I literally tumbled into his bushes and then rolled into his front yard.

In the least graceful way possible.

70

Before I could even sit up, Nash was beside me, gripping my shoulders and laughing hysterically.

"Are you okay?" he asked, trying to speak over his laughter.

"Is this funny to you?" I snarled.

"You literally just sprawled across my bushes and tumbled into the front yard. It's a little funny."

Before I could respond, he had one hand beneath my legs and the other behind my back as he easily lifted me into his arms.

"What the hell are you doing? Put me down right now!" I shouted.

"Stop yelling. You'll wake Cutler." He carried me up the steps and across his porch before walking into his house. He set me on his kitchen counter as he leaned forward, arms gripping the cold stone I was sitting on as he met my gaze. "You brought us the drinks; the least I can do is clean you up."

"No. The least you could do is not laugh and instead ask if I'm okay." I tried hard to cover my smile because it was pretty funny, even if I wouldn't admit it.

"Are you hurt?" he asked, as he pulled a bag of frozen peas from his freezer and handed it to me, before moving to the drawer beside the sink and grabbing a towel. He ran some water over it and wrung it out and then walked back over and dabbed at my bare legs.

"I'm fine. I'm not hurt. And I'm a doctor, remember? I can take care of myself." I tried to grab the towel from his large hand.

My God. Everything was large on this man. He was tall. His shoulders were broad. His arms were muscled, and his thighs were thick. And I could only imagine what lay beneath those joggers of his.

"Stop fighting me, woman. Why are you so stubborn?"

"Well, I barely know you, and you just acted like a caveman, with the way you picked me up and carried me inside. I'm not some damsel in distress."

The man clearly didn't get offended easily because he just flashed me that sexy smirk before returning his attention to my knee. "You've got a little cut here. Let me get you a bandage."

He moved to the cabinet beside the refrigerator, and I didn't argue this time. He was clearly determined to patch me up from my mortifying experience, and I wasn't in the mood to fight anymore.

I'd been so angry these last few months, and I was tired.

Tired of feeling betrayed and blindsided. Tired of feeling all this anger that I couldn't release.

He tore off the paper and looked me in the eye. "You barely know me, huh? What do you want to know? You already know that I'm a single dad, and I told you about Cutler's mother. Hit me with whatever you want. We're neighbors, and you shouldn't feel like you can't come into my house because you don't know me well enough. You're my son's doctor, after all. We should be friends, right?"

"I shouldn't have said that. It was rude. I'm just not used to a man picking me up and carrying me around." I shrugged.

He moved forward after placing the bandage on my knee, and he stood between my legs, catching me off guard again. His face was so close to mine that I couldn't move. "What are you used to, Emerson?"

Great question. What am I used to?

Bad sex. Zero loyalty. Lies. Betrayal. Need I say more?

My eyes zoned in on his plump lips. His gray eyes bored into mine. And I wanted to feel his mouth on mine. His lips. His tongue. I wanted to press my body to his bare chest and feel his arms wrapped around me.

His warm breath tickled my cheek. The tip of his nose grazed mine.

He was so close I could taste him.

Mint and pine and masculine, sexy man.

My hands moved to his chest, desperate to feel his muscles beneath my fingertips.

To feel something.

Anything.

It had been so long.

So long since I'd felt wanted.

This longing ache lay heavy on my chest.

I. Want. Him. To. Kiss. Me.

And just when I thought the night couldn't get any more embarrassing, he startled and pulled back. His thumb traced over my cheek, when I realized a tear had escaped my eye.

Scratch that. Multiple tears had escaped my eyes.

I was crying.

I was freaking crying after eating shit in his front yard.

Could this night get any worse?

"Hey. Are you okay?" The concern in his eyes had my chest squeezing.

I pushed down off the counter to stand and swiped at my face. "Yes. I'm sorry. I shouldn't be here. I just—I need to go. Thanks for the bandage."

He narrowed his gaze, and I turned to leave.

I couldn't get out of there quick enough.

What the hell was that?

He'd almost kissed me. And more alarming—I'd wanted him to.

I shook my head after I ran through the yard and walked through my door. Winnie was still lying on the couch in a ball, and she lifted her head.

"Don't judge me, Winiford," I said, as I moved to the kitchen and poured myself a glass of wine.

My phone vibrated on the counter, and I picked it up.

UNKNOWN NUMBER

Hey. It's your neighbor, Nash. Just making sure you're okay.

73

> Hey. How did you get my number?

I chewed on my thumbnail, thrilled that for the first time in months, an unknown number was from someone I wanted to talk to. I decided to change his contact info so I'd have it saved. I liked to put people in under names that I'd remember. I thought it over before I came up with a good name for him. The heart was my favorite organ that I'd studied in medical school, and the fact that it was his name, and he claimed it only beat for his little boy . . . it was the sweetest thing I'd ever heard.

BEATING HEART

> I ask if you're okay and you reply with a question about me having your number? 😵

> Sorry. I'm fine. Maybe just a little embarrassed.

I picked up my wineglass and took a sip.

BEATING HEART

> Nothing to be embarrassed about. That fall was epic. You ate shit and landed in a bush, followed by an Olympic-worthy dismount and roll into the grass.

> I texted Doc Dolby and thanked him for having you bring over those drinks for Cutler, and asked for your number so I could thank you.

> You didn't tell him that I did some fancy gymnast move off your front porch?

BEATING HEART

> Nah. I thought I'd save that to torture you with.

> Good to know.

BEATING HEART

> I hope I didn't do anything to make you uncomfortable. I shouldn't have stood so close, and I apologize if I crossed a line that I shouldn't have crossed.

> Stop. That wasn't it. I wasn't embarrassed that you were standing close. I'm not afraid of you, if that's what you're worried about.

BEATING HEART

> So what was with the tears?

I took another sip of wine and thought it over. I had nothing to lose. I wasn't staying here. I'd avoided talking about it for so long; maybe it would help to actually get it out. But I also didn't want everyone in town to know my story. Nash didn't strike me as a gossipy guy though. I moved to the couch, wineglass in hand, and dropped down beside Winnie.

BEATING HEART

Did I freak you out again? Do you have a thing against crying?

No. I was getting myself a glass of wine and moving to the couch. But I wouldn't say I'm particularly proud that it appeared you were about to kiss me and then pulled back because you thought I was crying.

I chuckled because I knew that would get a response.

BEATING HEART

Oh, I thought you were crying, huh? Those weren't real tears, Chadwick?

They weren't real tears. I think they were probably just a sign of my enemies leaving my body.

BEATING HEART

Wow. That's heavy. Tell me more.

I'm kidding. Listen, it's complicated. I think I got lost in the moment for a minute, and it felt good to feel that. It's been a while.

BEATING HEART

> I can't imagine it being more complicated than the fact that I have a kid with a woman who bailed. Shit happens to all of us. Don't be embarrassed to talk about it. My life is far from perfect.

I let out a deep breath and took another big gulp of wine.

> What are we, friends now? I thought you couldn't stand me.

BEATING HEART

> I think I stopped being annoyed by you fairly quickly. We can be friends if you want.

> Are you sure you want to be friends with an outsider? I don't live here, and I'm not staying.

BEATING HEART

> I'm more than aware. But I can't sleep because I'm worried Cutler will wake up and get sick, so I'm sitting in his room on the La-Z-Boy chair. Entertain me, friend.

> Fine. Prepare yourself.

BEATING HEART

I'm on pins and needles.

You're hilarious.

BEATING HEART

And you're deflecting. Tell me what you're running from. Why you came here. I know you're leaving, so you've got nothing to lose. We won't even remember each other this time next year. 😊

For someone who is determined to forget about me, you sure are interested in my story.

BEATING HEART

Spill it, woman.

I don't want anyone to know my business, so if you repeat it, I'll deny it and then egg your house.

BEATING HEART

I promise not to share anything aside from my Nest camera footage of you eating shit in my yard.

Deal.

My fiancé, the Stanford boyfriend, whom I started dating my senior year in high school and all through college and medical school, cheated on me, and we called off the wedding. Are you happy now? That's the big secret.

BEATING HEART

Of course, I'm not happy. I knew he was a dick. I could feel it in my bones when you mentioned him.

So you're a psychic now?

BEATING HEART

Who did he cheat on you with?

My maid of honor.

BEATING HEART

Oh, shit. You got a two-for-one deal. You found out that they were both assholes, so maybe you got lucky.

I think that's probably true. And it's been a few months, and I'm definitely over the sadness of it. But when I thought you were going to kiss me, it just made me realize it had been a while since I felt like anyone wanted to kiss me. And that is my strike three . . .

BEATING HEART

Meaning?

I fell in your yard. I cried when you were about to kiss me. And then I admitted that no one has wanted me since I called off my wedding with my loser ex. Three strikes. Drop the mic. I'm going to bed.

BEATING HEART

Hey, Chadwick?

I'm already sleeping.

BEATING HEART

That kiss would have been fan-fucking-tastic.

I sighed and pushed to my feet and padded my way down the hall to my room.

How could those six little words terrify me so much?

I think it's best we don't go there. I'm here to figure out what to do with my life, not make it more complicated.

BEATING HEART

Trust me, I've got no room in my life for complications. Let's write it off as a moment of weakness. Sweet dreams, Dr. Chadwick.

9

Nash

"Can I go to camp tomorrow?" Cutler asked.

For the fifth time in less than two minutes.

"Yes. As long as you're fever-free today and don't vomit anymore. But since you've been holding down the soup and crackers, I'm guessing you're on the mend." I settled beside him on the couch where he was watching his favorite Disney movie.

"J.T. must be so bored without me." He shoved another cracker into his mouth.

It was hard to believe that just eighteen hours ago, he was projectile vomiting for hours. He'd rebounded quickly after a good night's sleep, and he seemed to feel fine this morning.

I'd scoured the house with Lysol, so hopefully, this bug was long gone now.

"I'm sure he'll survive for a day. He's got Coop and Tyce there, right?"

"Yeah. But he doesn't like when I'm gone. We're brothers, like you and my uncles."

I chuckled. "I get that. There's nothing better."

I glanced down when a text came through. I'd be lying if I didn't say I was disappointed that it wasn't from Emerson.

We'd had a moment. One that had caught me off guard.

But having her here in my kitchen . . . Those jade eyes. Those plump lips.

It was too much.

This pull that lived between us.

She wanted to leave it alone, and I knew she was right. No sense starting something with a woman who wasn't staying. And I didn't do relationships anyway. I liked to keep things simple because my focus was on Cutler. So messing with my neighbor would be a dumbass move.

But still, I was disappointed the text wasn't from her.

Because maybe I'm a dumbass when it comes to my neighbor.

TARA

> How's the boy?

She texted me once or twice a year, and it always started this way. If I scrolled up through the conversation, this was what she always led with.

How's the boy?

Our son.

Her son.

I was torn somewhere between pissed off and relieved every time she messaged. *Pissed off, because he deserved better.*

Relieved, because he deserved better.

> Cutler is doing well.

I could mention that his sixth birthday had come and gone, and she hadn't called. But that would mean that I'd expected her to call. She had never called on his birthday. Or Christmas. Or any holiday, for that matter.

And that meant that I got to have him all the time.
Her loss was my win.
But I still felt bad that he didn't have a normal family life.
Not that she ever could have provided it.

TARA

> It still makes me smile that we chose that name for him.

It was her fucking claim to fame with me. She'd picked the name, and I'd liked it.

She brought it up every time I saw her. Maybe it was guilt because she had nothing else she could really bring up.

She did carry him and provide a home for nine months.

And that was the reason I tolerated her texts once or twice a year.

She gave me the best gift I could ever receive.

So, for that reason, she always got a pass from me.

> Yep. He's the best kid on the planet, no question there.

TARA

> I'm going to try to get to Magnolia Falls at the end of summer to see him. Do you think he would like that?

> I don't know. I'd keep your expectations low.

My phone rang immediately, and I groaned when I saw her name light up the screen.

83

"Yeah?" I grumped.

"What does that mean? We had an agreement that I could see him when I came through town," she said, using that whiny tone she always used when she wanted to get her way.

I pushed to my feet when Cutler glanced over at me, walked out to the back deck and pulled the door closed behind me. "And you can. I'm just saying, he's not three years old anymore. He has questions. He doesn't know you, and if you're coming just to stay for an hour, I wouldn't bother. It just confuses him."

"You could fix this, Nash. You could tell him that I love him but that I wanted a different life."

"It's not my job to make you look good. I tell him that you love him because I want *him* to feel good. Not because I give a flying fuck how it makes you look."

"What is with this attitude? I thought we had an agreement?"

"We do. I'm holding up my end. I'm raising my son. But I'm letting you know that things have shifted, so that you won't show up here and expect something different. He doesn't call you Mom anymore; he refers to you as Tara. He did that on his own. Kids at school talk. He sees his friends with their parents, and he knows that you aren't around. So you can't just expect him to be excited to see you."

She sighed. "He'll be fine when he sees me. Last time I saw him, he cuddled up on my lap. He knows instinctually that I'm his mama. It's a bond that we'll share no matter where we are."

"Tara, he was four years old the last time you saw him. It's been over two years. He's growing up. You can't just show up every couple of years and expect a relationship."

"I can show up whenever the hell I want to. He's my son, too," she snipped.

I ran a hand over my face, trying my best to keep calm. I didn't want to rock the boat. I got to have Cutler 100 percent of the time. If she wanted to roll into town for a few hours every couple of years, I could suck it up. This arrangement was a good one for me and Cutler. I didn't have to share him or have some strange dude playing stepfather to him.

"It's fine. I just wanted you to be prepared that he might be a little standoffish."

"I can win him over quickly. It's my superpower, right?" She chuckled, completely content now that she'd gotten her way. "Can I talk to him?"

"He's home sick from camp today. He's got the stomach flu."

"Well, then I'll cheer him up. I just want to say hello."

I walked back inside and paused the movie. "Hey, buddy. Your mama is on the phone, and she'd like to say hi."

His dark gaze locked with mine. "Tara?"

"Yep. Can she say hello?"

He shrugged, and I put her on speakerphone. I needed to hear what she was saying, so I could end the call if she upset him.

"Okay, he's here," I said.

"Hi, Cutler. It's Mama. How are you?"

"Fine. I threw up last night."

"Oh, gosh. I threw up a few nights ago, and it was the worst," she said with a laugh.

"You had the stomach buggers?"

"I had the tequila buggers." She chuckled, and I rolled my eyes. "I was telling your daddy that I'm going to try to get to Magnolia Falls at the end of summer, if I can."

"Why?" Cutler asked.

"Because I want to see my son, of course. I'm so proud of you. And I can't believe you're six years old already."

Cutler looked up at me. It was this weird, knowing look that he gave me. Like he understood who she was in a way. This kid was an old soul. He'd always been good at reading

85

people. He loved the people in his life fiercely, but he'd also learned that he needed to protect himself when it came to Tara.

"You can call me Beefcake. I don't like the name Cutler anymore."

"What? Cutler is the coolest name. I'm not calling you Beefcake."

His eyes widened. "I'm tired, Tara. I need to go rest."

"Wait. I don't want to argue. I'll call you Beefcake if you agree to call me Mama again. Deal?"

My chest squeezed when I saw the confusion on his face. Cutler wasn't playing a role. He was just an honest kid who had a big heart.

"He needs to go lie down, Tara," I said, taking her off of speakerphone.

"Okay. Tell little Beefcake I hope he feels better soon," she said with a laugh. "I'll let you know if I can make it there at the end of summer."

"I need to go. Keep me posted on when you're coming."

"I will. Hey, Nash," she said.

"Yep."

"Thanks for being a good dad to our son."

Hell, everything I did was for Cutler.

It was my honor to be his father.

"You got it. Bye."

I ended the call and propped a pillow on my lap, and he leaned down and rested his head there.

"You okay?"

"I hope Tara doesn't stay too long. I've got lots of plans at the end of summer with J.T. and my uncles and all my girls." He stared ahead at the TV, even though the sound was still muted.

I stroked his face, happy that his fever was gone. "Don't worry at all. We've got plenty of time for everything, okay?"

"Pops?"

"Yeah."

"I'm glad you're my dad."

Fuck me. My chest squeezed so tight it was hard to breathe.

"Thanks, buddy." I cleared my throat. "You are the best thing that has ever happened to me. I love you."

"I love you, too."

"Just like it was for you and Gramps when you were growing up, right?" he asked, his voice quiet.

"Yep. It was me and Gramps."

"Were you sad that you never met your mama?" he asked. We'd talked about it a few times over the last year. He'd suddenly become more curious about my mom's passing.

"Yeah, I was sad I never got to know her." She'd passed away during childbirth due to a complication. My father had gone to the hospital with his wife, whom he loved, and left with a newborn son all on his own.

"Gramps says that she made sure you were okay before she decided to leave with the angels, because he says she was an angel too."

I hadn't realized Cutler had talked to my father about it. "Is that what he said?"

"Yep."

"Sounds about right. But I had a great life with Gramps. You know that, right? Everyone's family is different, but as long as you're loved, that's all that matters."

"I know that, Pops. You and me didn't have mamas around, but we have a big family that loves us."

"We sure do." I continued stroking his hair away from his face as his eyes fell closed.

And he dozed off, and I just sat there staring at him.

This little dude brought so much joy into my life.

I dozed off on the couch right alongside him.

But I sprung forward in a jolt when a severe cramp hit my stomach. The room was dark, so it was clear that several hours had passed, and Cutler was lying there, watching a movie.

His eyes widened. "You've been asleep for a long time."

"Shit," I hissed as I ran to the bathroom, nearly crashing into the coffee table.

I barely made it to the toilet before I vomited violently.

Looks like the stomach buggers were back with a vengeance.

10

Emerson

I'd just gotten off work, and Winnie and I made our way home. I fed her while I heated up some leftover noodles and poured myself a glass of wine. I pulled up the recipe for the Rice Krispie treats with unicorn sprinkles I was going to make tonight. I promised Demi and Peyton I'd bring them tomorrow, and Lana and Petra were getting very used to me bringing in different baked goods for them a couple of days a week.

I'd enjoyed this time to myself. Swimming and baking and listening to music. No pressure from planning a wedding. No pressure from a fiancé reminding me that I worked too much during residency.

No pressure at all.

I was just living.

"Let's go outside, girl," I said.

Of course, she ran right over to Nash and Cutler's yard, looking for her favorite kid.

I was surprised they weren't out here, but maybe Cutler was still feeling bad.

I chewed on my thumbnail as I stared at their back door.

I was his pediatrician. The least I could do was check on him, right?

I was awkward after what had happened last night.

And we'd all but admitted that we were attracted to one another when we'd texted.

But we were neighbors.

We could be friendly.

I wasn't going to overthink it.

I walked toward the door, with Winnie on my heels, and knocked lightly.

The door opened so quickly, I startled. Cutler stood there, holding a washcloth in his hand, and his eyes were wide. "Hi, Dr. Emerson. Pops is real sick."

I heard loud heaving in the distance, and I hurried inside.

Me, Cutler, and Winnie walked down the hallway to the powder room, where Nash was on his knees and unloading everything in his stomach into the toilet. Winnie tried to get in there, and Nash tried to block her from sticking her head in the toilet.

"Winnie, out," I said, my voice firm, and my pup immediately hurried out of there. "Cutler, how about you take her out to the couch and sit with her, and I'll help your daddy, okay? I'll be out in a little bit."

He nodded and handed me the wet cloth, which melted my heart because he'd obviously been trying to comfort his father.

I wet the washcloth and wrung it out before dropping to my knees beside Nash, just as he'd heaved a few more times. I set the cool cloth on the back of his neck and ran my hand over his back. "You all right?"

"You don't want to get this. You should head home," he groaned.

"Trust me. I've got a steel immune system at this point. Don't worry about that."

He dry heaved several more times, but there was nothing

90

left in his stomach. He flushed the toilet and sat back, leaning against the wall, and reached for that damp washcloth and ran it over his face and mouth.

I settled beside him on the floor and glanced over at him to find him watching me.

"I'll bet you really want to kiss me now," he said, his voice tired, but I could hear the humor in his tone.

"Very funny. Are you okay?"

"Yep. I'll be fine. What time is it?"

"A little after seven," I said.

"Fuck," he said under his breath, trying to push to his feet. "I need to make Cutler dinner."

I put my hand on his shoulder. "Just stay put. I'll make him something to eat and grab you some Gatorade."

"I can call one of the guys. You don't need to be here."

"Stop being stubborn. It's the neighborly thing to do. You fixed my fence, after all." I smirked, before pushing to stand and making my way out to the family room.

I chuckled at the sight in front of me.

Winnie was sitting so close to Cutler, they were pressed against one another. They were both staring at the TV as Simba was singing his heart out on *The Lion King*.

"Hey, are you hungry?" I asked him.

"I had some more crackers already, but I'm a little hungry."

"How about some noodles with butter and toast?" I was hoping Nash had that here, but if not, I could run next door and grab some pasta and bread.

"Yes." Cutler fist-pumped his little arm. "I love noodles and butter."

I looked through the pantry and was surprised at how well-stocked it was. This was not the kitchen of a bachelor. This was the kitchen of a father.

One who fed his son well. The freezer was full of meat and fish. The refrigerator was packed with fruit and veggies and milk and eggs. The pantry was well-stocked with pasta and canned goods.

I pulled out a pot and got the water boiling before pouring both Cutler and Nash a cold glass of Gatorade.

"Drink this," I said, and I walked back down the hallway and handed Nash a glass. He was still sitting in the same spot in the bathroom, and I was glad that he hadn't thrown up anymore. "Just sip it slowly and let's see if it stays down."

"Thank you," he said.

I knew he was a proud man, and he probably hated asking for help. But he was sick, and I lived next door. I was happy to do it.

City life had been so different.

I'd lived in a high-rise, and I'd barely spoken to my neighbors over the years.

But this was the way I'd grown up.

Hell, my mom had Sunday dinners that were open to anyone who wanted to come. Half the town came to our Fourth of July party every year.

"You got it. I've got some water boiling, and I'm making Cutler some noodles. I'll wrap some up for you in case you're able to hold food down later tonight or tomorrow."

He nodded and then took a sip of the Gatorade before closing his eyes as his head rested against the wall.

I walked out and got the noodles cooking and poured them into a bowl with some butter before calling Cutler over to the table. Winnie had fallen asleep on the couch.

"This looks yummy. Pops makes the best noodles, too." He shoved a forkful into his mouth.

His dark hair was lying flat on his head, minus his usual gel, as he'd clearly been on the couch all day, and I took him in. He was such an adorable little boy with his chocolate brown eyes and cherub cheeks.

"You've held food down fine today?"

"Yep. Pops made me toast and a banana for breakfast and some soup and crackers for lunch."

He'd done the BRAT diet. Nash clearly knew how to care for a sick child.

"Good. And you rested a lot today?"

"Yep. We slept on the couch for a long time. Except when Tara called." He took a sip of water and then continued. "That's my mom. She's coming here at the end of summer, and she wants me to call her mom instead of Tara."

That was an odd request when you hadn't seen someone in a while. Obviously, I didn't know all the details, but I'd gathered enough from what Nash had shared to know she didn't come around much.

"How do you feel about that?"

"I don't know. I don't know her." He shrugged. "Do you know your mama?"

I sighed. "Yeah. My mom is great. But, I will say this. If my mom wasn't great, I'd be okay with her not being around, you know?"

"Really?"

"Yes. Really. I mean, you have this fabulous dad, and he loves you so much. And being surrounded by love is what's most important." I said.

He shrugged as he shoved some more noodles into his mouth and then took a minute to think over my words. "You only like fabulous people in your life too, Dr. Emerson?"

"First off, if we're sitting here eating noodles, I think you should just call me Emerson, okay? We're friends, right?"

His lips turned up in the corners, and he was so adorably perfect that I couldn't help but smile when I was around him. "We are friends, so I think I should give you a nickname, since you call me Beefcake."

"Okay. What do you want to call me?" I asked, as he looked deep in thought.

93

"I'm going to call you Sunny. Because the word sun is at the end of your name, and I think you feel like sunshine."

My heart melted.

"I like that name, Beefcake. Thank you." I patted his little hand. "And yes. I like to be surrounded by fabulous people, like you and my family."

"You want the other people to leave if they aren't being fabulous? Cause my camp counselor, Louisa, she says we should only be around people who fill our buckets."

"I like that. I had this, er, friend that I spent a lot of years with. But in the end, he wasn't a good friend to me. So I agree with Louisa. Let's keep people around who fill our buckets." I chuckled.

"But also, my pops and my uncles would beat your friend up if you wanted them to," he said.

I heard laughter coming from the bathroom, and I'd forgotten that Nash was close enough to hear our conversation.

"I don't need anyone to fight my battles, but thank you," I said, a bit louder than I'd been speaking before, and I heard him chuckle again from down the hallway.

"I'm happy you live next door to us, Sunny," Cutler spoke over a mouthful of noodles.

I reached for his hand. "Me too. This fresh start is exactly what I needed."

I cleaned up the dishes, and Nash came padding out of the bathroom wearing gray joggers and a white fitted tee.

Who looks this good after vomiting everything in their stomach?

Nash. Freaking. Heart.

His hair was a rumpled mess, but it only added to his appeal.

"Hey," he said, his voice gruff and tired. "Thanks for helping out. I'm all right now."

"Yeah? You sure?"

"Yes. You've done more than enough. I appreciate it." He cleared his throat and set his half-finished glass of Gatorade on the counter.

"All right. Well, you've got my number if anything comes up," I said, giving Cutler a hug before he jogged down the hallway when Nash told him to go get ready for bed.

"I do. We'll be good to go by morning."

I called for Winnie, who'd made herself completely at home as she lay on her back with her legs flayed out to the side like she owned the place.

"Winiford, come on, girl. Have some pride. Let's go."

Nash laughed as he followed me to the door, and my dog ran out ahead of me.

"She's always welcome. And hey, if you decide that you want to pull a Winnie and come lie on my couch like you own the place, my door is always open."

I laughed as I turned around when I got to the edge of the porch. He had his arms up, gripping the door frame, and his white tee lifted just the slightest bit, exposing a sliver of toned abs. I squeezed my thighs together as I tried to act unaffected.

My God, this man was so freaking sexy.

I hadn't had sex in months, and I was clearly missing it.

But just being in Nash's presence made me feel like a teenager with raging hormones.

"I hope you feel better." I reached for the railing. "I'm going to turn around this time so I don't fall into your bushes."

He chuckled. "Mind if I watch?"

I was hoping you would.

I shook my head; my cheeks heated at the thought of his eyes on me. When I got down to the grass, I glanced over my shoulder.

"Is that heart of yours beating now?"

He placed a hand on his chest. "It sure the fuck is."

"Goodnight, neighbor."

95

"'Night, Sunny," he said, and the nickname sounded sexy as hell coming from him.

I walked across the yard and pulled my back door open and looked back at his porch. He was still standing there.

"You're sick. Get in bed. Doctor's orders."

"Just waiting for you to get inside."

Such a gentleman.

A sexy-as-sin gentleman.

11

Nash

> Tara claims she's coming for a visit at the end of summer. I won't hold my breath, but I also need to be prepared for how that will affect Cutler.

RIVER

> Nice of her to show up whenever the fuck she feels like it. This would be a good time to get her to sign something. Make custody official. I can draft something up.

HAYES

> She should definitely sign something. She hasn't had anything to do with him since the day she left. And she doesn't contribute financially either, so it doesn't seem like a lot to ask for.

Yeah, it's just that things have been going smoothly, and I hate to rock the boat. She goes on the defense when she feels pushed into a corner.

ROMEO

She put herself in the fucking corner. Take your shot. You've done everything for that boy, and she doesn't have a leg to stand on.

KING

I'm with Nash on this one. Why rock the boat? She's letting him do it all on his own. Why start a fight when you don't need to?

Agreed.

RIVER

Because the law is the law. It doesn't matter if she hasn't done anything up to this point. She is his mother, and she could come around anytime she wants and demand things. I'm not saying she will. I'm just saying that it wouldn't hurt to have her sign something saying she does not want to pay child support or have any rights to her child.

HAYES

Agreed. The world is a cold-ass place. People are shitty. I say make her sign something.

KING

Hello, Sunshine. ☀️ The world isn't all bad, Hayes.

I instantly thought of the conversation between Cutler and Emerson. The name he'd decided to call her was so fitting. Even when she tried to keep to herself, there was just this bright light that she exuded.

Sunny.

HAYES

Well, it sure as fuck isn't all good either, so you need to be prepared for the hit before it comes.

ROMEO

That is something I always do as a fighter. Not a bad idea to take that approach in life.

I wasn't really coming here for legal advice. Just letting you know she may be coming to town, and Cutler may mention it to you. 🐷

KING

Did he tell you guys that the good doctor next door brought him and Cutler a little care package? Sounds like a little DROMANCE in the making.

> She brought Gatorade for Cutler. And what the fuck is a dromance?

KING

A doctor romance, you dicksicle. A.K.A. a dromance.

ROMEO

Is that a romance book thing?

KING

Nope. I think I invented it. But I will sure as shit be telling Saylor about it. Who doesn't love a good dromance?

RIVER

Someone who isn't dating a doctor?

HAYES

Someone who doesn't like dumbass wordplay?

ROMEO

Someone who married a coffee shop owner?

Someone who is not dating his kid's doctor. I'll meet you at the site in twenty minutes, dicklicker.

Kingston and I had a big day ahead of us with the renovation. Flooring was going in, and this was when things started to come together.

RIVER

Think about what I said, Nash.

All right. You can draft something up if she actually comes to town. I can try to just get her to sign it and keep things light. I can at least bring it up.

ROMEO

Preparing for the punch is always smart.

HAYES

Fuck yeah. The rug can be pulled out from beneath you at any time. Remember that.

KING

You cynical fuckers are bringing me down. See you soon, Nash. I'll grab coffees for us at Magnolia Beans. They are a lot more upbeat over there, and after this riveting conversation, I need some time with the ladies. 😌

RIVER

Stop being so dramatic. Are we still coming to your place this weekend for the Fourth of July barbecue, Nash?

My house on the water had a great view of the fireworks, and Cutler was looking forward to having a party.

Yep. Hot dogs, brewskies, fireworks, and some lake time. I think we could all use it.

ROMEO

Beans and I will be there. Will we be inviting the good doctor next door? I still haven't met her yet.

Well, I always let all the neighbors know, seeing as they'll all see us out there. So, I'll mention it to her, but I doubt she'll come. She likes to keep to herself.

KING

When she's not delivering care packages to you. 😌 Saylor and I will be there with Dandelion.

Kingston and Saylor had a goldendoodle that they treated like their child, and they took her everywhere with them now.

HAYES

I'm off this weekend, so I'll be there.

RIVER

Ruby and I could use some downtime. Looking forward to it.

I set my phone down and made my way to the renovation site. It was going to be a long day, and I was ready to make some progress on this project.

Once we were there, I spent all my time putting out fire after fire, so to speak. There was a leak issue in the men's restroom, and the flooring that we'd chosen didn't match the existing flooring. So now we were having to add another coat of stain to darken them up. The front door that Kingston had built at his shop was about an eighth of an inch too big, so we'd have to shave off the edges of the drywall to make it fit.

"Hey, Nash." Lucille and her husband, Dave, strode through the large opening where the front door would go once we fixed the issue.

"Hi. How's it going?" I asked.

"Well, we're anxious to get the doors open," Dave said, raising a brow. "It costs me a small fortune every day that this place isn't open. And there still seems to be a lot of work to do here."

"Correct. We gave you the timeline, and we're on track to finish in three weeks, as planned. We're on schedule, so I'm not sure what the problem is?"

"The problem is that we'd like to open the doors sooner

than planned." Lucille raised her chin and her brow all at the same time in a move meant to intimidate me.

It didn't work.

We had a timeline, and we were sticking to it.

It wasn't uncommon for clients to get impatient once we were in the middle of a project.

"Listen, we need to get this right, and we're on track to do so. But you can't change the timeline when we're three weeks out. It doesn't work that way." I shrugged.

"We're manifesting it," Lucille said, her tone harsher than I'd ever heard it. "And when you manifest, you don't have to get permission. It just happens."

I used my hand to cover my mouth to keep from laughing, because this was the first time I'd heard this reasoning when it came to changing the timeline.

"I can respect you putting all the positive mojo out into the universe, but that's not how construction works. We have every single minute of the workday thought out for the next three weeks, with a full team of guys working long hours at the site. All the manifesting in the world is not going to get the job done any sooner." I crossed my arms over my chest.

"That's disappointing. So, I'm going to ignore what you're saying and count on the doors opening in two weeks." Lucille stormed off, and Dave groaned.

"Sorry about that. She's just stressed about money right now, so she's got it in her head that if we open sooner, all will be good. But we're fine with the timeline as you have it. I just wanted to make sure we were on track," Dave said.

"If nothing major comes up, we should be good to go. I'm sorry we can't get you in here sooner. We're doing the best we can to get it done on time."

"I hear you, and that all sounds good. Thanks, Nash. It's really coming together, and I'm very pleased."

Just then, Lucille snapped her fingers from a few feet away.

"Let's go, Dave. I can't manifest when I'm standing in the middle of a construction site."

She whipped around and stormed off, growling at a few of the guys as she walked back outside.

Kingston walked over to me and did his typical dramatic shiver. "Yikes. I find that woman terrifying. She always looks so pissed off."

"Yeah, I do notice the way you always run to the bathroom whenever she stops by. Thanks for that, by the way."

He clapped me on the shoulder. "You're just much better at handling that kind of shit. I would have agreed to up the timeline, and that wouldn't be a good thing. So . . . you're welcome."

I rolled my eyes. "That's convenient. Are you ready to get the door in?"

"Yep. I just need your help to lift it."

"Let's do it."

We spent the rest of the day tackling one thing after another, and I was relieved when I got to the camp and picked up my boy.

I should have been concerned when his camp counselor told me she'd try to stop by our Fourth of July party. Cutler loved to invite everyone in town every time we had a get-together.

"I thought I told you that you needed to ask me before you invite people to things," I said as we drove toward home.

"Yeah, but she's real nice, Pops. She gave me an extra cookie at snack time."

I shook my head as we pulled into the driveway, and my head snapped in the direction of my neighbor's house. Emerson was out front in those damn jean shorts, bent over, planting flowers.

Cutler was out of the car and running that way as Winnie sprinted in his direction.

"Hey, what did I tell you about waiting for me before you jump out of the truck?" I grumped.

"Sorry, Pops! I want to say hi to Sunny and Winnie."

Emerson turned our way, pushing to stand and brushing her hands off to free them of the dirt.

"Hey," she said, as my son ran into her arms like they were long-lost family members. "How was camp?"

This fucking kid and his attachments to certain people.

Beautiful women seemed to be his thing.

He rambled on and on about all the things that happened at camp, and I crossed my arms over my chest, waiting for him to take a breath.

"Pops, did you tell Sunny about the fireworks party?"

Did I not just tell him that he wasn't allowed to invite people without asking?

I cleared my throat and shot him a warning look. "I haven't had a chance to do that."

"Oh, sorry. I'm not supposed to ask people to come to the party without talking to Pops first."

She smiled. "My parents had the same rule growing up, and I swear my brothers never listened. Everyone in town would show up at our parties, and my mom would get so aggravated with the boys. She finally just stopped fighting it and took on a the-more-the-merrier philosophy."

"I like that." My son glanced over at me, his hair disheveled from swimming in the lake at camp and his cheeks a little pink from the sun. No matter how much sunscreen I put on this kid, he still got tan everywhere, but his cheeks were always rosy. "The more the merrier, Pops. Did you hear that?"

"I did. I'm standing right next to you." I chuckled. "And of course, you like that. You aren't the one throwing the party."

Emerson's jade-green eyes locked with mine. "I'm guessing he's just the entertainment?"

"Something like that," I said, as Cutler started running

around the yard with Winnie. I scratched the back of my neck and squinted up as the sun was shining down on us. "You're welcome to come. It'll be a good group."

Why was I fucking nervous? I didn't get nervous around women. Not usually, at least.

Maybe I was prepared for her to turn me down.

Again.

"What exactly is a fireworks party?" she asked.

"It's a Fourth of July party. Good food. Good drinks. Good people."

"Sounds like a good time." She smiled. "It's probably always wise to have a doctor present with fireworks."

"Ah . . . so you'd be coming as a professional, then?"

"Seems like the neighborly thing to do." She smirked. "And how can I turn Cutler down?"

Well, you shut down that kiss with me fairly easily, didn't you?

"I'd be curious to see if our Magnolia Falls parties are as good as your Rosewood River parties."

"I'll definitely let you know. What can I bring?"

"A medical kit and a zipper to stop my kid from inviting everyone in town." I smiled because she was so damn pretty.

"Don't be mad at him for inviting me. I am your neighbor, after all. I would have seen the festivities going on."

"Not mad that he invited you, Sunny." I started walking backward toward my house. "Just mad he didn't let me do it first."

"That was a little flirty, neighbor."

"I try." I threw my hands in the air before turning to my son. "Come on, buddy. I need to get dinner going."

"Aww man, Pops. Winnie and I are having fun. Can't I stay out here a little longer?"

"I'm moving to the flowerpots on my back porch, and I can keep an eye on him if you want. I wouldn't mind the idea of

LAURA PAVLOV

wearing Winnie out right now. And she's bored watching me plant flowers. You'd be doing me a favor."

"Fine. Just until dinner. And stay away from the lake. You know the rules," I said. I wanted to invite her to eat with us, but she'd made it clear that she didn't want to complicate things.

She'd agreed to come to the party.

And for whatever ridiculous reason, I was on cloud fucking nine about it.

I doubted I'd be watching the endless fireworks that Kingston had purchased for us, as I had a feeling I'd be staring at my sexy neighbor all night.

Because regardless of whether or not she ever wanted to cross the line with me, if she was around, my eyes were on her.

12

Emerson

I thought I'd be upset to be here on the Fourth of July, seeing as I rarely missed the party my parents threw back home every summer. It was tradition, and I loved it. Collin and I never missed it. Actually, Farah never missed those parties either. She'd call herself the third wheel and make endless jokes about it.

In hindsight, Farah was not the third wheel at all.

Apparently, she was the spare tire that had replaced the one that Collin was bored with.

I shook it off.

It was still hard to wrap my head around the fact that two of the most important people in my life were no longer in my life.

How could they be?

They'd betrayed me in the worst way.

And with my now-canceled wedding date looming above me like a dark cloud, it was hitting me all over again. One more week, and I'd be able to put the whole thing in my rearview.

I shook it off and turned my attention to Demi and Peyton, who were walking my way. I'd just arrived here, and the party was in full swing. I'd had second thoughts when I'd heard the music and the laughter, wondering if I should have just stayed home and felt sorry for myself, baked some cupcakes or cookies, and let myself get lost in sugary goodness.

But Nash had texted and told me to stop hiding and get my ass over there.

So here I was.

I'd gotten to know a lot of locals already, as everyone had come by the office to meet me over the last few weeks. They didn't have kids, but that didn't stop them from dropping by, and they'd all made me feel very welcome.

"Hey, girl, we're so glad you're here," Peyton said.

Demi handed me a beer before clinking her bottle against mine. "I can't wait for you to meet Romeo."

"Well, my brothers will be very jealous. They're super fans of his. They were obsessed with that fight," I said.

"Says the girl who has a brother who happens to be one of the most famous hockey players in the league," Peyton added, because once they'd found out that my brother was Clark Chadwick, they'd all freaked out. I was used to it. Clark was a professional hockey player, and he'd really made a name for himself the last two years.

I chuckled, just as Peyton waved at someone and told us she'd be right back.

We both glanced over to see where she was going.

"That's my brother, Slade. I think she's crushing on him, but it's not something I want to talk about with her just yet." She laughed.

I shook my head. "Trust me. No one gets that more than me. I've lived it my entire life with my family."

A good-looking man walked over, and I assumed it was Romeo, as I remembered a photo my brothers had shown me.

"This is the infamous Dr. Chadwick, huh?" he asked,

extending his hand as the other arm looped around Demi's waist, and he pulled her close.

"Please, call me Emerson. You must be Romeo."

"Apparently, you've got some fans in Rosewood River, Golden Boy. They were invested in the fight," Demi said, glancing up at him, and my chest squeezed at the way they looked at one another.

Had Collin ever looked at me like that?

Like he couldn't live in a world that I didn't exist in?

Because that's what I was witnessing right now.

"Yeah? That's nice to hear. Thank you. And I'm a huge hockey fan, and Clark is a beast, so let him know he's got a fan here in Magnolia Falls." He wrapped both arms around his wife, her back to his chest. "My girl has been talking about you so much. We were hoping you'd show up today."

"Thank you. She makes the best coffee I've ever had, so she's stuck with me now. And she got me back on a horse after a few years of not riding much." I smiled at Demi. "And I was happy to come. It seems like the place to be."

"Just wait for the fireworks. King gets really into it, and it'll be a great show," Demi said.

Nash called Romeo over for something, and the next thing I knew, I was sitting in a chair with Demi, Peyton, and their best friends, Ruby and Saylor. I'd met Saylor when I'd popped into her bookstore a few times, and I'd met Ruby when I'd gone out riding with them on Demi's ranch. But today, I was getting to know them all better. I was enjoying myself and laughing endlessly, and it felt good.

Betrayal has a way of making you feel this need to protect yourself. Keep your guard up. And I'd been doing that for the last few months.

But today, my guard was down.

It was the first time in a long while that I was genuinely having a good time.

I wasn't faking it or forcing it.

And it felt damn good.

Maybe this was all part of healing.

"So, you're single, right?" Peyton asked as I sipped my beer. "Do you have your eye on any of our fine Magnolia Falls men?"

"Wow. You're really smooth. How do you even know she's single?" Ruby asked over her laughter.

"Please forgive her. She's just nosy by nature," Demi said, using her hand to cover her smile.

"Um, *she* can hear you. And I'm just getting to know our new bestie." Peyton chuckled.

The word bestie had my chest squeezing. My lifelong best friend had completely betrayed me. Was I the worst judge of character on the planet? Could I even trust if someone was really my friend anymore?

"Direct talk and intense questioning is Peyt's love language," Saylor said with a laugh. "She did it to me, too."

"That's okay. You can ask me anything. I'm currently single. I was engaged, and we called the wedding off a few months ago. So I'm not looking for Mr. Right, because I just spent years with Mr. Wrong. I can't be trusted." I shrugged, as if I hadn't just dropped a massive bomb on them.

They all gaped at me, Saylor's and Demi's eyes were as wide as saucers, Ruby's brows were pinched together as she studied me, and Peyton had one eyebrow raised. Clearly, they all had different reactions to the news.

"Well, I'm not even hiding my curiosity now. I need the deets." Peyton leaned forward and rested her elbows on her knees.

"She just told you that she called off her engagement. That's all the details you get," Demi said, shooting her a warning look. "And, Emerson, I'm so sorry that you've been going through that."

"So, I'm guessing you didn't come to Magnolia Falls for the small-town charm. You needed an escape, didn't you?" Ruby asked.

"Ruby's basically a therapist. She knows these things," Saylor said.

I took another pull from my beer and smiled at them. It felt good to talk about it, if I was being honest. My family, mostly my brothers, were so angry that any time the topic came up, they would tell me that they wanted to physically hurt Collin. And then *I* was calming *them* down.

My mother cried about it all the time, and then I felt the need to comfort her.

My father was so angry about it that he'd just wrap his arms around me and hug me every time he saw me, and I hated the pity.

My grandparents were crushed that the wedding had been called off, as it had been built into this grand event in Rosewood River. Two families that had lived there forever, tying the knot, so to speak.

Being here, in Magnolia Falls, felt different.

Safe.

I didn't have to defend anyone in the process of sharing what had happened. Even after all Collin and Farah had done, I didn't want to have everyone in town hating them for the rest of their lives.

It was me that they'd betrayed. Not the entire town of Rosewood River.

But small towns were funny that way. They may be gossipy, but the locals were fiercely protective and loyal.

And the rumor mill had been in full force ever since the wedding had been called off.

"I just needed to figure my life out. I needed a new plan, and I didn't want to do that back home in Rosewood River or in the city where everyone knew my story." I shrugged, because it was the truth.

113

"What you actually need is to find yourself an interim man. You know . . . a rebound. Give yourself the gift of having a fling. Cut loose. Otherwise, this escape was all for nothing," Peyton said.

"I swear you have no filter sometimes, Peyt. Maybe the whole goal was to be alone." Ruby reached for her drink and took a sip.

"Right. But she should still be pleasured." Peyton waggled her brows at me, and Demi spewed her beer all over her lap. "Escape by orgasm is the best kind of revenge there is."

"Peyton Francis, what the hell is wrong with you? She wasn't asking for your advice!" Demi shrieked.

"And she's a doctor!" Saylor said as she shook her head and winked at me.

"So what? Doctors need the dick sometimes, too."

Now it was my turn to laugh. And I laughed so freaking hard that tears pricked my eyes. And then they were falling down my cheeks as I continued laughing.

They were the first tears I'd shed over the situation that weren't sad tears.

"What's going on over here?" Nash asked, and I nearly jumped out of my chair at the sound of his deep voice and his hand landing on my shoulder.

"You know, baptism by fire, Peyton-style." Ruby chuckled.

"All right. Well, she's laughing, so that's a good sign. You aren't running her out of town just yet." He gave me a little squeeze. Maybe it was the three beers that I'd had since I'd arrived or the fact that I was more relaxed than I'd been in a very long time, but I melted a little at the gesture. Maybe all men weren't evil after all. Maybe just the one I'd planned to spend the rest of my life with was evil. "Do we need another round of beers over here?"

"Oh, hell yeah!" Peyton shouted, and his gaze locked with mine before he agreed to go grab us some more drinks and walked away.

"You are really on one tonight," Demi said, shaking her head at her best friend, as a big smile spread across her face.

"Well, speaking of hot men in Magnolia Falls. You're living next door to the most eligible bachelor in town," Peyton said.

"Nash is definitely a catch." Saylor took the last sip from her bottle and set it down at her feet. "And that could be perfect, since you aren't looking for anything. He's definitely all about raising Cutler, so I think he likes to keep it casual when he does get out, from what I've known of him over the years."

"Have none of you heard the rule, *don't shit where you eat*?" Ruby asked.

"I've heard it, but I can't really wrap my head around the meaning," Demi admitted, which was a call for more laughter.

"Agreed. It's a stupid saying." Peyton threw her hands in the air. "Plus, she can eat at home and go next door to take a shit."

Hysterical laughter bellowed around us just as Nash walked back over with five beers between his fingers and one brow raised as he took us in. "You ladies are having way too much fun over here. Fireworks in fifteen minutes. Get ready for a great show."

"Oh, we're ready for a show, all right!" Peyton shouted as he walked away. "So we agree. She can shit wherever the hell she wants to. And as far as the eating part. I say, let the man work his magic between your thighs. *Bon appétit, Nash Heart.*"

Now it was Saylor's turn to spew beer across her lap, after she'd just taken a sip from the bottle that Nash had handed her.

I leaned forward. "The meaning of *don't shit where you eat* is recommending that one doesn't have a fling with their neighbor, who's also the father of one of their patients."

"Thank you," Ruby said, flinging her thumb at Peyton. "I think this one took it a bit too literally."

"Whatever. I know what it means; I just think it's stupid. You live next door. It would be so convenient for a late-night booty call. And you're Beefcake's pediatrician; you aren't the psychologist for a mob boss who just confessed to all the murders he's committed. Pediatricians are allowed to mess around with the father of their patients, especially if he's a hot single dad."

"Ahhh . . . single dad romance is my absolute favorite," Saylor said.

This conversation definitely had my mind racing. Obviously, I'd wanted to kiss him the other night.

But where would that lead?

We were neighbors.

Friendly neighbors.

I was his kid's doctor.

I was moving in a few months.

I raised the beer to my lips and took a sip as they all waited for a response. "It's too messy. Too complicated."

"So you aren't saying that you don't want to do it? You're saying it's too . . ." Demi paused.

"Messy and complicated," Saylor finished her words.

"Listen, I'd climb that man like a tree if he looked at me the way he looked at you when you were coming across the yard earlier." Peyton's voice was lacking humor now.

"Stop. You're romanticizing things. He can't stand me most of the time."

"She's not romanticizing this." Demi leaned forward, and her gaze locked with mine. "She pointed it out, and we all turned and witnessed it."

My heart raced at the thought. I'd noticed the way that he looked at me, and I knew the way I felt when he was around. But that didn't mean we should act on it. "And how exactly does Nash Heart look at me?" My tone was all tease.

"Like he doesn't care if it's messy or complicated," Ruby said. "And that's not really his style. He's aloof most of the time with women because his singular focus is Cutler. But his eyes were on you, and he smiled right when you stepped off your porch."

"Nash doesn't get excited about women. He has hookups, and then he goes back to his normal responsibilities," Saylor said. "But something is different with you."

"I'm just a newbie in town. I know how small towns work. I've got several brothers who love when a newbie comes to town. The shiny new toy. Trust me, it'll wear off."

"Don't overthink it. You called off your engagement, right?" Peyton asked.

"Yes," I said, unsure where she was taking this.

"Well, we all know the best way to get over a man is to get under a new one. And your neighbor is not only the hottest single guy in town—next to Hayes—but he's also your neighbor. It couldn't be more perfect."

Thoughts of spending a night with Nash flooded my mind. Those toned abs I'd had a sneak peek of. Those muscular arms. The day-old scruff on his face. His wavy hair that I longed to run my fingers through.

Thick thighs.

Rough hands.

Did it just get hotter out here?

And then I remembered that I hadn't been with anyone other than Collin. I'd never had a fling. I didn't know how to separate sex from love.

I didn't know if I was capable.

"Everything you said is true. He's hot. He's funny and nice and snarky all at the same time, and I like it. And God knows I haven't had sex in so long, the lady parts are probably going to permanently close if I don't do something about that soon." I dangled the beer bottle from my fingers.

They all chuckled, yet I saw the empathy in their eyes as they looked at me.

117

"So, what's the problem?" Ruby asked.

"I'm not a fling girl. I've never had one," I admitted, feeling my cheeks flush. It was embarrassing, really. I'd only been with one man, and he hadn't even been faithful to me.

"Well, hells to the yes. It's the Fourth of freaking July. It's a great time to try something new, and what better day for some fireworks of your own?"

And with those words, the sky lit up in bright reds and pinks and oranges.

Everyone cheered, and I glanced over to find Nash's eyes on me.

And even though I felt the strongest pull toward this man, I knew I shouldn't act on it.

My life was already a mess.

No sense adding fuel to the fire.

13

Nash

I dropped Cutler off with J.T. His parents, Jay and Susannah, had become good friends, and I trusted them immensely. Our boys were both only children, so they were more like brothers at this point.

I understood it.

My Ride or Die guys were my brothers.

I'd finished work earlier than usual, and I wasn't used to having time on my hands.

All the guys were with their ladies tonight, and Hayes was at the firehouse.

So, I was on my own.

My phone rang, and I answered through my Bluetooth.

"Hey, Dad. How's it going?"

"It's good. I'm a little tired from being on the road, making the last of the deliveries for the week. But I'm heading home to crash. Just wanted to check on Cutler. The new asthma meds are working?"

My father had been a single dad, just like me. He'd worked hard his entire life as a truck driver, putting in long hours, and he'd been a tremendous role model. He and my mother had been ridiculously in love, and he'd never moved on after she'd passed away.

"Yeah. We haven't had any issues. He had to use his inhaler at camp a few times this week, but as long as we stay on top of it, use the peak flow meter every day, and be proactive, it's been going well."

"Listen to you. You sound like a doctor." He barked out a loud, weathered laugh. My father had smoked for as long as I could remember, and he had the husky voice to prove it. "Proud of you, son."

That had a lump forming in my throat. We didn't talk like that. I knew he loved me. Never doubted it for a minute. But he wasn't the emotional type, and I think losing my mother the way he had, made him guarded in a lot of ways. I'd worked hard to tell Cutler every day how much I loved him. He brought out a side of me that I hadn't even known existed before he'd come into the world.

"Thanks. Just trying to keep up on all of it."

"How are you going to handle Tara if she does show up in a few weeks? I never like it when she comes to town. It always has me a little anxious when she's here."

"Yeah. There's a good chance she'll flake on coming, but if she does, she never stays long. I'll let her spend a little time with Cutler, and she'll be on her way for another year or two. It's the best I can hope for," I said, as I pulled into my driveway, and a man standing on Emerson's porch caught my attention.

"All right. Keep me posted. I just got home, and I'm going to crash for the rest of the night. Talk to you tomorrow."

"Sounds good." I ended the call and climbed out of my truck.

Emerson had left the Fourth of July barbecue in the middle of the fireworks show last week, claiming she wasn't feeling well. I hadn't seen her since, aside from a quick wave, and I got the feeling she was avoiding me. We'd texted a few times, but it was just me checking on her and her checking on Cutler.

I got the message loud and clear.

She wasn't interested in making things complicated between us.

It was probably for the better. Even if I'd fucked my fist too many times to count since the day she'd moved in next door to me.

I should be going out tonight to try to get laid because I was desperate for some sort of release that didn't come from my own damn hand. Cutler was gone, and this was my window. But something had me walking toward the stranger standing on her porch.

Was this her ex?

"Hey. Are you looking for Emerson?" I asked, making my way up the three steps to her front door. We were eye to eye. He was tall, just like me. Dark hair. He wore jeans, a dress shirt, and a sports coat, but I didn't miss the cowboy boots on his feet. Sort of a mix of business and rancher. He didn't exactly scream Stanford grad. But I didn't attend college, so who was I to know how a smart dude dressed?

He turned to face me and narrowed his gaze. "I am. And you must be the neighbor. Cutler's dad, right? Is it Nash?"

She clearly talks to this dude often. I wanted to puff up my chest that she'd mentioned me, but then it hit me that maybe they were getting back together, and that's why she'd been avoiding me.

"Yeah. Nash Heart. And you are?" I raised a brow, trying to tune out the ridiculously loud music coming from the house.

"Easton Chadwick. Emerson's evil twin." He offered me a hand, and relief flooded for reasons I couldn't begin to explain. I had no claim over this girl.

I shook his hand. "Nice to meet you. What's going on in there?"

The windows rattled with the vibration of the loud music.

"Well, she didn't go to work today, which is very

121

uncharacteristic of my sister. I've called her a dozen times, called her office, and they said Doc Dolby came in today to cover for her. So I hopped on a helicopter and got my ass here because I was worried. And now she's not opening the door, and I've been banging on it for a good ten minutes."

"Wow. Must be nice to have access to jump on a helicopter with no notice."

"Yeah. We've got a brother with more money than he knows what to do with. So he's got all the toys, and he's willing to share," he said, but he knocked again and yelled her name.

"Do you think she's sick?" It was impossible to hide my concern.

"Probably not with that blaring music. All her years in pediatrics, between rotations and residency, she rarely gets sick. Her immune system is rock fucking solid."

All the blinds were pulled down, so we couldn't see what was going on inside. "What's with the music?"

He cleared his throat and shook his head before pounding on the door again. "Emerson's got a slight obsession with Beyoncé, and I do believe this is her new country song she's playing. On repeat."

"And you're worried?" I asked, because the dude had hopped on a helicopter and flown here when she didn't answer her phone. That seemed drastic, even for a concerned brother.

"Do you know what today is?" He turned to face me.

"Friday?"

He let out a long breath. "Today would have been Emerson's rehearsal dinner, and tomorrow would have been her wedding day. I talked to her last night, and she was fine. But today, she's gone radio silent. That isn't like her. My sister doesn't do that, at least not to me. Our parents are losing their shit and wanted to fly here, so I jumped in so I could see what was going on before all hell breaks loose at the Chadwick home."

Her fucking wedding day.

Now, I leaned forward and banged on the door.

"Should we break a window?" Easton asked, as he turned toward her flowerbeds, and I guessed he was looking for a rock.

"I've got a key, but I don't know if we should use it."

He whipped around. "You have a fucking key? Yes. We should definitely use it. She gave you a key?"

"No. The owners gave it to me. I've fixed things for them over the years when they've had issues."

"Dude. I need to make sure she's okay. Let's just open the door and find out what the hell is going on."

"It's a key to the back door. Come on." I hustled down the steps with him beside me, and we made our way around back. "You think she's still heartbroken over the dude?"

He barked out a laugh. "Hell no. I never thought she was that happy with him, if I'm being honest. And after what that fuckface did, she despises the asshole. But she had a plan, you know, and it got blown to shit. And I think she's more upset about Farah than Collin, which kind of says it all."

"That's her best friend?"

"Yeah, she's a real piece of work, too," he said when we paused at the back door. All the blinds were drawn on the back side of the house, too.

"You sure about this?" I asked one last time, and he nodded. I put the key in the door and pushed it open, and we both stood there, gaping at the scene before us.

Beyoncé's country song was blaring through her speaker, and Emerson was singing into a bottle of champagne. And that wasn't even the part that had my eyes going wide.

It was the fact that she was wearing a wedding gown as she danced around the room, belting out lyrics that didn't seem to go with the song. Winnie didn't move, she just lay on the couch with what looked like a wedding veil draped over her

LAURA PAVLOV

head. There were cupcakes lining the kitchen counter, and a batter-filled mixing bowl beside them.

"Holy shit. This is . . . *unexpected*," Easton said under his breath.

Neither of us spoke as we just took her in. Long brown waves fell down her back, and a satin gown hugged her curves down to her waist, where a full tulle skirt ran to the floor.

She didn't notice us as she took a long pull from her champagne bottle before turning it back into a microphone and singing loudly.

"This ain't Rosewood River. This is Magnolia Falls," she sang over hysterical laughter. The words did not go with the beat at all, but then she'd throw in a few, "ohhhhh, ohhhhhh, let's move to the right" before talking about someone not being an asshole and throwing their cards down. Her words were slurring, and she was cute as hell.

My chest squeezed as she spun around, lifting that full skirt and showing off her cowboy boots beneath her dress.

This city girl is all country.

Then she shouted with the music. "This ain't Rosewood River. This is Magnolia Falls, so hit the road, asshole."

The words certainly weren't the lyrics from the song, though she appeared to try to match Beyoncé's rhythm.

And I didn't give a fuck. I was too busy staring at the most beautiful woman I'd ever laid eyes on.

Emerson Chadwick might be a little bit broken, but she was strong and fierce in every way.

She whipped around, her hair flying all around her, and her eyes widened when she took us in. A big smile spread across her face. "What do you know . . .? It's two of my favorite guys."

"Damn. How'd you get up there with me already?" Her brother chuckled and moved toward the speaker and turned the volume down. "Hey, Emmy, how you doing?"

124

"I'm doing fan-freaking-tastic," she said, taking a long sip from the bottle. "But why'd you turn the music down? This is a dance party."

"I can see that," he said. "But I was worried about you."

"Worried about me?" Her gaze searched his before turning to look at me, her voice all tease now. "And were you worried about me, neighbor?"

"You've got Beyoncé on repeat, and your blinds are closed, and you're dancing around in a wedding dress." Easton glanced over his shoulder to see the cupcakes covering her entire counter. "You've baked enough cupcakes to feed a small country. Yeah, it's fair to say I'm worried."

"You know how much I love Beyoncé. And this new album is—"she paused to kiss her fingertips and flung her hand out before shouting, "—chef's freaking kisses!"

"What the fuck is chef's kisses?" Easton said over his laughter. "Emmy, you didn't go to work."

"Easton." She leaned closer to him, eyes wide. "You've missed work hundreds of times. I've never called in. Do I not get a pass just this once?"

"Yeah, you get a pass, girl. But I was worried about you." He wrapped his arms around her and hugged her before pulling back. "You all right?"

"Yeah." She moved to the couch and plopped down, a puddle of tulle and silk surrounding her. She looked like a little girl sitting that way. "Farah called this morning, and I don't know . . . I just felt sad after talking to her. So I put on my dress, because God knows I'll probably never wear a wedding gown after this fiasco. So I decided to day drink, bake, and dance." Her words were slurred but coherent.

"You decided to day drink?" He gaped at her with a wicked grin on his face. "You've shamed us our entire lives for day drinking. Said it was a waste of time."

She turned to look at me and patted the seat next to her,

125

and I moved to sit beside her. "He's referring to my brothers and my cousins. They love to have a good time. And you know what? I was wrong. Day drinking is underrated. I've had a damn good day. I drank half a bottle of wine, two shots of whiskey, and this fancy bottle of champagne."

"That is a recipe for a nightmare hangover. Have I taught you nothing about mixing booze?" he asked, as he moved to the kitchen and poured himself a whiskey and handed me one, as well. "If you can't beat 'em, join 'em."

I laughed and tipped my head back, letting the warm amber liquid move down my throat.

"Ahhh . . . thank you for joining the party," she said, before hiccupping three times and then falling back in a fit of laughter.

"What happened with Farah?" Easton asked, sitting in the chair across from us. Emerson had the place looking like something straight out of a magazine. The chair and couch were white, with floral throw pillows and a large area rug.

There were flowers and photos and colorful paintings on the walls. It looked like she'd lived here for years and not weeks. But it didn't surprise me.

This woman was different.

Special.

Her face hardened, and she set the bottle on the coffee table. "She said it meant nothing. It was a mistake." Another slew of hiccups escaped. "*A six-month mistake.* Apparently, that's how long they were sleeping together. And then she cried and said she missed me."

I could see the struggle there. The betrayal and the hurt.

"They're both assholes. They never deserved you. But I know it sucks. I get it, Emmy." I could feel the empathy pouring from her brother. It was impossible not to see how much he loved her and how much her pain was felt by him. "What can I do for you?"

"That's the thing, E. I'm not heartbroken, which is weird,

right? I dated him my entire adult life, and I'm not heartbroken. I'm angry. I'm disappointed. But the truth is, I feel like I dodged a bullet, and not just because he's a cheating pig, but because when I look back, I don't think I was happy these last few years. I think that's probably why he strayed. Because we were both settling." She shrugged. "But I wish it would have ended differently. He shouldn't have disrespected me." She paused, and no one said anything when she went on. "Even so, I wish we could have all remained friends, you know? And Farah's betrayal is just a punch to the gut."

Her hand rested beside mine on the couch, and my pinky finger stroked hers.

"Farah has been jealous of you our entire lives. We've all known it, seen it, but I hoped she'd outgrow it. Do I think she regrets it now that everything has blown up in her face? Hell yes. You were the best thing that ever happened to her, Emmy. You were a loyal, true friend," Easton said, and it was very clear how close these two were.

"Yeah. I know she needs a friend right now, but I can't be that person for her." She shook her head, looking between her brother and me. "And I feel bad because I'm happy about this new future of mine. They both seem to be lost and desperate to repair things, and I'm ready to leave my past behind me, you know?"

"I get that, and they'll have to live with the mistakes they've made," I said. "But you just keep doing your thing. Don't let anyone clip your wings."

"Fuck yeah. Spread those wings and fly, Emmy girl."

A wide grin spread across her face. "I should have known that the marriage would be a bust when he wouldn't agree to my one request at the reception."

"What was it?" I asked.

"We were supposed to get married in Rosewood River on the water. I told him I'd seen a photo shoot where the bride and groom waited until the photos were done and the reception was over, and then they jumped into the water in their dress and tux and took the final photos. I just thought it was a cute idea because we grew up on that river. But Collin thought the idea was appalling."

"Pretentious prick," Easton grumbled.

"So, who wants to go jump in the lake with me in this too fancy of a dress I'm wearing?" She waggled her brows.

Easton looked between us. "How about I order us dinner, and you take my sister out to the lake and make sure she doesn't drown in all that fabric?"

"I'm down," she said, turning to look at me. "What do you say, Heart?"

"Sure. If you want to swim in your wedding gown, who am I to tell you no?" I pushed to my feet.

"Burgers and wings good for everyone?" her brother asked.

She took one more swig from the bottle of champagne. "It's a perfect way to end the day. I'm glad you're here, E."

He nodded, and then she set the bottle down and turned to me. "You ready?"

"Born ready, Sunny."

14

Emerson

I held up the skirt of the dress and kicked my cowboy boots off on the patio, nearly losing my balance, most likely from the champagne I was still drinking. I'd cut off the hard liquor a while ago, but the bubbly stuff left me with a nice, lingering buzz. Nash steadied my shoulders until I was standing fine on my own two feet. Then he took off his shoes and jeans and tee, leaving him in nothing but a pair of navy briefs. I tried not to stare, but clearly, I still had a good buzz going, as I'd been boozing it up all day.

"If you keep staring at it, I can't control the way it'll react."

"Are you referring to your penis?" I chuckled.

"Can we not insult him by saying penis? I prefer dick. Cock. Shlong. Big daddy."

My head fell back in laughter. Nash Heart had turned my day around. Finding him and my brother standing at my back door had been unexpected. Normally, I'd hate being interrupted, maybe even a little embarrassed, when I was having a moment with Beyoncé. But today, I welcomed it.

Welcomed them.

Easton was a no-brainer. He'd been my other half my entire life.

But Nash, why did I want him there when I was having a pity party? I'd tried hard to avoid him all week. This pull that I felt toward him terrified me. But I'd been thrilled to see him standing there today.

"All right, let's do this," he said. And before I could respond, he scooped me up and tossed me over his shoulder, fireman-style. He ran toward the water as I laughed hysterically.

In all the years I'd been with Collin, he'd never picked me up or carried me. Not once. Not that I had asked him to or needed him to.

But this simple act of chivalry . . . it did something to me.

Maybe it was because of what today was supposed to be.

He charged into the lake, and we both crashed into the dark blue water. I went all the way under and found those abs beneath the surface as I swam toward him. He was reaching his hand out for me, and I took it. I came up, breaking through the surface with a gasp. The fabric was pooling around me, and it was heavier than I'd expected. But Nash was right there, pulling me closer.

I tried to find the bottom with my feet, but it was too deep. In one quick move, he tugged me up so my legs could wrap around his waist as he held me against his hard body.

And by hard body, I mean . . .

Hard.

Body.

Everywhere.

I could feel all of him, even with ten pounds of tulle and silk surrounding us. He was standing, his shoulders just above the surface of the water.

"You okay?" he asked, his voice gruff, as I pushed his wet hair away from his handsome face.

"Yes. I'm good. How freaked out are you right now?" I asked.

"Why would I be freaked out?"

"Oh, I don't know. You found your neighbor, who also happens to be your kid's doctor, dancing with a bottle of champagne and wearing a wedding dress. And now you're in the water with the crazed bride. I could see how that would freak someone out."

"Not freaked out at all, Sunny." His tongue swiped out along his bottom lip, and my drunken body reacted by pressing harder against him.

You're a doctor, for God's sake. Control yourself.

"No?"

"Nope. I live with a six-year-old. I've been puked on, changed shitty diapers, and been asked more rapid-fire questions than any man should ever be asked." His hands were on my waist and my back, and I couldn't even believe I was out here in my rejected wedding dress with my legs wrapped around him.

Who even am I?

"Well, thank you for showing up today and running into the water with me." My teeth sank into my bottom lip.

"Tell me about your call with Farah."

I startled at his words. He said it so casually, as if it were perfectly normal for him to be there for me. To listen to me.

"Do you have anyone that you've been friends with for so long that you can't imagine your life without them?"

"I do."

"Well, that's how it is with her. I can't remember a time in my life when she wasn't there. We didn't go to the same college, but we were only twenty minutes away from one another during that time. And she became a nurse, and I became a doctor, just like we'd always planned. And when I got my residency at UCSF, we celebrated that night because she was at the same hospital. Everyone there knows our story, so even my place of work became tainted by what happened." I paused and shook my head in disbelief. "We always said we'd work together and marry brothers and raise our kids together.

And now, everything is . . . different. And I swear, that loss is harder than breaking off the engagement with Collin. I don't miss him the way that I miss my best friend."

He listened intently, and it felt good to get it off my chest. If I said this to Easton, he would fly off the handle and tell me what a piece of shit Farah was. And I knew that it was true, but it didn't mean that it didn't hurt.

"I get that. Betrayal is tough, especially when it comes from someone you love. I don't trust easily. I keep my circle small. And if one of my best friends did to me what she did to you, it would kill me. So I get it."

"Really? Thank you. That makes me feel better."

"Of course. And that doesn't mean you should forgive her. That's up to you. Personally, once my trust is broken, it's hard to turn that around. But you have a history with her, and it's normal that it's hard."

"I want to hate her, and a part of me does. I know there is no going back after what happened. But when I heard her voice today, I remembered five-year-old Farah, the girl I ate lunch with every single day in kindergarten. And I remembered ten-year-old Farah, who slept over at my house almost every single night the summer before we started fifth grade. And sixteen-year-old Farah, who got her driver's license on her birthday and came straight to my volleyball game and waited for me to finish before we went to her birthday dinner. She was such a huge part of my life."

"And she always will be. Regardless of whether or not you have her in your life moving forward, you'll always have those memories."

I couldn't stop staring at his mouth. His plump lips. The chiseled jaw peppered in day-old scruff. My hands moved to his strong shoulders, gently tracing along each muscle until I moved it along the tattoo. Dark ink in a beautiful scroll that I'd been so curious about.

Ride or die. Brothers till the end. Loyalty always. Forever my friend.

"What does this mean?"

"River, Romeo, Hayes, King, and I all have it inked on our skin as a reminder of our friendship."

A lump formed in my throat. "You do understand, don't you?"

He knew what it was like to trust someone so deeply that you'd walk through fire for them. So, he understood how deep this wound had cut me. I felt it in the way his gaze met mine, and it comforted me.

"I do."

My teeth sank into my bottom lip. "I'm glad I moved next door to you, Nash Heart."

"Me too." He chuckled.

"Remember the other day when you seemed like you were going to kiss me, and I ran out of your house like a bat out of hell?"

This sexy grin spread across his handsome face. "I remember."

"I wanted you to kiss me."

"I know you did."

My head fell back on a laugh. "Well, don't get cocky about it."

"Not cocky, just a straight shooter. I wanted to kiss you. You wanted to kiss me."

"You make it sound so simple." My gaze locked with his.

"Listen, Emerson, I know you came here to get away from everything. And I'm sure that finding out that your fiancé and your best friend were having an affair and then calling off your wedding is a lot to process. I get it. So I'm not here to complicate your life. My life is pretty simple. I'm an open book. My world revolves around my little boy, and I like it that way. I know you're not staying, and I also know that starting something up would complicate things."

"But?" I shook my head and chuckled. "I'm guessing there's a but in there."

"But . . . I like you. I like spending time with you. Hell, I even like irritating you." He laughed. "And yeah, I'd be lying if I said I didn't think about kissing you. All the fucking time."

I sucked in a breath. He was so honest and open. I wasn't used to that.

"I like spending time with you, too. And I wouldn't ever want to do anything to complicate things for Cutler. But obviously, I'm attracted to you, and it's getting harder and harder to avoid you."

He thrust forward just enough for me to feel him beneath me.

"Speaking of hard," he said, his voice teasing. "It doesn't have to be complicated. Cutler is already invested in you. We're neighbors and friends. It's not like I'd have to introduce you to him. The kid is already crazy about you, and he knows you're only here temporarily. So I don't see how kissing you causes anyone any stress. Hell, maybe it'll suck, and we'll never want to do it again."

My heart raced as his eyes zeroed in on my lips.

"That's a good point. But I don't have a lot to compare it to. I've literally only been with one man in my life." I shrugged. I was putting it all out there. I didn't feel judged by Nash.

I felt safe.

"He's a dumb fucking dude to have messed this up. But if it means I get to kiss you, then I'm certainly not complaining."

"So, what are you waiting for?" I whispered, just as the sun moved behind the clouds and the sky darkened, as if it were preparing for this moment.

His hand moved to the back of my head, tangling in my hair, as he pulled my mouth down to his. His lips were soft but firm, and he took control immediately. His tongue slipped inside and found mine as he groaned into my mouth. He tilted my head, taking the kiss deeper, and I melted against his body.

The man could kiss. His hands were everywhere, rocking me against him as my hips started to move. My fingers tugged at his hair, urging him closer, like I couldn't get enough.

I'd never been kissed like this.

I ground up against him, riding up and down his erection, as we made out like teenagers in the middle of the lake. My breaths were coming faster, and I was so turned on that I couldn't think straight.

I bucked against him faster.

Harder.

Feeling every inch of his desire between my thighs.

It was too much and not enough all at the same time.

I was panting now as my entire body started to tingle. My head fell back, and his lips found my neck as he continued moving me up and down his shaft. Even with our clothes on and all this fabric between us, I could feel everything.

Every inch of him.

He was long and thick and hard.

I was dry humping him like it was my day job.

"That's it, baby. Let go." His words were a balm to my tattered heart.

Bright lights exploded behind my eyes like bursts of sunshine, and his name was a whisper in the breeze moving around us.

I went over the edge in a way I didn't even know I needed.

I continued riding out every last bit of pleasure as I held onto this man like he was my lifeline.

As if I'd needed to let everything go.

Let myself go.

Let myself feel good again.

I waited for my breathing to calm before I raised my head and looked at him. He had this ridiculously sexy grin on his face, his hair was wet and disheveled, and his gray eyes were locked with mine.

"Hey," I said.

"Hey yourself," he said, his tongue sliding out along his bottom lip.

"What are you thinking?" I asked, because I wondered if he thought the fact that I'd just ridden him like a professional bull rider, dressed in a wedding gown, had come off as a little desperate.

"I'm thinking that you're fucking beautiful. Even if I just get to look at you for a short time, I'll take it."

I sucked in a breath. "You really are a straight shooter, huh?"

"I am. Always have been."

"So, do you make girls orgasm just by kissing them often?" I teased, feeling my cheeks heat. "I'm sorry. Clearly, it's been a while for me."

"Hey," he said, his hand moving beneath my chin as he turned me to face him. "Don't do that."

"Don't do what?"

"Apologize for what just happened. I fucking loved it. Loved seeing you come apart. Loved knowing I could make you come while fully dressed." He smirked. "And no. I don't make out with a lot of women."

"What do you mean?"

"I mean, I've never stood in the water, making out with a woman like this. I'm a dad. I don't get out a ton, and when I do, it's usually a casual hookup. Nothing deep. So we get down to business pretty quickly."

I chuckled. "Down to business, huh? So what was this? You didn't get down to business at all."

"Today is about you. And I'm just glad that I could make you feel good on a day that was tough. I mean, Beyoncé on repeat and a bottle of champagne were a good start, but a lake orgasm is a strong finale."

"Lake orgasms are clearly underrated," I said, shaking my head.

"And you're beautiful."

Three simple words. *And you're beautiful.* They had a lump forming in my throat. It felt like he knew exactly what I needed to hear sometimes. I didn't know how it was possible, but I wasn't questioning it.

"Thank you," I said, just as the shouting from my back porch had us both turning.

"Dinner's here!" Easton's voice boomed.

Nash shifted me so I was on his back. "Hold on. I'll swim us in. This dress is going to be heavy for you to try to move in."

And he swam me to shore.

Like a knight in shining armor.

My sexy, off-limits neighbor was full of surprises.

15

Nash

Emerson had wrapped herself in a towel that had been on the dock, and I'd held the skirt of her dress up to help her get up to her house. I said I needed to run next door to get dressed because I sure as hell was not going to walk inside that house with a raging boner in front of her brother.

But that fucking kiss had done me in. I'd trained myself to go for long windows of time without sex ever since Cutler was born. But I was rock-hard and in need of relief. So a quick shower where I could have a minute with my hand was exactly what I needed. It didn't take long. Thoughts of the way her head fell back on a gasp, the way her tight little body rocked against mine, desperate for relief. The way her lips parted for me when I'd kissed her.

Quickest shower-slash-hand job of my life.

I was dressed and knocking on her back door in no time.

Easton opened the door, one brow raised, as if he knew exactly what I'd just been up to.

"All good, buddy?" he asked.

"Yep. Just needed to catch a quick shower."

"I'll bet you did." He chuckled. "I hope you're hungry."

I didn't see Emerson anywhere, so I assumed she was showering as well. Easton had cleaned the place up, and he had a large bag of takeout food from The Golden Goose on the kitchen table.

"Thanks for grabbing food for me, too."

"Thanks for being there for my sister. She's been through a lot," he said, handing me a beer.

"Of course. She's been really good to my boy."

"She talks about Cutler every time I speak to her. Says he's the coolest kid she's ever met, which is saying a lot because she's been around a ton of kids, being in pediatrics." He sat at the table and motioned for me to do the same.

"He's a cool little dude, no doubt about it."

"You raise him on your own?" he asked, before taking a long pull from his bottle.

"Yep. His mom took off shortly after he was born, so it's just been me and him, and I've had a lot of support from friends and my father. We do all right."

"And you own a construction company?"

I nodded. "I do. My buddy and I opened it together, and we've built a ton of the properties in town over the years."

"That's pretty damn cool."

"Thanks. You're a lawyer, huh?" I asked. "Twin siblings and one is a doctor, and one is a lawyer. That's quite the impressive package."

He barked out a laugh. "Nah. Emmy's the impressive one, trust me. She was top of her class and always driven. A fucking rock star at her sport. She probably didn't mention that she'd even approached trying out for the Olympic team at one point."

"Wow. No, she didn't mention it. I'm guessing that would have interfered with her dreams of being a doctor?"

"Yeah. She's just determined, you know? At everything she does. Always has been. I was more of a fuck-up before I found

139

my way. I wasn't the best student, but I'm damn good in a courtroom." He held his bottle up, and I clinked mine against his.

"She claims she was a bit of a troublemaker as a kid, but I find that hard to believe."

"You need to fucking believe that one. She worked hard to keep up with her brothers and cousins, being the only girl. The mailman banned all of us kids from the post office for a few years when we were young, because she'd been turning on the sprinklers every time he walked up to our door with the mail. He'd run off to the other side of the yard, and she'd turn those on," he said, over a fit of laughter. "This went on for a whole summer until he figured out someone was messing with the timers. We were all hellions, but she was the clever one when it came to pranking people. So watch your back."

"Good to know."

"Are you out here shit talking me, E? Don't listen to this guy," Emerson said, as she strolled out to the kitchen wearing a white tank top and a pair of fitted joggers. Her hair was long and damp, and her face was clean of makeup. Fucking stunning. "There was a wanted sign with Easton's picture on it hanging on several storefronts in Rosewood River when we were maybe ten years old."

Damn. This was my kind of guy.

"That was Mr. fucking Harley raising hell because he blamed me for his pig going missing. I was framed."

They were both laughing hysterically now, and I had no idea what they were talking about, but I couldn't help but laugh along with them.

"Easton," Emerson said, her voice serious.

"Emerson."

"You dressed Mr. Pinkleton in my tutu and rhinestone tank top. He's a farmer. What did you think he would do?" Tears were streaming down her face as she tried to stop her laughter, and they explained that Mr. Pinkleton was Mr. Harley's pig.

"Bridger and Clark stole the damn pig and dared me to dress it up." He shrugged, and she explained those were their other brothers. "You know I can't slack on a dare."

"Well, our cousins, Axel and Archer, were supposed to be the lookout guys, and they left his gate open," Emerson said, turning her attention to me as Easton and I dove into our burgers. "His chickens got out, and his pig was his prized possession, so having Mr. Pinkleton show up in that outfit put the old man over the edge. He made these wanted signs with Easton's photo and hung them on store windows all over town."

"I was ten years old and not hiding. I lived next door to the asshole. He was being dramatic, and he got my ass grounded for two weeks that summer. I'm the one who gathered all his chickens and put them back where they belonged. And Mr. Pinkleton sure as hell didn't mind that outfit one bit."

I barked out a laugh and shook my head.

"You guys sound like you got yourselves into plenty of trouble as kids," I said, reaching for my beer.

"I'm guessing you were a bit of a hellion, too?" Easton said, with a wicked grin on his face as he looked at me.

"What gives you that impression?"

"I don't know. You carried my sister out to the water in a wedding gown. You're clearly not an overthinker. She couldn't even get her prick of an ex to agree to jump into the water for a photo after their wedding. You went willingly. I'm guessing you know how to have a good time."

"Well, I wasn't exactly a Boy Scout," I said, trying to hide my smile.

We spent the next hour sharing stories about both Rosewood River and Magnolia Falls. Emerson wanted to know how I'd met my four best friends, who were more like brothers to me. We'd grown up together and always had one another's backs. She told her brother about our matching Ride or Die tattoos, and I shared that RoD was the name of my construction company.

I guessed, in a way, I had a big family, too. They weren't blood, but they were family.

No doubt about it.

After we finished eating, I figured they'd want some time alone, since her brother was flying home late tonight, so I pushed to my feet and helped clean up our trash. "Thanks for dinner. I'm going to head home and get some sleep."

"Cutler's spending the night at J.T.'s?" Emerson asked.

"Yeah. I'll pick him up in the morning."

She nodded, taking a sip from her water bottle. She'd stopped drinking and was clearly starting to sober up after eating. "Well, thanks for—everything."

"Of course. I appreciate the burger." I moved toward her brother, who was standing now, and extended a hand. "Good to meet you."

"Yeah. You, too. Thanks for using that key and not forcing me to break a window."

"That's a bit dramatic," Emerson said, as she followed me to the door and surprised me when she stepped outside and pulled the door closed behind her.

"You walking me home, Sunny?" I said, my voice all tease.

"I just wanted to thank you for jumping into the water with me and, you know, the kiss and the—"

"You're a doctor. Say it. Thank you for the magnificent orgasm." I chuckled.

Her teeth sank into that juicy bottom lip, and damn if I didn't want to tug her close and kiss her again. I wasn't sure if this was a one-and-done, and she'd want to pretend it never happened.

"Thank you for the magnificent orgasm, Nash Heart."

"Was that so difficult?"

"Actually, no. Neither was the orgasm." She winked. "But you should know, that's never happened from a little make-out sesh." She stepped closer, her chest bumping into mine as we stood on her back porch.

"That's because you've been kissing a fucking dickhead for the last decade. A real man can make you come with his lips, his fingers, and his cock."

"Holy shit," she whispered. "You've got a filthy mouth."

"And I think you like it."

"What if I wanted to kiss you again?" she asked.

"It wouldn't be very neighborly to deny you. But keep in mind, your brother is on the other side of that window, so I don't think he'd appreciate the show that went on out in the water." I smirked.

She pushed up onto her tiptoes and wrapped her arms around my neck as she tugged me down. Her lips were on mine, gentle at first, before her tongue slipped in. My dick sprung to life immediately, and my arms wrapped around her as I tilted her head back and took the kiss deeper.

I couldn't get enough of this woman.

When she pulled back, I was stunned that my first thought was that I missed her.

Missed her lips on mine.

Missed the way her fingers ran through my hair.

"Let's just sit with this for a minute, all right?" she whispered. "But I like kissing you, Nash Heart."

"I like it, too," I said, and smacked her on the ass when she turned around, and she squealed at the contact. "'Night, Sunny."

She waved before pulling open the door and stepping inside.

And I knew I was fucked. Because normally, a woman telling me she liked kissing me would freak me out. But this woman was different. And I couldn't wait to kiss her again.

LAURA PAVLOV

Lucky for me, I was exhausted, and I fell asleep quickly.
When I woke up, I was surprised I'd slept in later than usual. I
sent a text to J.T.'s dad, Jay, and let him know I'd grab donuts
and head over to pick up Cutler.

I'd promised to take Cutler out on the boat today, and we
were going to cruise over and meet up with everyone over at
Kingston's house.

I got him changed into his swimsuit and covered in a shit
ton of sunscreen before walking out the back door. I glanced
over at Emerson's house and saw Winnie sitting on the back
porch and a pitcher of lemonade on the table. Had she seen us
and run inside to hide?

Was she going to avoid me again after that fucking kiss?

Cutler was already running toward Winnie, and I didn't
stop him. I had a bone to pick with my neighbor. Not to
mention, the bone I'd been dealing with since we'd made out
like teenagers last night. I'd been rock-hard ever since, and
she wasn't going to ignore me when I was dealing with an
uncomfortable boner.

I followed Cutler up to the porch and noticed the door was
wide open. I peeked my head in. "Hey, Emerson, are you here?"

She came around the corner, wearing a pink bikini top and
a pair of jean shorts, and my mouth went dry immediately.
"Hey, what's up?"

I told Cutler to stay on the porch with Winnie and stepped
toward her. "I saw Winnie and the lemonade, and I wondered
if you ran into the house to avoid me."

The corners of her lips turned up, and she raised a brow.
"Why would I avoid you?"

"Because it's kind of your thing. But I'm about done with it.
It was a kiss. Don't make it bigger than it is and get all weird
and hide out in here every time I'm outside for another week.
It's ridiculous." I didn't hide my irritation. This woman was so
far under my skin I couldn't see straight.

She raised a brow. "Wow. All right. Good to know. But that's not what I was doing."

"What were you doing?"

"Well, I saw your truck pull up, and I was going to get my phone to text you and see if you and Cutler wanted to hang out today. I thought I'd be hungover, but instead, I feel damn good. Maybe it was the kiss or the magnificent orgasm . . . even if you're claiming that it *wasn't* a big deal. It was kind of a big deal to me." She chuckled and held up her phone, just as mine vibrated in my pocket. I pulled it out.

CHADWICK

What are you and Cutler up to today, neighbor?

I typed out a quick text, and she glanced down at her phone.

We're taking the boat over to King's to swim and hang out on the water. You're coming with us.

She chuckled and started typing, even though we were standing close enough that I could lean down and kiss her.

And damn, did I want to.

CHADWICK

Are you always so bossy?

Yes. Get over it. I want you to come with us. Do you need me to beg? Because I will.

CHADWICK

No need. All you had to do was ask, and I would have said yes.

Good to know, for future reference.

CHADWICK

Okay. I'm ready.

Let's go.

We both laughed, and she was cute as hell. I pulled the door open.

"Sunny's coming with us," I said, and my son started jumping up and down.

"Can Winnie come, too?"

"Sure. Uncle King said that Dandelion needs a friend. They can play together." Kingston's puppy had a ton of energy, and I knew he'd be thrilled if we brought someone to wear her out.

"Yes!" Cutler punched his fist to the sky with excitement.

Emerson grabbed a beach bag and filled it with a few things before looking over at us. "You have the inhaler?"

"Yep," I said, motioning to my backpack. But damn, if I didn't like the way she looked out for my boy.

And as we walked toward the dock, Cutler's hand slipped into Emerson's, and my fucking chest squeezed so tight it was hard to breathe.

She fit in with us perfectly.

Like she belonged here.

And that was scary as hell.

16

Emerson

We took the boat over to Kingston's house, and Cutler reached for my hand when I stepped off and onto the dock there. He seemed thrilled to have me and Winnie tagging along, and I was surprised that I'd wanted to come.

But I did.

I was tired of sitting alone and sulking about a life plan that had gone amiss.

It was time to move forward.

And not just by being angry and throwing myself into work.

It was time to move forward by living my best life.

Today was supposed to be my wedding day, and for whatever reason, it no longer felt like a loss. I was exactly where I wanted to be.

"Winnie!" Demi called out when my pup charged toward her, Saylor, and Peyton.

"Dandelion is going to be so happy that you brought her," Saylor said.

And in a blur, both dogs were running in circles and wrestling around on the grass. Cutler took off after them, and we all laughed at how quickly they seemed to be fast friends.

"Winnie's never going to want to go back to city living after spending six months here," Ruby said, giving me this knowing look as she continued. "Trust me. I never thought I'd stay, but this place has a way of growing on you."

I'm already realizing that.

"I'm glad you're here," Demi said, as we made our way to sit on the Adirondack chairs on the patio.

"Cutler, we're taking out the jet skis," Nash called after him, and then his eyes found mine. "Are you fine here?"

"Look at you, being all attentive and thoughtful," Kingston said as he waggled his brows.

Nash flashed him the bird, and everyone chuckled.

"I'm fine. Thank you."

He dropped his backpack next to my chair, and they all took off and piled onto the jet skis and paddle boards that Kingston had on his dock. I watched as Nash put a life jacket on Cutler and then took his hand and helped him onto the jet ski where he sat in front of his father.

"Are you telling me that you don't find it sexy, seeing the way that man fathers little Beefcake?" Peyton said.

I smiled and shook my head. "I don't think there's a woman on the planet with a pulse that doesn't find that man sexy."

"Oh. We're admitting it now. I like it," Ruby said, as Saylor handed us each a bottle of water from the cooler before sitting back down.

"Just speaking the truth," I said. "I've never denied that he's gorgeous."

"I heard you stayed home sick yesterday?" Demi asked. "No one misses a beat in Magnolia Falls. Oscar Daily let me know you hadn't gone to work first thing in the morning when he stopped in for his coffee." We all shared a laugh because the man didn't have young kids, but he somehow seemed to know everything going on with everyone in town.

I sighed and filled them in on the entire fiasco that was my day yesterday.

"So, today would have been your wedding day?" Saylor had so much empathy in her gaze when she asked the question, it made my chest squeeze.

"Yeah. But I'm happy that I'm sitting here with all of you instead of walking down the aisle. And, in a weird way, after jumping into the water in my wedding gown yesterday, I feel like I've got closure with everything." I chuckled.

"It's okay if you're feeling sad today. You can talk to us," Demi said, as Winnie and Dandelion came over and settled on the patio together, lying down and sprawling out in front of us.

"I'm actually feeling really good. It's not the wedding or even Collin that I struggle with at this point. In the end, it's Farah that I'm most hurt by, which doesn't make a lot of sense. I was planning to spend my whole life with Collin, yet I feel sort of relieved that it all blew up. But getting her call yesterday . . . that hit me hard."

"Do you want my opinion?" Ruby asked, and everyone leaned forward, resting their elbows on their knees like they couldn't wait to hear what she was going to say.

"Sure. I'd love to wrap my head around this."

"Well, from what you've shared, it's the betrayal that hurt more than the fact that you lost the love of your life, which tells me that he wasn't really that person for you. But either way, having a man that you thought you would spend the rest of your life with betray you with your lifelong best friend—yeah, that'll leave a mark. Of course, it hurts." She took a sip of water, and her gaze locked with mine, as if she were asking if I wanted more.

I nodded. "That makes sense."

"Do you want my theory on this?" she asked.

"Oh, I love it when Ruby gives us her theories. She's always spot on," Peyton said, and they all nodded in agreement.

"Sure. Lay it on me."

"I think you dated Collin for most of your adult life. He was your only boyfriend, so you had nothing to compare him to. You made plans when you guys were young, and you held up your end of the bargain. Sort of like the mentality, *if it ain't broke, don't fix it*." She shrugged, and I nodded, following her easily. It all made sense. "You were busy becoming a doctor and working hard, and you settled because he didn't give you a reason not to."

"Until he became a complete dickhead and banged your bestie." Peyton raised a brow. "Hello! Wake-up call. They actually did you a favor, even though it probably didn't feel that way at first."

I laughed because there was some truth to her words, but the way they went about it definitely didn't feel like a favor. "I'm sure they could have handled it better, but I get what you're saying."

"You dodged a bullet," Saylor said.

"Agreed." Demi squeezed my hand. "And we scored by getting the best doctor in town."

"Have you started applying to other hospitals yet? I know you said you aren't planning on staying, but I'm still hoping this town grows on you." Saylor pushed to her feet and smiled.

"I did hear back from a few hospitals, and I have some interviews set up over the next couple of weeks. But Boston Children's is my top choice. It's where I wanted to do my residency, but Collin didn't want to leave San Francisco because his job was there, and our families were not far, being in Rosewood River." I shook my head because that decision had all been based around this future that I was so hellbent on having at the time. But, at the end of the day, I allowed that to steer me, and that was on me. I wouldn't make that mistake again. Moving forward, all decisions will be my own.

"Anyway, they called, and I have an interview with them in a few weeks."

They all squealed and clapped and shared their enthusiasm with me before Saylor went inside to bring the veggie and fruit platters outside for us to munch on.

Something caught my attention in my peripheral, and I don't know how I knew, but the way Nash shouted my name—I just knew. I was already moving and reaching for the inhaler in his backpack as I sprinted toward the dock.

He pulled up on the jet ski and lifted Cutler off just as I arrived. He was gasping and struggling for air, and I dropped to the ground as Nash set him on my lap and I shook the inhaler.

"This is going to help. We're going to take four puffs, okay?" I kept my voice calm as his back melded against my chest. I held the device to his lips, and we counted out as he breathed in the medication.

Nash hovered above us, knees bent and eyes panicked.

Water dripped from his body, splashing against my arm, but I kept my focus on Cutler.

With each puff, I felt his breathing slow slightly, but it meant that it was working. Cutler's little hand wrapped around my forearm as if he wanted to hold me there.

"I'm not going anywhere, I promise. You're okay. That's what the medication is for." My heart raced, but my voice continued to stay calm.

It was important.

Nash's gray gaze found mine.

He's okay. This is normal with asthma. You did everything right by bringing him right back here.

I didn't say the words, but I knew he understood them because he nodded slightly.

I hadn't even realized everyone had gathered around now, as I'd tuned everything out but Cutler and Nash.

River, Kingston, Romeo, and Hayes were all surrounding Nash, and I glanced over my shoulder to see Ruby, Saylor, Peyton, and Demi all standing there, watching with concern.

I stroked Cutler's damp hair away from his face as his breathing began to slow.

"He's okay," I said, and I could feel the silent relief coming off their bodies. Cutler surprised me when he turned slightly and nestled his head beneath my chin. I wrapped my arms around him. "You're all right. I promise you are."

Nash was just watching me. Watching his son. Concern was still laced in that soulful gaze of his as he moved closer and ran a hand down Cutler's back.

"You all right, buddy?"

Cutler nodded in response but didn't speak just yet. It was a scary feeling when you couldn't catch your breath, and my guess was that he was just taking a minute until he felt confident enough to talk.

"What happened?" River asked. "I just saw you pull him out of the water before I even realized what was happening."

"He wanted to swim," Nash said, and now those concerned eyes were riddled with guilt. That was the thing with asthma: It could come out of nowhere. And parents would feel horrible and responsible, even though it wasn't their fault at all. Nash had a plan in place, and he'd stuck to it. In the future, I would recommend carrying the inhaler in a waterproof bag and taking it with him, but he was close enough that he made it back in plenty of time. Cutler's lips weren't blue; his color was still there. He just needed the medication for quick relief. "He was jumping around in the water, and he started coughing at first. I could tell something was wrong, so I got him out of there immediately, and I was glad I did, because he started wheezing as soon as I got him on the jet ski."

"What triggers it?" Ruby asked, as she dropped to sit beside me and kissed his cheek.

"It could be seasonal allergies, the pollen from the trees, or he could have a cold starting. It's hard to know. And he might not have another flare-up for weeks or months." I looked up at Nash, who was looking away at the water, deep in thought. I reached for his arm and tapped it, waiting for him to look at me. "You did everything right. He's fine."

He nodded and let out a long breath. "I should have brought the inhaler with me."

"It wasn't necessary today, but it wouldn't hurt in the future. You can get a waterproof bag and keep it on you, just in case. But it wouldn't have made a huge difference. His breathing relaxed immediately. This is a stronger medication than he had before, and it works quickly."

"Pops," Cutler whispered.

"Yeah?"

"Stop worrying. I just like hugging my girl, Sunny." His voice was tired but laced with humor, and laughter erupted around us.

"That's our boy," Romeo said.

Kingston sighed and leaned his head back against the dock, as if the relief was overwhelming him. Saylor went and settled on his lap.

And we all just sat there in the sunshine, me holding the sweetest boy on the planet, and all my new friends surrounding us.

Cutler slowly came back to life, and he put his hand on my cheek. "You know you're my girl forever now."

I nodded. "I like the sound of that."

"Damn. Beefcake is locking down his girls even when he's not feeling a hundred percent," River said with a chuckle.

We all moved to our feet to make our way back to the yard, because Kingston said he'd get the food going on the grill. And just like that, Cutler was walking with Saylor to go see Winnie and Dandelion.

"Hey, take it easy, buddy," Nash called out. He and I were the last two still standing on the dock, and the back of his hand grazed mine where we stood, and he just stared at me.

My teeth sank into my bottom lip, and I glanced toward the yard as I watched everyone carry out the food and place it on the big outdoor table where we'd be eating. Cutler was sitting on the patio with Saylor and the dogs. I turned back to look at Nash. "Hey, are you okay?"

He gave me that quick, simple nod I was learning was his way of answering without speaking, but then he surprised me. "Thank you. Thank you so fucking much."

"Nash." I shook my head. He was giving me way too much credit.

"Emerson."

I chuckled. "You did everything right."

"No. You made this one a hell of a lot better than the last one. There was no ambulance this time. You knew exactly what to do. You're not only a damn good doctor, but you're a damn good woman."

"Well, now you're just making me blush."

"I like making you blush." His tongue peeked out and dipped into the corner of his lips as he smiled. "I know today is a tough day for you, but I'm glad you decided to hang out with us."

"I mean, you did jump into the water with me yesterday; it's the least I could do."

"Yeah. I'm still thinking about what happened out in that water." He leaned forward and whispered against my ear. His breath tickled my skin, and I squeezed my eyes closed and did everything I could to control my breathing.

"That was pretty fun, huh?"

He pulled back to look at me. "Have dinner with me and Cutler tonight."

My heart raced at his words. I'd kissed him last night. I was here today.

I wasn't ready for anything serious. Hell, I didn't know if I'd ever be ready for anything serious again.

My life was still up in the air.

But I let my heart do the talking. My stupid, silly heart that had led me astray in the past.

But the words were out of my mouth before I could stop them. "I'd love to."

17

Nash

KING

Emerson is great. We needed a doctor in the group. So try not to fuck this up.

RIVER

No pressure there at all.

First of all, she was supposed to be marrying someone else today. Second, she isn't staying in Magnolia Falls. Third, I don't do relationships. I'm a father, remember? That's a full-time job.

ROMEO

That's what I thought when I met Demi.

KING

You thought you were a father?

ROMEO

No, dickweed. I thought I didn't do relationships.

HAYES

Well, you're married, Golden Boy, so you were clearly wrong about that. But I get it. I don't do relationships either. Too messy. And I'm not even a single dad.

RIVER

You're just a grumpy dickhead.

HAYES

Truth. And I like it that way.

KING

Well, I was the ultimate playboy, and I fell hard and fast for my girl. So, never say never.

HAYES

How about you stop talking about my sister on the group thread.

KING

Speaking of your sister, I need everyone's help. I want to propose, but it needs to be grand. Big. Memorable.

RIVER

Proposal by sticky note?

ROMEO

Those sticky notes did work out for you, but he wants something big. King, how about you take her out on the boat?

KING

Too basic.

Take her horseback riding somewhere overlooking the water.

KING

Sorry. I just fell asleep. Way too boring.

HAYES

She loves that shit you do with your whole dandelion shtick. Take her out to that field full of allergens out by Demi's parents' ranch and propose to her there. You two can make all sorts of sappy wishes on those weeds.

KING

Hayes? Did someone kidnap you and steal your phone? This is what I'm talking about. I'll take her to the dandelion field, send her on a scavenger hunt, and then have one of those planes fly overhead and write the words: "Will you marry me, Dandelion?" in the sky. Followed by champagne out in the field. Maybe a little sexy time so that I make it memorable.

HAYES

I'm going to beat the shit out of you when I see you next.

ROMEO

RIVER

Dude has a death wish. Everything else sounds good. Slightly over the top, but it's very . . . you.

Agreed. I've got to go.

ROMEO

Yes, your neighbor who you aren't dating, but seem to be spending an awful lot of time with, is coming over for dinner, right?

KING

After spending the whole day together.

RIVER

Sounds kind of like a relationship. And this may be her wedding day, but the wedding was called off a few months ago. She seems like she's over it. Make your move.

HAYES

Hey, maybe she just wants something casual. That plays into your hands.

KING

She's dated one dude in her life, and she was supposed to marry him. She doesn't strike me as a casual girl.

HAYES

Go plant some dandelions, dickmunch.

RIVER

Don't overthink it. See where it goes. If all else fails, tell her you like her on a sticky note. Because we can all tell that you like her.

I set my phone down and looked over at Cutler, who was doing a puzzle on the coffee table. He found this new love for puzzles a few months ago. When the kid wasn't running around outside, this was what he wanted to do.

I loved the concentration and how intently he focused. It's how I felt when I was building and creating something with my hands. I loved taking an old, rundown shack and turning it into a home.

Maybe my boy inherited some of that creativity from me. I had pasta boiling on the stovetop and the meatballs in the oven. This was Cutler's favorite meal and one of the few things I made well, aside from barbecue.

At least I thought I did, but this was all according to a six-year-old, so for all I knew, my cooking was shit.

My phone vibrated, and I was surprised to see another text from Tara. This was way more communication than we'd had since the day she'd left.

TARA

Hey, I'm still planning to come in a few weeks. I'm looking into an Airbnb, unless you'd be cool with me staying with you?

What the actual fuck?

That's not an option.

TARA

I wish you had a little more faith in me. I think Cutler would enjoy spending time with me.

I ignored the comment because she wasn't in a position to ask me to trust her. She didn't know shit about parenting

161

or kids or Cutler, for that matter. She didn't know that he loved puzzles and that he loved to swim and play baseball. She didn't know about his asthma or the scares we'd had over the last few months. She didn't know that he ate his cereal dry unless I allowed him to have chocolate milk on his Cheerios, which, apparently, he got at his uncles' homes whenever he stayed over there. She didn't know that he loved to ride horses and that he had a heart that was so big it concerned me because I wondered how I was going to protect this kid from getting it broken in the future. She didn't know that he was a massive flirt and a jokester and that he'd been collecting baseball cards for the last two years. She didn't know that at every parent-teacher conference I'd ever attended, I'd been told that my son always looked out for the kids who weren't included.

My boy was a fucking rock star.

I knew it. My father knew it. My friends knew it. All the people in Cutler's life knew it.

But she wasn't one of them, so it pissed me off that she would have the audacity to tell me how things would go down.

Maybe River was right, and it was time to force her hand legally, so we wouldn't have to jump through hoops on the rarity that she came to town.

There was a knock on the back door, and Cutler went running in that direction. The only thing that could distract him from his puzzle right now was Emerson and Winnie.

I wiped my hands on the towel and made my way toward the door. My stomach was twisting a little bit, which surprised me. Women didn't make me nervous. But I sure as hell didn't date a whole lot anymore, and I hadn't had a woman over to my house for dinner since the day Cutler was born.

So maybe I *was* fucking nervous.

I definitely liked her. But I also knew the score. I was a single dad, and my priority would always be my kid. I didn't

162

have room in my life for relationships. She was supposed to be marrying someone else today, so she wasn't looking for anything either. She'd be leaving town in a few months, so there was no point getting attached.

Yet here we were.

My kid loved her. She was his pediatrician. She lived next door.

She'd known exactly what to do today when I'd freaked out after I'd noticed his change in breathing.

And I couldn't get that fucking kiss from yesterday out of my head.

It was just a damn kiss.

So what if it was the best kiss I'd ever had?

It. Meant. Nothing.

"What did you make us?" Cutler asked, as I came around the corner and took her in. She wore a little white top with spaghetti straps tied in bows on her golden shoulders. A matching skirt that slung low on her hips, and the slightest bit of tanned, toned abs were showing with her arms raised, holding some sort of plate in her hands. My mouth was dry at just the sight of her. When was the last time I was this awestruck by a woman?

Probably never.

I didn't know what it was about her, but I was reacting in ways that were foreign to me. I reached for the plate she was holding, and her jade eyes locked with mine. Long brown waves fell around her shoulders, and her lips parted when my fingers grazed hers.

"Thank you," she said, before turning her attention back to Cutler. "I made you my favorite unicorn Rice Krispie treats. They're my specialty."

"You're a doctor *and* a baker?" Cutler asked.

"Baking is one of my guilty pleasures. When I was in medical school, and then during residency, it was how I'd spend my time off. Just trying out different recipes and turning off my brain for a few hours."

"Hey, Pops, do I know how to turn off my brain?" Cutler asked. "And how come we never bake?"

They both followed me into the kitchen, and I set the Rice Krispie treats down on the counter before turning off the pasta and pouring the noodles into a strainer, as they both sat down at the kitchen island across from me.

"Well, we don't bake because I don't know how to. I can make spaghetti and macaroni and cheese, and I'm good on the barbecue. That's as far as my kitchen skills go. But if I'd known I could turn off my brain if I baked, I might have tried it sooner." I chuckled as I turned toward Emerson. "What can I get you to drink?"

I was surprised when she said she'd have a beer, which was what I was drinking. I figured she'd ask for a glass of wine, which is why I'd set a few bottles out on the counter for her.

"Can I take Winnie to my bedroom to show her my baseball card collection?" Cutler asked.

"Sure. Dinner will be ready in about ten minutes."

"Yes!" he shouted as he ran down the hall, with Winnie on his heels. "Wait till you try the 'sketti and meatballs. My grandpa says my pops has got the best balls in town."

Emerson spewed beer across the counter and then jumped to her feet with surprise. I barked out a laugh and grabbed some paper towels, making my way over to her and wiping the counter before pausing as I stood in front of her. My gaze locked with hers. "Do my balls make you nervous?"

She pinned her bottom lip between her teeth. "Everything about you makes me nervous."

That was unexpected. I raised a brow. "I guess the feeling's mutual then."

"Are you saying I make you nervous?" she said, her tone teasing.

"Something like that." My thumb grazed along her bottom lip, and damn if I didn't want to kiss her right here, right now.

We stood there flirting with one another for a few minutes before I heard footsteps coming down the hallway.

"Is dinner ready, Pops?" Cutler yelled. I stepped back, and Emerson cleared her throat before reaching for her beer.

"It's ready. Let me get this onto the table." I plated the food, and Emerson came around and grabbed the salad and garlic bread and carried it out to the table for me.

"Why do I always have to have the plain milk with dinner?" my son asked, and I shot him a warning look. I didn't do the whiny bullshit, and he knew it. He was only asking because we had company, so he was pushing his luck.

"Cutler," I said, my voice firm, as we all took our seats.

"Pops. You know I like for you to call me Beefcake."

"Fine. You know the rules, Beefcake. Don't try to work me over just because we've got a pretty lady at the table."

"She is pretty, isn't she?" he said.

"*She* can hear you, you know?" Emerson said with a laugh. "Thank you for saying I'm pretty. Now, tell me what the rule is about the milk."

"I only get chocolate milk on Friday night. We do pizza and chocolate milk. But the other nights, I have to have plain milk." Cutler made a face, and he had a big milk mustache on his lip. "But when I go to my uncles' houses, I always get the chocolate milk."

"Which uncle breaks the rule?" she asked, as she placed some salad on her plate.

"All of them." My boy twirled his noodles around his fork and popped it into his mouth.

"Bunch of traitors," I said, my eyes zeroing in on her mouth when she groaned after taking her first bite of a meatball.

"Don't you think my pops has the best balls?" Cutler said, as he looked at her too.

165

She finished chewing, a wide grin on her face, as she nodded. "Yep. He's definitely got the best balls in town."

Loud laughter escaped my mouth, and Cutler shook his head and smiled before talking over a mouthful of food. "I've never heard you laugh so much before. I think you like Sunny and Winnie just as much as I do."

"They're fine," I said, my voice pure humor.

"Pops didn't like you when you first moved in, but now I see him looking over at your house all the time when we're outside."

When did Cutler start throwing me under the fucking bus?
I raised a brow and looked at him.

"What? You know it's true, Pops," he said over his laughter. I leaned forward and wiped the milk mustache from his lip.

"Maybe I'm just making sure the fence can hold Winnie in the yard," I said.

More laughter.

These two thought the whole thing was hilarious.

"I think you're right, Beefcake. I think he's looking for us." Emerson spun her pasta around her fork, just like my son did. "And I'd be lying if I said I wasn't looking over here all the time, too."

I took a pull from my bottle as my gaze locked with hers.

I liked the idea of her looking over here more than I should.

It had been a long time since I'd wanted a woman like this.

And there was no doubt about it.

I wanted this woman something fierce.

18

Emerson

I worked on the puzzle with Cutler and Nash while Winnie fell asleep on their couch. We had Rice Krispie treats, and they both gave me way too much credit by acting like I'd cured a freaking deadly disease because I put colorful sprinkles in them and called them unicorn Krispies. Cutler made me promise to teach him how to make them sometime soon.

Nash went to bathe his son, and I'd thought that was my cue to leave, but he'd asked me to stay. So I'd done the dishes and taken Winnie out back before settling on his couch.

"Sunny, I came to say goodnight. Pops said I can't ask you to read me a book though, so I'm just giving you a hug." Cutler looked like the cutest thing I'd ever laid eyes on. His pajamas were covered in little hot dogs, and his hair was damp and slicked back in his typical fashion. He had large dark eyes and these pink little cheeks and the cutest button nose.

"Hey. I told you not to ask her," Nash grumped, shaking his head at his son.

"I didn't ask. I just told her that I wasn't allowed to ask her." He waggled his brows and leaned forward to hug me. He smelled like coconut and sunshine, and I imagined the coconut

167

was his body wash and shampoo, and the sunshine was just a Cutler Heart thing.

"What if I would like to read him a book?" I asked, pushing to my feet.

"Unbelievable." Nash threw his hands in the air. "You're too slick for your own good, Beefcake."

"And you've got the best balls in town, Pops."

My head fell back in laughter. This little boy was like a breath of fresh air for me. After the bitterness I'd felt these last few months, being here, around Nash and his son, it was exactly what I'd needed.

I had a new perspective on life in a way. I wasn't mopey and sad anymore.

And today should be the day that I felt the most down in the dumps.

But as I walked down the hallway toward Cutler's bedroom, I felt anything but.

I felt like I'd dodged a bullet. Of course, the way the bullet had just missed me was an unpleasant experience, but I was grateful to be exactly where I was today.

I kicked off my sandals and hopped onto the bed beside Cutler, him beneath the covers and me on top. Nash sat in the chair beside the bed, and Winnie jumped up on his lap as if she were a lapdog, which she very much was not. We all laughed, and I turned the first page on his latest Junie B. Jones book. He chuckled a few times as I read two chapters.

His eyes were heavy, and his little hand was wrapped around mine, and I freaking loved it. He was so cuddly and cute, and I was happy to be in here, reading to him.

Nash pushed to his feet, helping Winnie off his lap before she jumped up on the foot of Cutler's bed.

"Can Winnie stay in here until Sunny goes home?" Cutler whispered, his voice sleepy. Nash glanced over at me as I climbed off the bed. I gave him a nod, and he agreed to let her stay for a little bit. I kissed Cutler on the cheek and patted my pup on the head as I followed Nash out of the room and down the hallway.

We'd barely made it to the kitchen, when he spun me around, pressed my back against the wall beside the refrigerator, and stepped closer.

"Did you really need to read two chapters?" His voice was gruff, eyes zoned in on my mouth.

I laughed. "Two chapters seemed fair."

"Do you know how badly I've wanted to kiss you for the last few hours? Hell, all fucking day. Do you have any idea how crazy you're making me?"

My tongue wet my bottom lip because my mouth went dry. "Tell me."

"Well, you come over here looking like a fucking vision, wearing this pretty white skirt and top," he said, his fingers tracing along the sliver of skin exposed on my stomach. His fingers were calloused, yet they moved so lightly, and I loved the feel against my skin. "Groaning when you ate my cooking and torturing me."

"Well, you do have the best balls in town, neighbor. Even gramps thinks so," I said, my voice laced with humor, even though my heart raced at his nearness.

At his touch.

At the look in his eyes as he watched me.

"I know today is a tough day for you, and I sure as shit don't want to push you. Hell, I don't know what I have to offer you, Emerson. But I know that I desperately want to kiss you again." His fingers continued the soothing motion back and forth along my skin, his other hand moving to the side of my neck.

"Today hasn't been tough at all, which is surprising. I don't know what that says about me."

"Maybe it says that you're moving forward," he said.

My hand moved to his chest, feeling the beat of his heart beneath my palm.

Beating heart.

I wanted to make him feel the way he made me feel.

I knew it couldn't go anywhere. We both had our reasons. But getting lost in this man right now was just too easy.

And exactly what I wanted.

What I needed.

"How about you? Are you moving forward?" I asked, desperate for his mouth to be on mine right now.

Apparently, I had zero patience when it came to Nash Heart.

"I've never had a woman for dinner with my son. I've never made out with a woman in the middle of the lake. I've never wanted anyone the way that I want you, and that's the fucking truth. I don't know what it means, but I know what I'm feeling is different."

I sucked in a breath at his words.

This is temporary. Don't get ahead of yourself. He's just attracted to you.

"I want you, too." I searched his gaze. "I've only been with one man, Nash. And I thought it was forever, and I was really wrong. So maybe not knowing what this is, is a good change for me. I want you. You want me. Why torture ourselves?"

His mouth was on mine, and he pressed his body into mine. I could feel every hard edge and muscle. My hands moved along his shoulders and down his arms.

He was strong and masculine, and I freaking loved the feel of his weight against me. He took control of the kiss, his tongue slipping into my mouth as it tangled with mine.

Desperate and needy.

It was different from the kiss yesterday.

We were both all in now.

There was no hesitation.

No apprehension.

We wanted this.

I ground my hips against him, and he reached behind me, his hands cupping my ass and lifting me up. My legs came around his waist, just like they had out in the water. But this time, there was very little fabric between us, and I felt everything.

Everything.

He carried me down the hallway, his lips never leaving mine. Before I processed what was happening, he walked into his bedroom and closed the door quietly, before dropping me onto his bed.

I was overwhelmed with feelings. I wanted him. Wanted this. But I hadn't been with any man other than the one who had betrayed me in the worst way. All these thoughts were racing through my mind, and Nash must have picked up on it.

"Hey," he said, leaning over me from where he stood at the foot of the bed. "Don't go overthinking this. I didn't bring you in here to have sex."

Well, those weren't the words I wanted to hear either. I raised a brow. "And why not?"

"Because you were supposed to marry another man today. Because you've only been with one dickhead in your life, and we're not going to rush this. I just wanted to bring you somewhere that I could make you feel good without worrying that a nosy six-year-old or an overzealous Bernedoodle would walk in on us."

"You're not having sex with me because my ex is a dickhead?" I pouted.

He ran his rough fingers along my jaw. "I'm not having sex with you *tonight*. And not because of him, but because there's no need to rush. This is new. We don't know what it is. So we'll take our time."

"I thought you didn't do relationships. Isn't this sort of your shtick? Casual sex. One-night stands. Flings. Hookups.

171

Whatever the kids are calling it these days," I said with a chuckle.

Had I ever been this comfortable with a man?

I'd dated Collin for more than a decade, and it was never like this. It was never easy and playful.

"Did you literally just list every description for a hookup that you know?"

"Yes, I believe I did."

He leaned down and nipped at my bottom lip before kissing me hard and groaning into my mouth. And just like that, my body was on fire again. My fingers tangled in his hair. I couldn't get enough.

I wanted more.

He pulled back and smirked. "Yes, casual hookups are normally my thing. Not that I do them a lot, but when I do go out and have some fun, it's always casual. But this feels different." He held up his hand to stop me. "I know you aren't staying, but while you're here, I want to do this right."

"You don't have to treat me like a porcelain doll. I'll be fine. I've made it clear that I want this. I want you."

"And you'll have me. But you've been fucked over enough for one lifetime. How about you let me treat you the way you deserve to be treated? Even if it's just for a few weeks or a few months."

A lump formed in my throat, and I nodded. "Fine. I can get on board with your chivalrous plan. So why are we here?"

"I said I was going to make you feel good, and I meant it. I can do that without sticking my dick in you, or didn't your ex ever show you how that's done?"

My breaths were coming faster now, as the anticipation of what he planned was building. "Well, you do have the best balls in town."

A wide grin spread across his face. "And the best tongue, too. Do you trust me?"

I shouldn't trust anyone, but I did trust this man. Maybe I was a fool. Maybe I'd get burned again. But I didn't care in the moment. I nodded, and his mouth was on mine again.

He kissed me until my lips ached. I bucked up against him, desperate for release, as we made out and dry-humped like horny teenagers. And just when I was ready to lose my mind, his hand moved to the hem of my skirt. Fingers slid up my thighs, and he slid my panties to the side and dipped in.

"Fuck," he hissed. "You're soaked."

My eyes fell closed at the feel of his fingers on my clit, teasing me the way they circled and then sliding down to my entrance.

"Nash," I groaned into his mouth before he pulled back.

"I know, baby. You're desperate to feel good. I've known it since the first time I saw you. I knew you needed to let go. And I can make you do that, if you trust me."

"I trust you," I whispered. "Now stop teasing me."

His free hand moved to my shoulder and slipped the strap of my blouse down my arm before doing it to the other side. I wasn't wearing a bra because I didn't have a whole lot there to cover, and I sure as hell hadn't realized I'd be lying like this in his bed. But I wasn't complaining because I'd never felt so good.

He sucked in a breath as his eyes raked over my breasts. My nipples were rock-hard, eager for his mouth on them. His fingers were stroking me between my thighs, and the sensation was almost too much.

"Look at those pretty pink nipples and perfect tits. Fuck, Emerson. You're so beautiful it's hard to look at you sometimes."

The irony was not lost on me.

I'd never felt more beautiful in my life than I did when this man was looking at me.

I barely knew him, yet he made me feel seen.

LAURA PAVLOV

His mouth covered my breast, tongue flicking my nipple, just as his finger slipped inside me, and I nearly lunged off the bed. He chuckled against my chest before moving to the other side, taking turns licking and tasting and driving me mad.

He did this for the longest time, sliding in a second finger and moving in and out in the perfect rhythm.

Over and over.

His mouth on my breasts, his fingers between my thighs.

I was panting and sweaty and desperate for release as I started to buck against him faster.

"Nash, please."

"Does this pretty little pussy want to come on my fingers?" he asked, pulling back to look at me, and his filthy mouth had me panting with desire.

"Yes," I said with a gasp.

He chuckled as he watched me, and he pumped his fingers faster as his thumb pressed against my clit, knowing exactly what I needed.

"Let go, baby. I've got you," he whispered, his gaze locked with mine as I rocked against him.

My teeth sank into my bottom lip, and I exploded.

White lights lit up the darkness behind my eyelids as my entire body shook and quaked. Pleasure lit every inch of me, and I cried out his name as I went over the edge.

It was the most powerful orgasm I'd ever experienced.

And I wished this night would never end.

19

Nash

I stared down at her.

Cheeks flushed.

Lips parted.

Hair falling around her, forming a goddamn halo, looking like an angel.

I couldn't look away. I stroked her hair away from her pretty face as her gaze locked with mine.

"Wow. Dinner with the best balls in town, and now you're giving out nightcap orgasms. I've never lived next door to someone who was quite so neighborly."

"Well, I've fixed the electrical and a water leak for the Halls a few times, but you're the first neighbor I've shared my fabulous balls with and graced with an orgasm."

"Speaking of balls," she said, tugging me down and rolling onto her side to face me. "How about I return the favor?"

I groaned when she slipped her hand into my gray joggers and stroked me over my briefs.

"I'd hate to deprive you of these spectacular balls." My voice was gruff.

She quickly shoved my joggers and my briefs down my

LAURA PAVLOV

thighs, and my dick sprung to life. Her eyes widened as she took me in, wrapping her hand around my shaft, moving it up and down as I rolled onto my back.

"Fuck," I hissed, because it felt too damn good. "Just like that."

She moved to her knees, bottom lip pinned between her teeth, as her heated gaze watched me. My hips started moving as she pumped harder.

Faster.

I reached up and wrapped my hand around her neck and tugged her down. I needed my mouth on hers. Now.

My lips crashed into hers, tongue slipping in when her lips parted for me. I fucked her mouth while I fucked her hand.

And nothing had ever felt better.

I moaned into her mouth as she continued working me with her hand.

My body tensed just as the most powerful orgasm shot through every inch of me. I erupted as a guttural sound left my throat, and I came hard.

She didn't pull back.

Didn't care that I was making a fucking mess.

She continued kissing me and running her hand up and down my shaft as I rode out every last bit of pleasure.

Once my breathing slowed, and she pulled back to look at me, she just smiled with this sexy look that had my chest squeezing in response. She pushed to her feet and moved to the bathroom, and I heard the water turn on. She came back with a damp washcloth and cleaned me up. I reached for it, but she pulled back.

I pushed the hair back from her face. "You don't need to do that. I can do it."

"I want to do it. You've done more for me over the last two days than you even realize." Her eyes were slightly wet with emotion, and she blinked a few times and looked away.

176

"Hey," I said, reaching up to turn her chin so she'd meet my gaze. "What's going on in that head of yours?"

She sighed and reached for my hand and placed it on her chest, over her heart. "You know how you said your heart only beat for Cutler?"

"Yeah."

"Well, for the last few months, I didn't know if mine would ever beat again. But can you feel that strong heartbeat there?" she asked, keeping her hand over mine. "I know this is just two neighbors having some fun, and it can't go anywhere, but I don't know . . . I feel like you've brought me back to life in a way, Nash. So, if this all ends right now, today, thank you for doing that."

Her words hit me hard. I understood that feeling when you weren't sure you'd ever feel anything again. I'd been closed off for a long time. Focused on Cutler. On giving him a good life.

I didn't regret a thing.

I'd walk through fire over and over until my skin was pure ash for that boy. But I wouldn't lie; it felt good to like the woman who was currently sitting beside me in my bed. Normally, I was one foot out the door.

I didn't feel any of that with Emerson.

"How about this—" I said, slipping the hair behind her ear before tucking my dick back into my pants and sitting forward. "We take it one day at a time. I know you came here to heal and to put the past behind you. There are no expectations here. But I'm also not going to lie and say I don't like being with you. So how about we just enjoy things for right now?"

She nodded, the corners of her lips turning up. "I can do that. I just don't want to confuse Cutler."

"You live next door. You're his doctor. He won't be confused. I've taught him to be neighborly," I said, waggling my brows, and she laughed and pushed to her feet. She moved to the bathroom, and I heard the water turn on again before she came out and clasped her fingers together.

"Okay. Well, thanks for a great dinner." She smirked. "I need to be up early. I'm going to grab Winnie and head home."

I nodded, and it surprised me that I was disappointed she was leaving. Of course, she was leaving. We weren't dating. We were friendly neighbors. Who enjoyed making out and trading orgasms.

Nothing more.

I'd never allowed a woman to stay the night in my home with my son here.

But as I followed her down the hallway, and she tiptoed into Cutler's room and patted Winnie to follow her out, I wondered what it would be like if she were here.

All the time.

Where the fuck did that come from?

When she got to the door, she turned around, and I was on her once again. I pinned her there beneath my weight and kissed her hard.

She was breathless when she pulled back and looked up at me. "I know we're not overthinking this, but I need to say something. I need to say it for myself. And it's okay if you want to run for the hills. I'd understand."

"Tell me."

"Well, if we are going to continue, you know, trading the orgasms," she said, pausing to look at me with those jade-green, intoxicating eyes.

"I plan on trading many more before you leave town." I ran the tip of my nose against hers.

"Well, obviously, you know my story. I've only been with one guy for the past too many years." She chuckled, but I could tell she was nervous by the way she was biting her lip.

"Agreed. You wasted a lot of time on an asshole."

"So, I'm all about having fun right now, but I'm not a girl who bounces around. It's just not who I am. And after what Collin did, I only have one rule that I just can't bend on. And I know this is casual and temporary and all of that."

"Emerson." I put my finger on her lips to stop her. "You don't need to explain anything. Tell me what the rule is."

"You can't be trading orgasms with someone else while we're—exploring things." She looked away as if she had no right to ask me to be monogamous with her.

I placed my thumb and pointer finger on each side of her chin and turned her to look at me. "That goes without saying. It's you and me having some fun. But only you and me."

I saw the relief in her eyes, and she nodded. "And if you wake up tomorrow and you're done exploring with me, just please tell me. I want us to be open with one another."

"Done. Same with you. We keep it casual and we're honest with one another. And while we're messing around, we don't mess around with anyone else. I couldn't agree more."

"Not a bad way to spend my almost wedding night, huh?"

"Hooking up with your neighbor instead of walking down the aisle with a douchebag? It's a win for sure."

Her head tipped back in laughter. "All right. I need to go."

My tongue dipped out and slid across my bottom lip as I pulled the door open. "I'll walk you out."

"It's Magnolia Falls, and I have a large dog with me."

"You have a giant stuffed animal, not a guard dog. And maybe I just want to enjoy the view of watching you walk away."

"So smooth." She shook her head as she walked down the steps and across the grass. And I did exactly what I said I would.

I watched her walk away.

Reminding myself that she'd be walking away permanently in a few months.

But for whatever reason, I just didn't care.

I'd always trusted my gut, and my gut was telling me to enjoy this time with her.

I waited until she was inside her house and she'd closed the door behind her, and I made my way back inside.

Once the house was locked up and I turned all the lights off, I made my way to my room. My phone was vibrating, and I knew exactly who it would be. I sat on the edge of my bed and opened the text chain from my boys to catch up.

KING

> I'm guessing dinner is going well. We haven't heard from Nash in hours.

ROMEO

> I think he likes her. I saw the way he was looking at her all day.

HAYES

> That doesn't change the fact that she's leaving in a few months. He's wise to be cautious.

RIVER

> You assholes do realize it's a group text, and he's going to see this, right?

KING

>

> Of course, we do, dicknugget. We're talking it through. I like that he actually likes someone. I was starting to worry that he might be broken.

I barked out a laugh. We really had no filter with one another, but calling me broken on a group chat was next level.

HAYES

He's not broken. He's damaged.

ROMEO

He's not broken or damaged. He's just cautious. He's raising a kid on his own. It's a full-time job.

RIVER

He's going to really enjoy catching up on these messages. 😵

KING

Cautious is a better word. And rightfully so. But he also deserves to be happy.

HAYES

I've got news for you. You can be happy without having the same woman in your bed every night. Nash does just fine.

KING

You can't just have flings for the rest of your life. Eventually, everyone wants to settle down.

HAYES

You were the one who was never going to settle down. Now you're an expert on relationships? 👆

RIVER

Listen, Nash is in a different place than we are. None of us have a kid to raise, nor are we doing it as a single parent. So, if he wants to have flings for the rest of his life, he can do that. He makes his own rules.

ROMEO

I have something to tell you, but I'd rather tell you when I know Nash is here.

RIVER

If you are going to get back in that ring and fight again, I'm going to lose my shit. I can't go through it again.

ROMEO

You can't watch ME get hit over and over?

RIVER

Correct.

HAYES

I fucking agree. It's the one and only time I've experienced human tears. They were coming from my eyes when you went down during that fight and crawled back to your feet. Fuck no. Not going there again.

KING

Sorry, dude. I agree. I don't support it. Plus, your face is just too pretty to look at right now. I don't like seeing it all swollen and discolored. It freaks me out.

ROMEO

Thanks. Well, lucky for me, and apparently all of you, I'm not getting back in the ring.

RIVER

Tell us.

ROMEO

Not until Nash is here.

For fuck's sake. I'm here. I'm slightly offended that I'm being psychoanalyzed, but I'll let it go. But I'm glad you aren't getting back in the ring again. I can't stomach seeing grumpy Hayes whimpering like a big ole baby.

HAYES

Real men cry. At least that's what King told me.

KING

My work here is done. Mic drop.

RIVER

We're waiting, Romeo.

ROMEO

Cutler is going to have a sibling or a cousin or a bestie. I'm not sure what it is since we are technically not blood-related.

KING

Nash is pregnant? 🤓 🤭

STFU. Beans is pregnant?

ROMEO

She is. We just took a test. She said we can't tell anyone yet because you're supposed to wait a few months. But she knows we don't keep secrets.

HAYES

Congrats, brother. Happy for you both.

RIVER

Fucking amazing. Cutler is going to be really happy about this, too.

KING

Holy shit. What if Romeo has a daughter, and Cutler falls in love with her? 😵

ROMEO

If I have a daughter, she won't be allowed to date until she's forty. But if Cutler wants to wait that long, he'd be my first choice.

This is really amazing, Ro. Cutler is going to watch out for that little girl or boy like a big brother. I won't tell him yet, because we all know little dude can't keep a secret. I'll let you and Demi tell him. I'm really happy for you.

My chest squeezed the slightest bit at the thought. Cutler had changed my life in so many ways—all of them for the better.

I'd become a man the day my son came into the world.

A father.

And even though it hadn't always been easy, it had been the greatest joy of my life.

And I was fucking thrilled for my friend to experience it. He and Demi would be amazing parents. That little voice in my head was always there, reminding me that I was failing my boy by not giving him a traditional family.

185

LAURA PAVLOV

But at the end of the day, he was loved. Deeply and fully. And hopefully, that would be enough.

KING

Damn. Romeo's going to be a dad. We're all growing up, aren't we?

RIVER

Yep. When is this big, grand dandelion proposal going to happen?

KING

Soon. I'll send you the details. We're all meeting at Whiskey Falls after. The girls and I are planning a little surprise party for Saylor after we get engaged.

HAYES

Pending she says yes.

KING

She says yes every night. 😉

HAYES

Sleep with one eye open, lover boy. 🖐

ROMEO

Excited for you, brother. Will you be inviting Emerson to the engagement party?

RIVER

Nice segue, Ro. Bringing us full circle.
How was the date?

It wasn't a date. It was dinner with my
neighbor.

KING

So nothing happened? No frisky time? 🔥

HAYES

Are you fucking drunk? What is wrong
with you?

KING

Just asking what everyone wants to know.

I never kiss and tell.

KING

I'm a vault. You tell me everything.

RIVER

You're a fucking broken vault, brother.

ROMEO

They don't call you Loose Lips Pierce for
nothing.

HAYES

You're worse than Cutler.

KING

He's evading. Obviously something happened, or he wouldn't have anything to hide.

RIVER

I think he likes her. He's being all secretive and gentlemanly now.

ROMEO

He definitely likes her.

HAYES

I think you're right.

KING

Of course I'm right. I called it weeks ago. He definitely likes her.

I chuckled and set my phone down. I wasn't going to respond. I ran a hand down my face and thought about it.

They were right.

They knew me well.

I definitely liked her.

20

Emerson

The next few weeks flew by in a blur. I was busy at work, and the locals were now treating me like I'd lived here my entire life. Oscar, who owned the local market, stopped by to see me almost daily with different ailments. It didn't matter that I was a pediatrician. He ignored me every single time that I reminded him about it.

This town had an open-door policy, and the locals did not hesitate to stop by.

"Hey," Lana said as she peeked her head into my office, and I hit send on the email to Boston Children's Hospital. I'd just confirmed the remote interview I had scheduled with them early next week. "Midge Longhorn is here, and I reminded her that this is a pediatric office, but she just brushed me off. She said you'd see her if I told you that it was an emergency."

I'd gotten to know Midge as I had eaten at her restaurant, The Golden Goose, several times over the last few weeks. Cutler and Nash loved the place, and seeing as I spent all my free time with them, we ate there often.

Did I mention I spend a lot of time with my neighbor?

LAURA PAVLOV

We traded kisses and orgasms like it was our day job. We'd yet to have sex, as Nash thought we should take it slow.

I didn't know if he was protecting me or himself at this point.

Because I was ready.

I'd never been so turned on by a man, and after years of having a dull sex life, I was ready to jump the man's bones.

But I wouldn't beg.

"Did she say what was wrong?"

"Nope. Just that she was adamant about seeing you."

I sighed and glanced down at my watch. I was meeting Demi, Ruby, Saylor, and Peyton at Whiskey Creek tonight for a happy hour girls' night. We'd grown close, and it had helped to heal the pain I still felt when I thought about Farah. I sent a quick text to them in our group chat, letting them know I would be running a little late due to Midge showing up unexpectedly.

"Okay, I'll meet her in room one. I know you need to head out, so I'll lock up. I'll see you tomorrow?"

"You're a saint. I'm going to continue to spend every day that you're here convincing you to stay."

I smiled and closed my laptop, before making my way down the hall to room one just as Midge arrived, holding a lollipop in her hand with a wicked grin on her face. "Thanks for seeing me, Dr. Chadwick. Doc Dolby never let me just drop in."

"Well, it's definitely better to make an appointment, but seeing as this is a pediatric office, I don't think that would have worked either."

"I can't go to see Davis Ward about this issue."

Davis was the family medicine doctor in Magnolia Falls, and he'd seemed pleasant enough the two times I'd met him.

"Why not? What's going on?"

"I don't know what's going on, but I know what isn't going on. Does that make sense?" The older woman raised a brow.

"No. It doesn't make sense to me, so how about you just say it?" I sat on the rolling chair and wheeled myself directly in front of her.

"*Doug* is what's not going on." Nash had filled me in that Doug Callan was her ex-husband and now boyfriend. They'd recently moved in together, and it was the talk of the town. Apparently, Midge had divorced Doug many years ago and married his brother, Dennis Callan, who also happened to be the minister in town. She'd then divorced Dennis after a very short marriage, and she and Doug had remained enemies up until recently.

Ahhh . . . the joys of small-town living. Everyone knew your business.

"Again, I'm going to need you to clarify."

"Doug and I are only having sex five days a week," she said, crossing her arms over her chest.

My eyes widened as I gaped at her. "That sounds like a lot of sex to me. What's the problem?"

"The problem is, I went a lot of years without it. And now, I want it every day. So I'm hoping you can help me with that."

"Are you asking for medication?" I cleared my throat, because this conversation was unexpected, and I was completely caught off guard.

"No. His package is working just fine. I think we just need to spice things up, you know? I was hoping you could give me some tips."

"Some tips?" I repeated her words, fighting the urge to follow it with, *that's what she said.*

Raunchy humor came with being surrounded by my brothers and cousins.

"Yes. Why do you seem so surprised?"

"Um, because I'm a pediatrician, and I'm single." I shrugged.

"Oh, please. Everyone knows you and Nash are bumping pleasantries. That man has been single since Cutler's mom left

191

town. Everyone has tried to tie him down, and then what do you know . . . our new doc happens to be a single, hot woman who lives next door. So, I could use some pointers, you know, from the younger generation. I need Doug to look at me the way Nash looks at you. How do you seduce your man?"

"I—er, I," I stammered, pushing to my feet and pacing around the room. "I don't know that I've ever really seduced a man."

"That's your tip? You just happen to be gorgeous, so you don't have to try?" She threw her hands in the air.

"No. That's not what I'm saying." I leaned against the counter and placed my hands on my hips. "It seems like you're having an awful lot of sex, but I guess if you want more, you should just ask for it."

"Ask for it? I thought you were going to tell me to wear something sexy or do some sort of dance for the man."

"I mean, if that's your thing, go for it," I said over my laughter. "But as a modern-day woman, I think you should just ask for what you want."

Maybe I should take my own advice. I want Nash, and I am done waiting.

"Is that what you do? Ask for what you want?"

I chewed on my thumbnail as I looked at her. Her gray hair was tied back in a knot at the nape of her neck. "It's a new thing for me, and I'm working on it."

"Fine. I'm going to go home and demand that man make mad, passionate love to me again tonight."

I closed my eyes and sighed, because sex talk with Midge Longhorn was not what I'd expected when I arrived at work today.

"I never said demand. I said that you should ask for what you want." I walked to the door, and she followed me down the hall.

"Got it. Should I call you tomorrow and get on your schedule so we can follow up?" She smirked.

"Sure. Make it during lunchtime and bring me a grilled cheese and tomato soup."

"I can do that. Have a good night." She waved as she pushed through the door, and I locked it behind her.

I grabbed my purse and slipped out the back door, walking the short distance to Whiskey Falls bar. I loved Magnolia Falls, as it reminded me a lot of home back in Rosewood River. Hell, this whole town was growing on me. Ruby's father, Lionel, owned the bar, and I'd met the girls there one other time over the last few weeks.

"There she is!" Peyton shouted when I walked in.

The place was fairly busy for a weeknight, and this was definitely the most popular hangout for locals.

"Hi," I said, making my way around the table and hugging each one of them. "Sorry, I'm late."

"Your text said that Midge was there? Why in the world would she be coming to a pediatric office?" Demi asked as she reached for her water. I noticed everyone else had wine, and she normally did as well, so maybe she just wasn't drinking tonight.

"Well, I feel like there is doctor-patient confidentiality, but seeing as Midge isn't technically my patient, and I didn't really give her any medical advice, I can tell you. But it has to be in the absolute vault."

"Vault. I love that," Peyton said.

"She's specifically speaking to you, because we all know how chatty you are," Ruby said, as she sipped her wine and tried to hide her smile behind her glass as she directed the comment to Peyton.

"It's a small town. Everyone knows everyone's business. I'm not responsible for that." Peyton chuckled. "Tell us."

"Well, she wanted advice on how to spice up her sex life. They already have a lot of sex. Like five nights a week. But Midge wants more," I said, as I leaned into the table and whispered it to them.

Demi spewed water across the table.

Saylor's mouth gaped open.

Ruby's head fell back in a fit of laughter.

And Peyton's eyes danced with excitement.

"Stop it right now," Demi said after she cleaned herself up. "She went to the pediatrician for sex advice?"

"You cannot make this shit up. Magnolia Falls is a town full of quirky-ass people. The woman married Doug Callan, then divorced him and married his brother, Dennis. Then she divorced Dennis and proceeded to steal a few local dogs, only to wind up back with Doug and Johnny Cash, and now she's looking for sex advice."

"I thought Johnny Cash was dead." Peyton sipped her wine.

More laughter erupted around the table.

"He is. Johnny Cash is what Midge named her dog. Apparently, she had a thing for the man back in the day."

"Okay, we all know Midge's story. I want to know what the good doctor told her to do," Demi asked, just as a bunch of appetizers arrived and were set in the center of the table.

"I told her to ask for what she wants. What was I supposed to say?"

"I think that's perfect advice," Saylor said.

Ruby nodded, reaching for some chicken fingers and tater tots and placing them on her plate. "Agreed. I always ask for what I want."

Peyton raised a brow and looked at me. "Do you ask for what you want, Dr. Chadwick?"

"You made that sound so freaking creepy," Demi said over her laughter as she mimicked her words in a raspy whisper. "*Do you ask for what you want, Dr. Chadwick?*"

Now it was my turn to laugh because they were all funny as hell, and I loved being around them.

They were staring at me and waiting for an answer.

"It's something I'm working on. I clearly didn't focus on what I wanted in the past. I've told you my relationship with Collin was perfect on paper, but in hindsight, it was lacking. Like we were going through the motions. I think I was so focused on school and work, and I own my part in that. It was more of a friendship, and there was no passion."

"But you and Nash seem awfully passionate," Peyton said, as she waggled her brows. "Come on, something is going on there. You guys appear to hang out all the time, but are you doing the dirty deed?"

"Normally, I would call you out for being inappropriate, but I'm actually dying to know what the story is there. You, Nash, and Cutler seem awfully cozy when I see you together. There's definitely passion there, because of the way he looks at you," Demi said, before fanning her face. "It's hot."

My teeth sank into my bottom lip as Ruby jumped in. "You don't have to tell us anything. We're just happy to see you having fun."

"I don't mind talking about it. I used to tell Farah everything, and it feels weird now, because I don't have my confidant, you know?"

"Because your confidant was banging your fiancé," Ruby said, not making any effort to hide her annoyance. "She doesn't deserve your friendship, Emerson."

I nodded. "I know. But it's weird because we've shared our secrets since we were little girls. And I'm dying to talk to someone about this," I said, as the server brought over the glass of wine that I'd ordered.

"You can trust us. Our lips are sealed. We already know Midge's dirty little secret," Peyton said, reaching for a few onion rings.

"Obviously, Nash is focused on Cutler. He doesn't do relationships, and I'm just getting out of a disaster of a relationship. The only one I've ever even had. So we're just having fun, I guess." I sipped my wine and felt my cheeks heat at the thought of him.

"By having fun, do you mean he's rocking your world? That man is one hard-bodied hotty. All tan and golden and sexy." Peyton shrugged, and we all gaped at her. "What? You know it's true. And he clearly likes you because you spend so much time together. It's always just been him and Cutler and the guys. He's different with you."

"She's right," Demi, Saylor, and Ruby all said at the same time, which made me laugh.

"We just make out like teenagers every night, and I think he's afraid to take things further because I've been honest about Collin being the only man I've ever been with. So he probably feels like it'll be too much for me." I wasn't about to admit that the man gave me daily orgasms just by touching me. We'd never had sex, but we'd done everything else. And it was all I could think about most days.

"Would it be too much for you? To have sex without knowing where it's going to lead? Is that an issue for you?" Ruby asked.

"Always the therapist." Peyton flicked her thumb at Ruby.

"It's a fair question," I said. "And no. I don't know what the future holds for me for the first time in my life. I have an interview with Boston Children's in a few weeks, and hopefully I'll figure out where I'm going when my contract is up here. Nash and I have both been honest about what we have to offer, but we aren't spending time with other people, so it's not like it's a one-night hookup type of thing."

"Those are my favorite," Peyton said, bumping me with her shoulder and waggling her brows at me.

"So, why not go for it? Have some fun. He's a good man. You clearly really enjoy being around one another," Saylor said.

I nodded. "Let's just say that he's usually the one to stop

things. And I've been sort of waiting for him to make the next move, but it just hasn't happened yet. Maybe he doesn't want to go there."

Ruby rolled her eyes before tossing a tot into her mouth. "Please. That man looks at you like he's ready to strip you naked in front of all of us. We've all noticed. Knowing Nash, he's trying to be respectful. Why not take your own advice and ask for what you want?"

"Yes. I think you should definitely do that." Demi rubbed her hands together.

"Yeah. It's not a bad idea." I took a bite of my chicken finger and thought it over.

"I think you should go for it." Saylor took a sip of her wine.

"Just tell the man that you want him, and then get on your knees and crawl to him and beg for it," Peyton said, and we all turned and gaped at her. "What? That would be so hot."

"Maybe for some. I think I'd prefer to tell River to get on his knees and crawl to me and beg for it. In fact, I think I'll give that a shot tonight." A wicked grin spread across Ruby's face.

"Oh, I guess that's what happens when you've got two alphas under one roof. So what do you think, Emerson? Are you going to crawl to him and beg for it, or make him crawl to you?" Peyton raised a brow.

I reached for an onion ring and took a bite as I thought it over. "I think I'm going to just tell him how I feel and see what happens."

"That's a brilliant idea," Demi said, and she smirked. "Not that I have anything against anyone getting down on their knees."

"King would love if I demanded that he get on his knees," Saylor said over a fit of laughter, and we all joined in.

We paused and ordered another round of drinks, and Demi just asked for a refill of her water.

"What is going on with you?" Peyton asked. "It's a girls' night."

"Well, there's something I wanted to tell you, and I was waiting for us to all be together."

Peyton fell forward, resting her head in her hands. "Oh, my gosh. This is it, isn't it?"

Demi smiled, and her eyes watered. "It is. I'm preggers. My sexy boxer husband put a baby in me."

High-pitched squeals left everyone's mouths, and we each took turns hugging her.

And in that moment, it hit me.

Life was full of ups and downs.

I'd been down for a while, but it felt like things were turning around.

And I was ready to ask for what I wanted.

I may not know what the future holds, but I know what I want in this moment.

And he happened to live right next door to me.

21

Nash

I rubbed my hands together, suddenly feeling like a pathetic bastard. I was sitting out back on my Adirondack chair, my gaze moving between the water and my neighbor's house, waiting for a light to turn on or for her to come walking out back. I'd never been like this.

Not when I had my first high school girlfriend.

Or my second or third.

Not when the mother of my child and I were giving it a try.

Not until right now.

Maybe it was the fact that she wasn't staying, and that made it safe.

This attraction. This pull. It was keeping me up at night.

Every time I kissed Emerson Chadwick, it was like someone set me on fire. Like I was coming alive in a different way for the first time in a very long time.

And we'd made out like horny teens for the last few weeks. I'd always made it a point to please the woman I was with. But pleasing Emerson—it was different.

It did something to me.

I'd held back because I knew she'd only ever been with one

dude, and he'd betrayed her in the worst way. I knew she was still healing, and I didn't want to be the asshole that pushed her.

This had to happen on her terms, and it was fucking killing me.

But I hadn't seen her today, and Cutler had gotten a last-minute invite to J.T.'s to sleep over, and I'd had dinner over there with them. But since I'd been home, I'd found myself staring at Emerson's house on and off for the last hour.

I'd checked my phone numerous times, and I hadn't heard from her.

I needed to shake this off.

We were friends who made out at the end of each day and liked each other, and that was it.

Nothing more.

At least, for *her*, it was nothing more.

But for me, it felt like everything.

Like it was hard to breathe when she wasn't around.

What the fuck is happening to me?

I pushed to my feet.

She owed me nothing.

I walked toward my deck just as I heard movement next door, and Winnie came charging toward me.

"Nash?" Emerson's voice carried from a few feet away. It was dark, and the stars and moon overhead were providing the only light illuminating her.

She wore a skirt and a blouse, and I'd known she'd gone to meet the girls right from work, so she must just be getting home now. Her feet were bare, and as I moved closer, I noticed her cheeks were a little flushed.

"Hey, you're home."

"Yeah. You weren't waiting for me, were you?" Her voice was all tease.

I shoved my hands into my pockets to stop from pulling her closer as she moved right in front of me.

Don't be so desperate, asshole.

"What? No. I was just sitting out by the water," I said, the lie slipping from my lips easily to avoid embarrassment.

The embarrassment of admitting that I was crazy about her. She wasn't mine. I had no claim.

"Well, I was coming out here in hopes you were having a nightcap."

"Oh, yeah?"

"Yeah." She nodded, moving closer. "Is Cutler sleeping?"

I shook my head slowly, my gaze locking with hers. "Nope."

"Nope?"

I leaned down, kissing her neck, craving her in a way I couldn't wrap my head around. I nipped at her ear before whispering. "He got invited to sleep over at J.T.'s."

She tipped her head back. "Really? And you weren't waiting for me, being in that big house all alone?"

My dick sprung to life at her words. "Maybe I was waiting for you, Sunny. Maybe I even texted you twice because I couldn't wait to see you."

What the fuck did I have to lose at this point? My pride? I didn't give a fuck.

"Really?" She rubbed the tip of her nose against mine as she pushed up on her tiptoes. "I didn't know that. My phone died, and I was going to come knock on your door to tell you something. Something that couldn't wait until morning."

"Tell me." I reached around her waist with one hand, dipping lower to graze her perfectly peach-shaped ass. I fucking loved her body. Hell, I loved her face. Her hair. Her laugh. Her witty banter and her sense of humor. Her goofy obsession with baking.

I was so fucked.

"I want you, Nash Heart. No more holding back. We don't have to know what it means. I just need to know that you want me the way that I want you. That's all I need."

My hand moved to the side of her neck, my thumb tracing her bottom lip. "I fucking want you, Emerson. There's no question about it."

"Then do something about it."

"You sure about this?" I lifted her easily, and her skirt bunched around her waist as her legs wrapped around my middle.

"I'm sure. Stop being such a gentleman and show me what I've been missing."

"My house or yours?"

Her hands were on each side of my face. Those jade-green eyes bored into mine. "Mine."

Her head fell back in laughter when I started jogging toward her back porch. Winnie was on my heels, and I pushed the door open and moved inside, kicking the door closed behind me. My mouth was on hers, and I dropped to sit on her couch, with her straddling me. My hands were in her hair. I fucking loved kissing this woman. I'd never kissed a woman like this before. We'd been doing this song and dance for weeks, and normally, I'd tire of this quickly.

But Emerson was different.

Everything about her was different.

She pulled back to look at me. Her lips turned up in the corners as she flashed me this sexy smile. "Where should we go?"

I chuckled. She was nervous. It was cute as hell. "Where do you want to go?"

"Well, I've only ever done the deed in the bedroom, so . . ." She shrugged.

"Done the deed? That dude clearly failed you, if that's what you're calling it. And if you've done it in the bedroom, then I say we go anywhere but the bedroom first." I paused and then groaned. "Fuck. I don't have a condom in my wallet. I need to run to my house to grab a few."

"Grab a few? I've never needed more than one." Her cheeks pinked. "But I've got a whole box in my nightstand drawer. I'm a doctor, remember?"

I barked out a laugh as I stroked her long waves away from her face. "You're a pediatrician."

"A pediatrician with a super-hot neighbor living next door. It's been a while for me, so I guess I've been thinking about this, about you." She shrugged again.

"I've been thinking about you too, beautiful. Every fucking day since you moved next door."

She sucked in a breath, and her eyes were wet with emotion. "I don't know what this is," she whispered.

"Maybe you're not supposed to." I leaned forward and kissed her. "Maybe you're just supposed to enjoy this for now."

She nodded, pushing to her feet. "I'll be right back."

She hurried down the hallway toward her bedroom before coming back with the box of condoms, and she tossed it to me. I stared at the box and smiled. "Magnum large-size condoms, huh?"

"In my medical opinion, these were necessary."

"I think it was a wise choice, Dr. Chadwick." I tossed the box beside me and tugged her down onto my lap again, her legs falling on each side of me as her skirt gathered around her waist. My lips were on hers, and my hand moved between her lean, toned thighs. I groaned into her mouth as my fingers dipped beneath the lacy fabric and found her soaked. "Goddamn, woman. I need to be inside you right fucking now."

She nodded and pushed up to stand, unzipping her skirt and letting it fall to the floor. I tugged at the hem of her top, and she raised her arms so I could pull it over her head, my fingers tracing over the peach lace that covered her gorgeous tits.

"Do you know how many times I've thought about seeing you this way?" I reached behind her, unclasping her bra and

203

staring in awe as it fell to the floor. "How are you so fucking perfect?"

She sighed, teeth pinning that bottom lip beneath them, as if my words overwhelmed her. I ran my fingers over her pink, perky nipples, my mouth watering at the sight. I leaned forward, flicking her hard peaks with my tongue, and then I covered her breasts with my mouth one at a time, teasing her with my tongue as her head fell back and her breaths came fast. My fingers moved to the edge of her matching panties, and I slowly slid them down her thighs. She lifted one leg at a time as she stepped out of them.

Her hands moved to my shoulders, and she pushed back, forcing me to look up at her. "Clothes off. I want to see you."

Hell, being naked never bothered me. I only put clothes on at home because I had Cutler there. I reached over my shoulder and yanked my tee over my head before lifting us both to stand. She unbuttoned my shorts while I kicked off my flip-flops, and she tugged my briefs down my legs, tossing them into a pile on the floor.

I chuckled as I dropped back down and reached for the condoms. She quickly snatched them from me, pulling out the foil packet, tearing off the top, and waggling her brows as she leaned down. "I want to do it. But wow. You and I both know there is no way that's going to fit."

I leaned back against the couch, watching as she rolled the latex over my throbbing erection before I pulled her down to me. Her knees were on each side of me as my dick teased her entrance. "Trust me. You can take it, beautiful. You're on top, so you set the pace."

Her tongue slid along her bottom lip as she reached down and gripped my cock in her hand, positioning me right where she wanted me.

So fucking sexy, I had to force myself not to come right there.

Just looking at her was difficult.

She moved the slightest bit and gasped at the intrusion and then slid down about an inch, pausing to catch her breath.

I reached up and wrapped my hand in all that beautiful hair before tugging her down until my mouth crashed into hers. And I kissed her for the longest time, fighting every urge to thrust forward.

She pulled back, lips swollen and parted, as her gaze locked with mine, and she slid down a little further. Slowly at first, then she'd pause and let her body adjust before she'd move again.

It was so hot. So sexy.

"I love watching the way you take me. Like that fucking pussy was made for me."

Her hands found mine, our fingers intertwining, as she closed her eyes and moved again.

And again.

And I watched as she took me. Inch by inch.

I could barely breathe at the feel of her.

Tight and wet and perfect.

"Fuck, Emerson," I hissed. "You feel so fucking good."

"Mmmm," she said, as she started to slide up and down my shaft, finding her rhythm.

Her tits bounced just a bit as she moved, and her hands broke free from mine as she arched back, resting her palms on the backs of my thighs for leverage.

She rode me, slowly at first. I sat forward, my lips covering her breasts and licking and sucking like my life depended on it.

My hands wrapped around her tiny waist as I helped to guide her.

Up and down.

Faster and faster.

Our breaths the only audible sound in the room.

"Nash." My name left her lips in a desperate whisper. "I'm so close."

My thumb moved to her clit, knowing exactly what she needed. I leaned back, just watching as my cock drove in and out of her. Her eyes fell closed, head tipped back, lips parted, as she arched her beautiful body, and her long hair tickled the tops of my thighs.

I'd never seen anything or anyone more beautiful.

And I just watched as she came apart above me.

Like a fucking angel.

Her body flushed and shaking as she exploded around me. I couldn't hold back any longer. I drove into her.

Once.

Twice.

And a guttural sound left my throat as I followed her into oblivion. Both of us were heaving for air as we rode out every last bit of pleasure.

Her body fell limp against mine. I could feel her heart racing against my chest.

I wrapped my arms around her and held her there.

Relaxed and sated.

And I wanted to keep her right there for as long as I could.

Wanting things I shouldn't.

Needing things I shouldn't.

But for tonight, I'd let myself go there.

Just for tonight.

22

Emerson

I lay there, trying to catch my breath for so long, it was getting embarrassing. I pulled back to look at him.

"Hey," I whispered.

"Hey, beautiful. How do you feel?"

"That was amazing. I think we should do that again as often as possible," I said, my voice sultry and unrecognizable.

Hello, fabulous orgasm. It's been a while.

"We can do it anytime you want. My dick has an open-door policy when it comes to you." He stroked his fingers along the side of my face.

Nash shifted me off his lap and set me on the couch before walking the short distance to the bathroom. I heard the toilet flush, so I knew he'd disposed of the condom. He strode back toward me, with only the moonlight shining in through the windows illuminating his large, muscled body. He had no shame in the way he confidently moved in my direction, probably because he was some sort of chiseled Adonis. He pulled on his briefs before reaching for the blanket on my couch and wrapping it around me and settling me on his lap again.

LAURA PAVLOV

There was such a comfort between us. One I couldn't explain because I hadn't known him for that long. But somehow, it felt as if I'd known him forever.

"Thank you for this," I whispered, as emotion took over. "It hasn't been like this in a long time, if ever, actually. So thank you for showing me how good it can be."

His thumb swiped at the single tear rolling down my cheek, and I cringed at how ridiculous I was being.

"Sometimes moving forward is hard, even when you know you should. So, if I'm able to help you see that you deserve better—that you deserve the fucking moon and the stars and all that shit—then I'm happy to do it." His gray gaze locked with mine. "Maybe you just needed to see how good it could be when you aren't in a bed."

"Oh, you think it's the location, huh?" I chuckled, completely comfortable that I happened to still be stark naked while sitting on my couch. I'd never had that comfort before now. Collin was all about being proper and following rules— well, until he was banging my best friend, which seemed like a pretty big rule to break.

I liked that I didn't have to worry about anyone questioning what I wanted anymore.

Questioning how hard I worked.

Questioning the amount of time I spent with my family.

"I think it's just time that you do what you want. From what you've told me, you haven't done that in a long time. I think it's damn good that you've been set free," he said, and his words hit me right in the chest.

"Sometimes I feel guilty, you know?" I whispered.

"About what? He's the one who should feel guilty, not you."

Nash had a confidence that I envied. I'd noticed it the first time that I met him. He wasn't trying to impress anyone. He didn't overthink his words. He knew who he was. What he wanted. And he made no attempt to dim that for anyone.

"I guess I just didn't know what a relief it was going to be to have my heart broken." A loud laugh escaped my lips. "I mean, there were deposits put down for a wedding that the whole town was going to be attending. There were plans made and a future that I had laid out for myself. A job I thought I'd be taking but that I walked away from. And yes, my fiancé and my best friend definitely broke my heart. And they have to carry the weight of their choices." I looked away for a minute as I gathered my thoughts. He didn't rush me or push me for more. He waited. "And sometimes I feel bad because I'm happier now than I've been in a long time. I just didn't know I wasn't happy before, because he was all that I knew. But even being alone these last few months, it's been freeing."

"It doesn't change what they did, but I think it'll make it easier to forgive and move forward, knowing that you're happy."

"How about you? Do you forgive easily?"

"I don't normally let people get close enough that there'd be a reason to forgive, if that makes sense." His eyes were so earnest and genuine. "I keep my circle small for a reason. My focus is Cutler. I'm close to my father. And my friends are my family."

"What about Tara? Do you forgive her for leaving?" I asked, because I wanted to know more. He was raising his son with so much love, and I wondered how he didn't resent her for leaving Cutler. Leaving him.

He sighed, and I saw several emotions cross his gaze in just a few quick seconds. "Tara is the one who's missing out. If she'd stuck around and stayed in town, I'd be sharing custody of Cutler, and I don't think I could have handled that. So sure, it pisses me off that she left him. I don't have a whole lot of respect for her anymore. But I'm grateful at the same time, because he's my greatest joy. And there would be no Cutler without her, right? So how can I hate her for that?"

I nodded. "I understand that. You have one amazing little boy."

"I know I do. I'm a lucky man," he said. "And apparently, you're baking unicorn Krispies with him tomorrow?"

"Yep. He's never made them. How is that possible?" I laughed.

"I don't really bake." He tugged me down and kissed me. "But thank you for doing that for him."

And before I knew what was happening, he was on his feet, carrying me toward the bedroom. And I was hoping it was time for round two.

Because I couldn't get enough of Nash Heart.

* * *

I couldn't remember a time that I'd felt more relaxed. More at peace. Nash had spent the night with me last night. We'd had sex for a second time in my bed. We'd then had sex in the shower together this morning, which was also new for me. Collin thought sex and showers were hypocritical. He believed you showered to get clean and start your day.

I'd thought I felt the same.

But now I knew differently.

One should always have sex in the shower before starting their day.

I felt like I was on top of the freaking world.

My not-serious relationship was proving to be better than the only real relationship I'd ever had.

And today, I was showing Cutler how to make unicorn Krispies, and we'd made a batch of red velvet cupcakes because he'd said those were his favorite. And I was having the best time.

"I can't believe you told Pops he couldn't stay," Cutler said over a fit of laughter, as he continued stirring the chocolate batter in the mixing bowl.

"Well, this is our thing, right? I can't teach you the secrets of baking with your dad all up in our business." I smirked as I lined the cupcake tins with paper.

"I think he was happy to take Winnie on the boat, anyway." He dipped his finger into the bowl and popped it into his mouth, his eyes going wide when I caught him.

I dipped my finger in and mimicked him, and he relaxed. "No sense baking if you can't test the goods, right?"

"Yes! I knew you were my girl before, but now it feels like you're my girl and my best friend. Just don't tell J.T."

I chuckled. "You really are the cutest, Beefcake. So why'd you want to learn to bake the unicorn Krispies?"

"Well, there's this girl in my class named Jolie." He set his spoon on the paper towel beside the bowl, and I showed him how to ladle the batter into the little cups.

"And Jolie likes unicorn Krispies?" I asked, helping him dip the ladle into the batter and maneuver it into the cups. He was very cautious and careful, and it impressed me. My grown brothers and cousins couldn't fill a cupcake tin with batter to save their lives, so this was surprising.

"Every year, we do a special day for each kid in the class, and it's called Star Student Day. Jolie brings cupcakes every single year on her special day. Her mama makes them. And then her mom and dad wear these T-shirts that say Jolie's mom and Jolie's dad on them when they walk her into school. So I thought maybe if I learned how to make treats of my own, me and Pops could bring something for the class this year on my special day. And no one has ever brought unicorn Krispies."

A lump so thick it nearly choked me formed in my throat. It physically hurt me to know that he was hurting about anything. Because Cutler Heart was so loved and adored, but

211

sometimes, it was easy to look around and compare yourself to what you think you should have, and it could be very painful.

"I'll bet you could get your dad to bring in just about anything you wanted him to. And I'm sure he would wear any T-shirt you chose for him," I said, as I watched him meticulously fill the last cupcake paper.

"I know he would. And he bought cookies for me last year. But we never made homemade before." He paused and thought about it. "And Pops can't bring me to school with a mama, because I don't have one."

I turned to look at him as he set the ladle down on the paper towel, as if he hadn't said something heavy at all. He was just speaking the truth.

"But I bet everyone doesn't have both parents bringing them to school on their special day, right?" I knew there was talk of Tara coming to visit soon, but I wasn't going to bring that up, because, according to Nash, she wasn't someone they could count on at all.

He looked up at me with those big brown eyes, almost like he felt empathy for me because he sensed my sadness about the conversation. "Nope. They don't all have both parents bringing them to school every day, but all the kids in my class do have two parents. But everyone knows I've got the best pops in town. But one time I'd like to have two people bring me to school so I can say I've got two as well."

It was like a dagger to the heart.

"I get that. Wanting to be like everyone else. I don't know if I told you, but I was planning this big wedding for the longest time. And then in the end, I had to call it off. I've never known anyone who called off their wedding. It's kind of embarrassing that I had to tell everyone it wasn't going to happen, but guess what, Beefcake?" I took the pan and moved it onto the top rack of the oven before setting the timer.

"What?" he asked, as he bent down, hands on his knees, as he peered into the oven.

"I'm doing just fine. It's the reason that I came here and met you, right?" I closed the oven door and smiled at him. "And just because I'm different doesn't mean it's bad."

"Why'd you call off the wedding?" he asked, his little eyebrows cinched with concern.

"Well, the groom that I picked found himself another lady." It was my lame attempt at telling the truth to soothe his pain, but it seemed to be working.

"I've got a lot of girls, Sunny. But I can't believe someone wouldn't want to marry you. You're my special girl. You know how to take care of sick kids, and you bake the best Krispies and cupcakes, and you ride horses, and you're a real good swimmer, too. You've got the best dog, and you're very pretty." He reached for my hand. "But you're also the nicest girl I know. You want me to have my uncles go beat that guy up for you? My uncle Ro is the champion, and they're all real strong. My pops could beat just about anyone in a fight, except for maybe Uncle Ro."

"No," I said over my laughter. "I'm happy about it now. I just meant that sometimes being different from everyone around you isn't a bad thing. Maybe it just means we're special."

"Pops always says that I'm special. And he's like me. He didn't have a mama either, and he's the best pops." He beamed up at me as I moved to get another bowl so we could start the icing. Nash had told me that he lost his mother in childbirth, and I couldn't even imagine how hard that had to be on both him and his father. "Did your mama bring cupcakes when you were the star student at school?"

I pulled the step stool back up to the counter for him since we were going to make the icing next. I measured out the butter and dropped it into the bowl. "My parents are really

213

great. But," I said, holding up my phone to show him a photo of all of us together. "They've got five kids, and then I told you I've got my cousins who grew up right next door to me. So my mom couldn't always bake cupcakes for all of us for every occasion. We got special treats on our birthday, and that was great."

He studied the photo, and his head fell back in laughter. "Man, Sunny. You've got so many brothers and cousins, and they're all boys. Did you wish for a girl sometimes?"

"Nope. I had a best friend named Farah, and she was more like a sister to me back then." I cleared my throat. The pain always hit hard when I talked about Farah. "And now that we're talking about this, I just remembered something."

"What?" he asked.

"Farah's mama always brought all the treats on the first day of school and on her birthday and her half birthday. She didn't have any siblings, so her parents really spoiled her."

"And did you ever feel bad about that?"

"Nope. Because I had such a good family, just like you do. Farah was always really lonely because her parents were very busy. But they'd always throw her fancy parties and bring her special treats, but they didn't spend a lot of time with her. And sometimes, things look good on the outside, but it's more about feeling good on the inside."

"I always feel good on the inside. My girl, Ruby, taught me about that." He took the measuring cup that I'd filled with powdered sugar and carefully poured it into the mixing bowl. "Do you think Farah was sad on the inside because she was wishing she could spend more time with her family?"

My chest was heavy. That girl practically lived at our house when we were growing up. "I think she might have been. So always remember, being loved is most important. It's not about how something looks, Beefcake. It's about how it feels."

"I feel happy when I'm with you, Sunny. I'll bet this is how

Jolie feels when she bakes with her mama." The words left his mouth so casually, I sat there gaping at him with surprise. I loved how honest he was. How he just said how he felt.

The door sprung open, and Winnie came running in before I could respond to Cutler.

"It smells like cupcakes, and I'm getting hungry," Nash said, with a big grin on his face. "I'm done being kicked out of the cool kids' baking club."

I shook my head and chuckled as Cutler charged at him, and his father scooped him up effortlessly.

"Sunny is the bestest baker and the bestest girl, Pops. We better hope she stays a long time, because she makes me feel real good on the inside."

Nash barked out a laugh, and so did I. "Yep. She makes me feel good on the inside, too."

With that, he winked at me, and I could feel the heat climbing my neck.

This man had such an effect on me, and I didn't know what to make of it.

But I'd decided not to overthink it, and I was just going to enjoy myself.

Because I couldn't get enough of Nash or his little boy.

23

Nash

"You did this on purpose," Kingston whined, and I used my hand to cover my mouth. "What is she, some sort of Olympic volleyball player?"

"My Sunny is the bestest player I've ever seen." Cutler was jumping up and down after Emerson and I smoked Kingston and Romeo in the final round of volleyball. She high-fived my son before bending down and wrapping her arms around him and kissing his cheek. These two were thick as thieves these days. I also didn't miss the way she was always assessing Cutler's breathing when we were outside being active. She'd study him the same way that I did, checking for signs of breathing struggles. I'm sure it had a lot to do with her being a doctor, but my gut told me that it had even more to do with her loving my boy. And I had no doubt that she did.

"Hey, you never asked. You were the one who suggested we play volleyball, seeing as I already smoked your ass at baseball a few weeks ago." I laughed as Emerson came up beside me, hair in a long ponytail on top of her head, short shorts showing off her long, toned legs.

She was already the most beautiful woman I'd ever laid eyes on, but I'd be lying if I didn't admit that seeing her smoke all the guys in volleyball was even sexier.

She made it all look so effortless.

Romeo and Demi had a beach area down near the water on their new property, and they'd put in a volleyball court. Kingston was one of those dudes who was basically good at all sports, and he felt pretty confident that he'd dominate at this one. But I hadn't mentioned the fact that Emerson played college volleyball. And I'd loved watching all of them gape at her as we played game after game as partners, taking every single team out.

"Damn, girl, you're smart and athletic. That was badass," Ruby said, as she handed Emerson a bottle of water.

River sauntered over and handed me a beer as Ruby and Emerson led Cutler over to where Demi, Peyton, and Saylor were sitting a few feet away.

"Of course, Heart dates the girl who can treat his son's asthma and kick King's ass on the volleyball court. Always the overachiever, this one." River clinked his bottle with mine. Normally, I'd get defensive about him claiming we were dating. But the truth was, we spent every free minute together. We weren't with anyone else. So call it what you want.

A relationship. Dating. I wasn't going to deny any of it anymore.

We settled around the firepit, and Hayes was next, because these guys loved to dish out shit. "So much for keeping it casual. You look at the girl like she hangs the fucking moon."

Because she may as well hang the moon.

We'd been spending a lot of time together because she lived next door, and hell, we just liked hanging out. It wasn't just sex for us.

At least it wasn't for me. Which was a foreign concept to me.

But yes, the sex was mind-blowing.

Apparently, Emerson hadn't been having a whole lot of sex with her ex over the last few years, and she'd gone a few months since she'd had any at all, so she was making up for lost time.

And I didn't get out much, as it was difficult as a single dad, so I hadn't had consistent sex in—well, six years. Since the day my son came into the world and everything changed.

But now it was the three of us, cooking dinners together and doing puzzles with Cutler. We watched movies every night and sat out on the lake while my son played with Winnie.

When we weren't at work, we were together.

And when my boy was sleeping, we were sneaking down the hall to my room to have sex.

Fan-fucking-tastic sex.

And I was here for it.

For as long as she was.

"Whatever. We're friends. She's my neighbor, and she's cool. And fucking beautiful. And smart, and—" I glanced up to see all of them gaping at me.

Romeo clapped his hands together once and barked out a laugh. "Look at our boy. He's growing up."

I flipped him the bird. "We're having fun. It's nothing serious."

"Then why the fuck would you not tell me she's an Olympic volleyball player? If it's not serious and you've known me my whole life, why would you do me dirty that way?" Kingston said over his laughter.

"She played collegiate volleyball." I chuckled.

"I love that you think anyone who beats you has to be an Olympic athlete." Hayes smirked.

"Well, you were recruited to play college ball, and you're a fucking firefighter. You're in fabulous shape. How the hell did she beat you?" Kingston pressed. Hayes had been offered a college football scholarship right out of high school, but he'd turned it down to become a firefighter and to support his younger sister, Saylor.

"Well, I don't spend a lot of time diving for balls anymore. I try to put out burning buildings, you asshole. Stop pouting. The girl beat you. Maybe you're not that good."

"Saylor thinks I'm the best at everything." King puffed out his chest, and laughter filled the air around us.

"So, we've got the big proposal this weekend. People spend less time prepping for a wedding than you did for this damn engagement." River kept his voice low, making sure no one else could hear us.

"Hey. Go big or go home. And you all have the plan for after and where to meet, right?"

"You sent us a fucking itinerary. Of course, we know the plan," Hayes grumped before turning to me and raising a brow. "Let me guess, you're next?"

I coughed and covered my mouth before shaking my hand in front of me. "You're fucking crazy. She's not staying. We're just having fun."

"But if she were staying?" Romeo asked.

"She's not. So, there's no sense going there," I said, glancing over when the sound of my son's laughter pulled my attention away.

Emerson was tickling Cutler as he sat on her lap, and his head was back, mouth open, as he bellowed out in joy.

"Yeah. Just having fun, my ass," River said under his breath.

I took another pull from my bottle and pushed the thought away.

She was leaving. We knew what this was.

I was the king of keeping it casual.

I'd be fine when she left.

"Just enjoy it, brother. You deserve to have some fun. And Emerson is cool as hell. Don't overthink it." Romeo shrugged.

Yeah, he was right. I wasn't going to overthink it.

"You're just saying that because she told you that her brothers and her cousins are obsessed with you, Golden Boy," Kingston said as he shook his head. "I saw his head double in size right in front of me."

Romeo flipped him the bird and barked out a laugh. "And you jumped right in that selfie so fast with me, you didn't miss a beat."

Emerson had sent a selfie of her with Romeo to her family group text.

"Hey. I'm the photogenic one."

Emerson's brother, Easton, whom I'd already met, ended up FaceTiming his sister after she'd sent the photo.

"Yeah, well, her brother nearly lost his shit when he realized Lincoln Hendrix was Ro's brother," River said, with a wicked grin on his face. Romeo's brother, Lincoln, was the quarterback for the New York Thunderbirds.

"He played for San Francisco for years before heading to New York, so he's still got a lot of fans out this way." Romeo nodded, proud as hell of his brother. "And Clark Chadwick is a fucking legend on the ice, so they're clearly an athletic family."

Emerson's brother was one of the best centers in the league, and the guys had flipped out when they'd realized that he was her brother.

They were all teasing her about it now and giving her a hard time.

It was like Emerson had been part of this group forever.

She fit right in.

* * *

220

"I think you have the best style. There is no one cooler than you," Emerson said, as my son came out of the bathroom with his hair slicked back and enough gel to make it look like it had a glass coating over it.

"I think you're really cool," he said, walking straight over to her and placing a hand on her cheek. The kid had game, no doubt about it. But his relationship with Emerson was different than it was with anyone else. I wasn't sure what it was, but their connection was impossible to miss. He talked to her about everything. It had surprised me because normally he just liked to flirt and be funny, but he went deep with her. He talked about his mom and the disappointment he felt that she'd left. He talked about things that happened at school that bothered him. Things he didn't talk about with me. I'd hear them chatting when I was cooking dinner or when we were out on the boat and I was driving.

I was always listening.

It made me happy that he was so comfortable with her, but it also terrified me.

Tara had left him when he was a baby. I knew it hurt that he didn't have a mother in his life like all of his friends did. So, I'd always been cautious about who I let into his life. But I'd let her all the way in, and now I was fucking worried about how he'd handle it when she left.

With Tara, he didn't have an emotional attachment. He just had to deal with the fact that he didn't know her, and she hadn't stuck around.

With Emerson, there were feelings. Real feelings.

"No one has ever called me cool," she said over her laughter as she patted her legs, and he climbed onto her lap.

"You're a doctor, and you're pretty. You make me laugh, and you make the best cupcakes and unicorn Rice Krispie treats. You have pretty hair, and you can play all the sports as good as Pops and my uncles. That's cool, Sunny."

"Thanks, angel face," she said with a chuckle, because she had a nickname of her own for him now. "Maybe you can mention that to the boys today?"

Cutler wanted to meet her brothers and her cousins, so they were doing a Zoom call with all of them. They'd had it planned for days, and it was all my boy could talk about. And I was standing here like an asshole, not knowing what the hell to do.

Her laptop was open as she started typing something, which I assumed meant she was logging in. It only took a few seconds before she and Cutler started waving at the screen.

"Is this the infamous Beefcake?" one of the guys said.

"My Sunny calls me angel face."

"Angel face? That's lame, Emmy. Beefcake is probably the coolest handle I've ever heard. I'm Emmy's evil twin, Easton. Nice to meet you, buddy."

"Well, then, you can call him Beefcake, and I'll call him angel face." Emerson waggled her brows at my son, and he laughed.

"Nice to meet you, too. Tell me all of your names," my son said.

They went around saying their names, and Emerson raised a brow at me, waiting for me to come sit beside her, and I didn't know why the hell I was so nervous.

I sat in the seat next to them, and the conversation flowed easily. There was Easton, who I'd already met. Her superstar hockey player brother, Clark, who Cutler grilled endlessly about hockey. Rafe and Bridger rounded out her brothers, and then Axel and Archer were her cousins, and the group of them were funny as hell in the way they gave one another shit.

They were telling Cutler and me old war stories about Emerson and all the trouble they got into as kids. My son was laughing his ass off. They insisted we'd need to make a trip to Rosewood River sometime soon.

The lines were blurring.

I was doing my best not to overthink it, but it was getting more challenging.

Because when Emerson left, I didn't know how my son would handle it.

My job had always been to keep everything together.

But I wasn't so sure I could do that this time.

I was too invested.

I needed to pull back, but I didn't know how to do that.

And I already knew it was going to hurt like hell when she left.

24

Emerson

I'd been slammed at work, as all the kids had gone back to school, and now they were all getting sick. It was typical when school first started, and the weather was starting to change now. Doc Dolby had even come in for a few hours this week to help me with the overflow of patients, and I'd grown close to the man since I'd gotten here.

"I'm going to head out. You're doing an amazing job, Emerson. I'll be here tomorrow morning so you can focus on your interview with Boston Children's. I know that's the one you're most interested in."

It was the top pediatric hospital in the country. I'd been thrilled when they'd had an opening and offered me an interview.

It would be a fresh start.

One I'd longed for.

But the thought of leaving wasn't as exciting as it should be. I'd grown to love this town. The people. My life here.

Nash and Cutler.

All of it. I hadn't expected that. This was my interim place. My short-term stop to figure out what I wanted to do with my life.

But I was more confused now than ever.

I cleared my throat. "Yes. Thank you again for covering for me tomorrow. And you have a few prospects to take over your practice, right? How are those interviews going?"

Why was I holding my breath? Why was I nervous to hear that he'd found my replacement? I wanted the best for this place. Whoever replaced me would be taking care of Cutler. They had to be the best.

Because I loved that little boy in a way I'd never known possible. I missed him when I wasn't with him. I'd worried all day when he'd started school a few days ago. Doing my best not to overstep, I'd made baseball cupcakes for Nash to take to the classroom for him, and Cutler had thanked me no fewer than a hundred times.

I didn't go with Nash to drop him off or pick him up because it wasn't my place.

But I'd thought about him every second of the day and made Nash FaceTime me the minute he'd picked him up, so I could hear everything.

I couldn't even wait until I got off work and we had dinner that night.

That's how invested I was.

And it was no different with his father. My casual relationship had turned out to be the most fulfilling relationship I'd ever had.

Nash Heart had healed me. He'd put me back together, and I was the happiest I'd ever been in my life.

As corny as it sounded, this man completed me.

He was the yin to my yang.

The peanut butter to my jelly.

"Did you hear me, Emerson?" Doc asked, pulling me from my Nash-filled daze-slash-panic attack I felt every time I talked about leaving.

"I'm sorry. My brain is on overload. You said there are two great applicants, right?"

225

"Well, they are both wonderful. But neither one is you." His gaze softened. "But I want you to do whatever is best for you, all right? If you think that's Boston, then I support you. But if for any reason you're having second thoughts, you just have to let me know before I move forward with anyone else."

"Of course. But obviously, if they're interested in me, I'd be a fool not to take it." I shrugged, my heart racing at the thought.

Did I want them to offer me the job?

Of course, I did.

How could I not want this?

I'd interviewed with them for residency, and I'd been blown away by the program. I'd flown out there and spent a day touring the hospital and making rounds. But in the end, I hadn't ranked them as my first choice. Collin didn't want to move to the East Coast, and I'd gone against my better judgment and stayed in San Francisco. I'd loved the hospital there, too. It meant working with my best friend and starting my life with my fiancé.

And in the end, that decision had blown up in my face.

I wouldn't make that mistake twice.

"Can I give you a little advice from a man who's lived a lot longer than you?" he asked, hesitant with his question.

"Always."

"It's okay to change your plan. Rose and I never planned on coming back to Magnolia Falls after I completed my residency. But her mom got sick, and life happened, so we came back here with the intent of staying just a year. And then Rose got pregnant, and we wanted to stay near family." He had a look of nostalgia on his face, and it made my chest squeeze. "I had all these plans, and I was hung up on them for the wrong reasons. Life was happening right in front of my eyes, all while I was planning for a different one. The grass is not always greener, Emerson. And it seems like you were pretty unhappy

226

with that life you came from. I know you were just planning this as a stopover to figure out what you wanted to do next, but take the time to weigh all your options, all right? That's all I'm saying. Don't take that job just to prove that you *can* do it. Do what makes you happy. And if Boston makes you happy, you have my full support."

I pushed to my feet and came around my desk, closing the distance between us. I wrapped my arms around him, settling my cheek on his shoulder. "Thank you."

He gave me a few pats on the back and chuckled when I stepped back. "You smile a lot more now than you did when you first arrived. Remember, you can do good work anywhere that your heart is full."

I nodded, pushing down the lump that was forming in my throat.

"I know. This place sure has grown on me."

"Magnolia Falls or a certain father and son?" He squeezed my shoulder. "Don't run from joy, Emerson. Just because one person let you down, doesn't mean everyone will."

I swear, Magnolia Falls was no different from Rosewood River.

Everyone knew your business. But they were also rooting for you, so it was hard to be annoyed.

I shook it off. I was interviewing with the most incredible hospital tomorrow. I needed to keep my head on straight. The last time I let myself get distracted, it didn't work out so well for me.

"Thank you. I'll see you tomorrow after the interview." I walked back behind my desk as he made his way out the door with a wave.

I pulled up the potential interview questions that they might ask me and got to work on answering them.

I called it a day when Petra reminded me it was getting late, and I walked out with her. She was still laughing about the changes we'd seen in Carrie Peters since the first time I'd met her. She'd been in today for a wellness check, and she didn't scratch or bite anyone, nor did she have an attitude. Her mom still didn't seem to care for me, but that didn't matter. I'd made progress with Carrie, and that felt like a win.

"You've got a gift. I'm going to call you the tiny human whisperer," Petra said.

A compliment from Petra was something I didn't take for granted, because they didn't come often. But she and I had grown close since our rocky start a few months ago.

I waved goodbye and made my way toward home, with Winnie striding beside me.

I waved at a few locals as they passed by and came to a stop when Janelle was locking up Magnolia Blooms.

She had a big bouquet of pink tulips in her hand. "I was just hurrying over to your office to catch you before you left. I wanted to give you these."

"What are these for?" I gasped as she handed me the enormous bouquet.

"Big day tomorrow. I heard you've got a big interview. I ran into Nash and Cutler earlier and they were telling me about it." She smiled. My heart squeezed that they'd told her about the interview. I stopped into her floral shop often to get fresh blooms for my house, and we'd grown close, too. How had I let that happen? I'd grown close with half the locals here.

"I can't believe they told you and that you did this for me. Thank you."

"Even if I don't want you to leave, I know you deserve whatever it is you want in life, Emerson. So I support that because I support you." She kissed my cheek and made her way to her car, as she lived a little further from downtown. "And, I've got to say. Your boys are awfully proud of you."

My boys.

I waved goodbye and made my way down my street, walking up to the front porch to find a note taped on the door.

Sunny,
I gots the best surprise for you. Come over when you get home.
I love you.
Beefcake

My chest squeezed for maybe the millionth time today, and I pushed inside the house. I fed Winnie and made my way down the hall to change my clothes real quick. The evenings were getting cooler outside, especially by the water, so I slipped into a pair of jeans and my favorite navy hoodie. Winnie and I walked the short distance next door. The back door was open, and music was booming from inside.

Is that Beyoncé filling my ears?

"Hello?" I called out, as my dog ran inside like she lived there.

"Sunny!" Cutler came running toward me. He was wearing a white tee that had something written on it with a Sharpie. He jumped into my arms. "We've got a surprise for you."

I looked over to see Nash coming from the kitchen with a big smile on his face and a white tee that also had writing on it.

"Apparently, tomorrow is the equivalent of your star student day, and he wanted you to have a shirt like Jolie," Nash said, as he glanced down at his shirt. *Sunny's my girl.*

Cutler jumped down and pointed at his shirt, which also read, *Sunny's my girl.*

My heart squeezed so tight I felt like it might explode through my chest.

"It's your big day tomorrow, Sunny." Cutler grabbed my hand as I took in dozens of rainbow-colored balloons hanging from the ceiling and he pointed at the poster board taped to the wall that read *Happy Star Student Day, Sunny.*

229

This had become a topic for Cutler and me ever since he'd opened up to me about it. I'd agreed to make the unicorn Rice Krispie treats for his star student day in two weeks. We'd talked to Nash and explained that store-bought treats were fine most of the time, but homemade treats were a must on your special day.

I took it all in, shaking my head in disbelief as I bent down and hugged Cutler tight.

I hugged him like my life depended on it. Like if I let go, he would disappear.

"Sunny, we've got more to show you." He pulled from my embrace, and I felt the loss of him the minute he hurried to the kitchen.

"You're going to love this," Nash said against my ear. "The kid likes to go a little overboard for his girl, apparently."

His voice was light and full of tease, but nothing about this moment felt light to me.

Nash had completed me in ways I wasn't ready to say aloud yet, and so had his son.

These two had been the reason I smiled every day now.

"It's a meatloaf cake with my favorite spray cheese. Have you heard of Easy Cheese, Sunny?"

"Ummm . . . it's Easton's favorite road trip snack, so of course I have. Because cheese in a can is quite the invention, right?" I said, glancing down at the heart-shaped meatloaf on the large platter. The orange spray cheese made a zigzag line across the front, which I guessed was their attempt at making it look like a beating heart.

"Pops doesn't bake, so we made you a meatloaf cake with a heartbeat. Because you're a doctor, and me and Pops have beating hearts, '*parently*. And Pops says the heart is your favorite of the bodies."

"Organ. It's her favorite organ," Nash said, clearing his throat as his gaze locked with mine. "We didn't want to make it a boring circle. So, we went with a heart-shaped meatloaf. Pretty classy, eh?" he said, moving to the kitchen, acting like they hadn't gone completely overboard for me.

"It's perfect," I said over the lump in my throat. "Thank you so much."

"Hey." Nash carried the enormous meatloaf cake over to the table and stopped in front of me as Cutler wrestled on the couch with Winnie. He placed his thumb and finger on each side of my chin and turned my face until I was looking at him. "Don't go quiet on me. We're excited for you. You're going to crush it. I know how badly you want this. This is us supporting you, nothing more."

Had I completely scared him about showing any sort of emotion? He was always so quick to tell me that nothing was a big deal. Not to overthink it. Reminding me that there was an expiration date for us.

Was that for my benefit or his?

I shook my head and smiled. "I know. And I appreciate it. I'm not being quiet because I'm freaked out."

"Then what's going on in that head of yours, beautiful?" He leaned down and grazed my ear, keeping his voice low.

What was going on in that head of mine?

"Nothing. I just appreciate you both going to this effort," I said.

But it was so much more, and he knew it.

And for the first time in my life, I actually didn't know what I wanted.

And that scared the hell out of me.

25

Nash

KING

Nash is being a total dick today.

> You're working five feet from me, dickskunk. Why are you sending this in a group text?

KING

Because I want everyone to know.

> Of course you do.

ROMEO

King likes to share. What's going on?

RIVER

He's in a relationship for the first time in a very long time, and he doesn't know how to process those feelings.

HAYES

What kind of response is that, River? You sound like a fucking therapist.

KING

He's married to one, so now he's an expert.

RIVER

Hey, that's what Ruby told me when I said Nash seemed a little edgy when I saw him yesterday.

ROMEO

I don't think it's the relationship. I think it's the fact that he doesn't have control of what's going to happen with her. Where it's going or if it'll end when she leaves.

KING

Proud of you, Ro. That was very deep, brother.

You can all fuck off. I'm fine.

HAYES

That lame response is not going to support your claim of being fine. You don't sound fucking fine.

RIVER

Speak, asshole. You can talk to us.

Things are good. Really fucking good. But she's got interviews every week, and she's leaving. Today, she has an interview with a children's hospital in Boston. And that's where she wants to go.

KING

Maybe in the end, she won't want to leave. What makes you so sure?

Because she came here after she called off her wedding from the last dickhead she dated. I'm the fucking rebound guy. I'm not the forever guy. And I'm worried about Cutler. He's getting too fucking attached.

KING

You are nobody's rebound, brother. You're the gold standard. She's smart, and she knows it. But damn, I love the chowder in Boston.

HAYES

Who gives a shit about chowder, jackass?

RIVER

Anyway, it sounds like you and Cutler are both getting attached. And I think that terrifies the shit out of you. Don't run from it, brother. Fight for it.

ROMEO

Have you talked to her about staying?

KING

Of course, he hasn't. That would be too logical. Maybe you could write it on a sticky note?

I hope you get stung in the dick by a bee today, King. 🐝

HAYES

If this is the real deal, you better fight, brother. There are no second chances.

Let's talk at the gym today when we have lunch. I need to get to work.

RIVER

Remember, brother, we've got your back.

HAYES

Ride or die.

KING

Brothers till the end.

ROMEO

Loyalty always.

RIVER

Forever my friend.

I shook my head at the words tattooed on my shoulder. The words we'd always lived by. I knew they had my back, and it settled me.

I set my phone down and got back to hanging shiplap on the large wall of the dining room, which we were painting in a black satin finish.

I thought about what the guys had said, and I knew they were right. We were spending a ridiculous amount of time together. But Emerson had made it clear that she wasn't staying. She wanted a fresh start in a new city.

I was the interim guy.

A pit stop on the way to her next destination.

And I'd been fine with that because I wasn't looking for anything serious either.

But now I wasn't so sure. She fit perfectly into my life. Into my son's life.

The three of us just worked in a way I'd never experienced.

It hadn't been like this with Tara—ever.

She'd been miserable after Cutler was born.

Resentful and unhappy.

And I'd found my footing on my own, and I'd liked it that way. No room to be let down.

But I'd opened this door, and she'd surprised me.

Everything was better with Emerson in our world. And that scared the shit out of me because getting attached to her was dangerous.

And I had Cutler to think about.

My phone vibrated with another text, and I pulled it from my back pocket.

EMERSON

> Hey! Just finished the interview with Boston Children's, and it went really well. They said they were impressed when they read my letters of recommendation.

I scrubbed a hand over the back of my neck. She wanted this.

And I wanted her to be happy. Even if that meant I would be miserable.

That was why we'd gone all out last night. My son had been the one to remind me over and over that it was her big day coming up, and we needed to celebrate it. I knew her ex was the one who'd talked her out of doing her residency there, and I would not be that guy.

I would never hold her back.

If she decided to stay, it would be because she wanted to stay. Not because anyone guilted her or pressured her.

> Of course, they were impressed. You're fucking amazing, beautiful. They'd be fools to let you go.

So would I.

> **EMERSON**
>
> That was awfully sweet of you to say, neighbor. Do you think I should take it if they offer me the position?

> Does my opinion really matter in this decision?

It was a dick thing to say. I shouldn't have said it. But there was truth to my words. We'd put so many rules in place that I didn't know where the lines were.

I saw the three little dots move across the screen, and I waited.

> **EMERSON**
>
> Yes, actually. Your opinion matters to me.

My chest puffed out like I'd just won some big fight that I hadn't expected to win.

> **EMERSON**
>
> And King said that Boston has the best chowder. So maybe you'll come visit me. But Seattle Children's seems interested, too, and they're famous for their coffee, and I know you love your coffee.

I deflated in an instant. She was just being polite; she wasn't asking because she saw a future for us. I needed to pull my head out of my ass and remember what this was.

Temporary. We were just having fun.
So have some fucking fun, asshole.

> It's good to have options. I'm happy to help you work through it.

EMERSON

> Dinner tonight at my place?

This was getting too complicated. For me. For my boy. I needed to tread lightly.

> We're having dinner at my dad's tonight, and I want to get Cutler down early because it's a school night.

I'd planned on inviting her. My dad loved her, as they'd met twice over the last few weeks. But distance was necessary, and I needed to man up and protect my boy because this was going to hurt like hell when she left.

EMERSON

> Oh, okay. 👍

That wasn't a typical response from her, so I'd probably pissed her off. But she was the one who was one foot out the door. I needed to do the same.

* * *

"Why didn't Emerson come with us to Gramps' house for dinner?" Cutler asked for maybe the hundredth time tonight.

A reminder of how badly I'd fucked up. How easily I'd let this happen.

"Because tonight was just about us visiting your grandfather. We can't spend every night with Emerson. She's not staying forever. She's just here for a few more months."

"Pops, Emerson is my girl. It doesn't matter how long she stays. I'll still love her no matter where she lives," he said, and my fucking chest squeezed at his words.

My boy loved so deeply, and it scared the shit out of me. I'd known it, and I'd still let him get attached. I'd never made that mistake before now, and I was so fucking pissed at myself for allowing this.

"It's fine to love someone and let them go. As long as you know they're leaving." I cleared my throat as I turned down our street. The sun was just going down, and the temperatures always dropped this time of year in Magnolia Falls.

"You worry too much, Pops." He chuckled, and movement on Emerson's front porch pulled my attention.

There was a guy standing there with her, and the conversation looked heated. It was her stance that had me reacting. Her arms were crossed over her chest, her shoulders tense and eyes hard.

"Cutler, I need you to go sit on the chair on our front porch and wait for me. Do you understand?"

His eyes were as wide as saucers when I jumped out of the truck and helped him out and pointed to the porch. "I got it."

I was moving before I even stopped to think about it. Her voice was louder than I'd ever heard it, as she shouted something at him that I couldn't make out.

I was across the yard and up the stairs, with my hands gathered in his sweater as I pulled him back and shouted in his face. "Get the fuck away from her!"

"Who the hell are you?" he asked, shoving me back but not moving me at all.

This guy was weak, and I saw the fear in his eyes.

"I'm your worst fucking nightmare." I stepped in front of him, my face inches from his.

"Stop, Nash. I've got it handled," Emerson said, rushing to stand between us.

"Is this the fucking guy?" I asked, venom leaving my lips as I glared at him.

She squeezed her eyes shut and let out a long breath as she gave me the slightest nod. "Please let me handle this."

"I don't know who the fuck you are, but I came a long way to talk to her, so I suggest you go on home, *neighbor*." He raised a brow as he brushed the nonexistent wrinkles from his annoying-as-fuck V-neck sweater.

"Pops! Is Emerson okay?" Cutler called out from our front porch. I heard the concern, and so did she. Her gaze moved from me to our house next door, and she looked torn. Unsure what to do.

"I'm fine, angel face," she called out.

"Everything is okay, buddy. Stay right there!" I yelled over to him before turning back to her. "Do you want him to stay and me to go?"

She sighed, resting a hand on my forearm. "Let me handle this, okay?"

Her words stung. I held my hands up and took a step back as the asshole smirked at me.

"You heard her. She's fine. Go home."

"You're fucking lucky my boy is watching, or I'd lay you out right here, you weak motherfucker." I flipped him the bird and stormed toward my house.

Once we were inside, Cutler started firing off eight hundred fucking questions, just like I knew he would.

Who was the guy on Emerson's porch?

Why did I seem angry?

Why did he stay there?

241

Why isn't she coming over?

"Pops, you're not listening. Who's Emerson's friend?" he asked as I guided him to the bathroom and turned on the water in the tub.

It was a school night. I needed to stay focused.

"I don't know," I said, because I didn't have a better answer at the moment.

But my blood was boiling.

Did she want to talk to the asshole? Did she miss him? Would she consider going back to him?

I had a shit ton of questions of my own.

Like father, like son, apparently.

"Get undressed and hop into the tub," I said, trying hard to hide the anger from my tone. My son didn't need to be exposed to that.

He stepped into the bathtub and sat down, and I handed him his body wash and grabbed the cup to pour water over his head.

"I liked when Sunny gave me a bath last night."

I squeezed my eyes shut and tried to chill the fuck out. "Well, you're stuck with me tonight, kiddo."

"You're my favorite, Pops. I like being stuck with you." He scrubbed the shampoo into his hair, and his words settled me in a way. "But I like being stuck with Sunny, too."

And just like that, I was pissed off all over again.

I dropped to sit on the floor while he played around in the water, and I glanced down at my phone to see I'd missed a few texts.

TARA

Guess what?

Hello? Are you not going to guess?

NASH! Are you there?

She'd always had zero patience. Clearly, that hadn't changed because all three texts came in at the exact same time.

What is it? I'm trying to bathe my son.

TARA

I found an Airbnb. I'm coming back home to spend time with my boys in two weeks.

And just when I thought things couldn't get worse . . . Life managed to surprise me.

26

Emerson

"Who was that guy, Em?" Collin hissed from behind me as I stormed into my house, and Winnie followed us inside.

The nerve of this guy, just showing up here and thinking he was entitled to ask me anything.

"That is none of your damn business. What are you even doing here?" I dropped my purse on the counter and crossed my arms over my chest as I turned to face him.

It had been a long day at the office. I'd had a great interview, but then my text with Nash had left me feeling off. It was the first night in weeks that he hadn't wanted to hang out. All my insecurities were coming out in full force, and then I'd come home to find the devil himself standing on my front porch.

"Well, you won't take my calls, and I needed to speak to you." He looked different. Tired. Pale. Frazzled.

Although Nash definitely added to Collin's anxiety when he stormed over here like a freaking caveman.

It took all that I had not to kick Collin out and jump into Nash's arms. I'd missed him all day, and I'd been disappointed that I wouldn't be seeing him tonight, which was why I'd worked late.

But I needed this to end with Collin, so I'd have one final conversation with him if that would mean he would stop trying to reach me. I motioned for him to sit down on the couch, and I took the chair across from him, my dog lying right beside my chair protectively. "There is nothing more to talk about, Collin. You need to let this go and move on. I have."

"I can see that. So, are you fucking him?"

"I'm going to give you the next two minutes to tell me why you're here, and then I'm going to tell you to leave. My personal life is none of your damn business."

"So it means nothing that I've not been sleeping or eating because I miss you? You won't speak to me. You're clearly fucking some random dude. And I'm the bad guy?" He threw his hands in the air.

It was the strangest thing. I'd spent more than a decade with this man, yet sitting here, with him acting completely unhinged—it did nothing to me.

I felt nothing.

I was more anxious about Nash being upset.

A man I'd only known for a few months.

A man who made me feel—everything.

"Collin." My voice was completely calm and lacking any emotion. "I know how much you like to be the smartest guy in the room, and you like to wield it like some sort of trophy over everyone's heads. But it won't work here. *You are the bad guy* because you fucked my best friend for months before our wedding day."

"I lost my mind, Emerson. Your residency was a nightmare, and you were working such long hours, and I was—I don't know," he pushed to his feet and paced around the room, "I was lonely."

"You should have talked to me. But it wouldn't have changed anything, Collin. I was in my final year of residency. Those are the hours that I was required to work. And you were traveling all the time anyway. You didn't want to live together before we were married, so yeah, we were living separate lives. I get it. But I never once considered straying. I thought we were just going to get through those final challenging months, and after the wedding, we'd be on the other side of it," I said, as he dropped back down to sit across from me.

He buried his head in his hands, and Winnie lifted her head to look at him before setting it back down. "What can I do to fix this, Em?"

"You can't fix it. You can't talk your way out of it or throw money at it. The truth is, we weren't working, Collin. I was just too busy to realize it at the time. I didn't know anything different, and sure, we had some good times over the years. But we were spending less and less time together these last three years. We both played a part in that," I said, holding my hands up when he looked like he'd just found his opening. "But let me tell you what I didn't do. I didn't fuck another man while we were together. Let alone your best friend. It's irreparable, Collin."

"So you just waited until I was the bad guy, and then you fucked another man? Weeks after we were supposed to be married?" He raised a brow.

It hit me in that moment that this was what he always did. He was relentless when it came to winning an argument. And most of the time, people backed down. Hell, I'd probably backed down hundreds of times over the years because it just wasn't worth the fight.

"Oh, my gosh. This is what you do, Collin."

"What am I doing now?" he groaned.

"You just argue until you get your way."

"No, I don't. I'm just trying to win back the woman I love. This is me, fighting for you."

"It's a pattern. When you didn't want to live together, I thought it was ridiculous. We'd been dating for years. We were engaged. We were both paying rent at two expensive apartments in the city. But you wanted to wait. You insisted that it was the proper thing to do. And I'm guessing that was really convenient, considering you were fucking my best friend for six months." I shrugged, all of it hitting me like a ton of bricks now.

"I was trying to respect you by not living together first," he said.

A maniacal laugh escaped my mouth, and his eyes widened. "Respect me? Do you even hear yourself? You have zero respect for me after what you've done. Collin, there is no me and you. We are as done as anyone can get. And honestly, part of me wants to forgive you because I'm happy now. Happier than I think I've been in a very long time. And I want us both to be free of this anger. But the betrayal and the fact that you have ruined my relationship with my best friend—I don't know how to ever forgive you for that. You could have chosen anyone."

His eyes widened in shock. "So you don't care that I cheated. You care that I cheated with Farah?"

"In this moment . . . yes. Because you and I are done either way. It wouldn't have mattered who you'd cheated with; I would have walked away from you, regardless. We clearly had nothing worth fighting for because I've never once thought about trying to work it out with you since the moment that I found out what you did." My words were harsh but true. A lump formed in my throat. "I'm just sad that it had to end this way."

"So you aren't willing to go to relationship counseling with me?" he asked.

"No. There's nothing to fix here. We're better apart. I know it. You know it." My gaze locked with his. "What are you even fighting for? We weren't happy, or you wouldn't have strayed. This is just about winning for you, Collin. And there's nothing to win."

LAURA PAVLOV

"You're wrong, Em. You're the best thing that ever happened to me." He clasped his hands together.

"Well, if that's true, I'm sorry for you, because there's no turning back. But for me, that relationship was not the best thing that ever happened to me. Not even close. And you need to believe me when I tell you that we're done. I don't have anything else to say to you."

"You don't miss me? Miss us?" he pressed, and I was frustrated that he was still pushing.

"I don't." His eyes were locked with mine, and he finally nodded.

I could see it there in his light blue eyes. He finally got it. He knew it was over.

"You've never looked at me the way you were looking at him, Em," he whispered.

"What?"

"Your neighbor. I knew it the minute he came running over. I still thought I could fight for you. Make you see my point. But I lost before I even arrived here."

"Collin, you lost the minute I found out about you and Farah. You and me being done has nothing to do with Nash." I cleared my throat. "But I'd be lying if I didn't admit that he's shown me how good things can be. How it should be when you're with someone. You and I haven't had that in a very long time."

"Had what?"

"The loyalty. The passion. The friendship. The love. Any of it. We were just good on paper."

"Don't say that. I finally accept that it's over. But don't say we never had anything." He swiped at his cheek when a tear rolled down his face. "I'm sorry, Em. I'm so fucking sorry for what I did. I hope someday you'll be able to forgive me."

"I hope there's a time when we can all forgive and forget.

248

I'm just not there yet, and you need to stop calling and pushing, okay?"

He nodded. "Okay."

"Hey, Collin," I said, mustering the strength to say what I needed to say next.

"Yeah?"

"You must have had some kind of feelings for Farah to have carried on for as long as you did." I clasped my hands together, because I didn't want to care about her, but I still did.

"It was a mistake. It shouldn't have happened."

"But it did." I reminded him. "And I know she's going through a hard time, and I can't be there for her. But you should be. You two got into this together. And you've got all the support from your family. She's alone, and you know it. So if there were any feelings worth exploring, I think you should explore those with her. You and I can't repair what we had, but maybe you and her have something deeper than you want to admit."

"Wow. You're really done with me." His gaze searched mine. "You're in love with this guy, aren't you?"

I didn't answer him.

I didn't need to.

I sure as hell wasn't going to tell Collin something that I should be telling Nash.

"Just remember that you cared enough to carry on with her for months. She's alone right now, Collin, and if you're avoiding her because you think I'm going to care, you're wrong."

"I hear you loud and clear, Emerson. Do you think you can call your brothers and your cousins off the warpath? I'll agree to leave you alone, but I'd like to be able to go to Rosewood River without feeling threatened."

I rolled my eyes, even though I knew he was right. They

were an intimidating bunch, and I'm sure they wouldn't hesitate to scare the shit out of him.

"If it means we can move forward, yes. No more calls. No more texts from other phones. I'll ask my family to back off when they see you next."

He nodded and stood. "Thank you. I wanted to offer you the tickets for our honeymoon. I can't cancel it, and it's prepaid. You can go and get away for a bit. Seems like the least I could do."

"Thanks for the offer, but you can go ahead and use them. My getaway was coming here to Magnolia Falls, and it's been exactly what I needed."

"I can see that." He cracked his knuckles, a habit that he'd had for as long as I'd known him. He walked toward the door. "I want you to be happy, Em. You deserve it."

"I'm actually really happy, Collin. I wish things hadn't gone down the way that they did, but I think we're both better for it." I pulled the door open and paused. "I want you to know that I wish you the best. I don't wish you ill will. I may not be able to be your friend right now, and maybe I never will be, but I do want the best for you."

His eyes were wet with emotion, and he forced a smile. "I want the best for you, too. I need you to know that I will regret what I did to you for the rest of my life. I'm really sorry. Thanks for hearing me out today."

I nodded and watched as he walked to his car.

I hadn't wanted to speak to him, but I knew this was necessary and final.

And I didn't feel any sort of sadness about it. All I felt was relief.

But what surprised me the most was where my mind kept going.

I wasn't sad or heartbroken after seeing Collin. My boyfriend of ten years. My ex-fiancé and the man I was supposed to spend my life with.

Instead, all I could think about was the man next door.

The one who'd flown into a rage at the sight of my ex being here.

The man I missed if I didn't see him every single day.

The man, I realized in this moment, that I'd fallen in love with.

27

Nash

I got Cutler down to sleep and grabbed a beer from the refrigerator. I'd noticed the asshole's car was gone out front, but I hadn't heard from Emerson.

Maybe she was confused after seeing him.

Hell, for all I knew, she might have left with him.

This was why I didn't do attachments. I didn't have time to get worked up like this. I took a long pull from my beer as I paced around the living room.

Fuck.

Why was I so pissed off about him coming here?

It was none of my fucking business.

A light knock on the back door startled me from my thoughts, and I moved quickly across the room and yanked it open.

She was wearing a pair of jean shorts and a white hoodie, hair pulled back in a knot at the nape of her neck. The sky was lit by only the light from the moon and the stars overhead.

"So what was that about?" she asked. Her hands were on her hips, and she raised a brow.

"I could ask you the same thing."

"I didn't know he was coming. But you overreacted a bit, don't you think?"

I crossed my arms over my chest, mouth in a straight line as I stared at her. "Overreacted? I actually think I underreacted. I would have knocked his ass out if Cutler hadn't been standing on the porch next door, watching."

"Do you want to tell me why you wanted to knock him out?" she asked, stepping a little closer.

"Because he fucking hurt you. He doesn't deserve your time."

"Okay. But you do know that I can take care of myself, right?"

"I'm more than aware, Emerson. You remind me all the time," I hissed. "But sometimes I like to take care of you, so you'll just have to deal with it."

"Is that so?" Her lips turned up the slightest bit in the corners.

"That is so."

"And the only reason you were upset about him being here was because you knew that he hurt me?"

I narrowed my gaze as Winnie came jogging over from the grass and walked past me like she owned the place. But I hadn't invited Emerson in yet. I was trying to put distance there, right?

Hell, I don't know what the fuck I'm doing anymore.

"What other reason would there be?" I asked, my voice gruff as she moved closer, her chest bumping into mine as I looked down at her.

"It seemed like maybe you were jealous."

I chuckled and scrubbed a hand over the back of my neck. "I don't get jealous."

"Not even a little bit?" Her hands moved to my chest, and she tipped her head back to look up at me.

"Does it even fucking matter?" I hissed, suddenly angry again as I turned and stepped into my house, and she followed me inside.

"Yes, Nash. It fucking matters."

I was surprised to hear the anger in her voice. She was the one throwing all the mixed signals. She was the one leaving in a few months. She was the one who had just been chatting with her ex-fiancé. Why the fuck was she irritated?

"Listen, I overreacted. I saw him there, and I didn't like it."

"Why?" she pressed, following me to the kitchen, where I grabbed my beer and leaned against the counter. "Why didn't you like it?"

"I don't know."

She reached for the beer and took it from my hand, setting it on the counter beside me. "Yes, you do."

"What the fuck do you want from me, Emerson? I've been playing by your rules this whole fucking time."

Her eyes widened. "My rules? You were the one who said you don't do relationships. How are these *my* rules?"

"Fine. They were our rules. And it's just gotten—complicated."

"And you don't like complicated, right?" she asked, moving right in front of me again and fisting her fingers in my shirt.

"I don't know what I like anymore." I looked away because I couldn't look into those jade-green eyes and lie to her. I knew exactly what I wanted.

I want her. All of her.

"Nash," she said my name on a whisper. "Look at me."

I swallowed hard and turned to face her. Her eyes were wet with emotion, and her bottom lip trembled.

"Are you going back to him?" I finally asked, because I couldn't help myself.

She looked surprised by the question. "Is that what you think? You think I would go back to him?"

"I don't know. It's crossed my mind over the last hour while you've been over there with him."

"So you *were* jealous?" Her lips turned up in the corners as a tear ran down her cheek.

"Tell me what happened."

"He apologized. Maybe he needed more closure, I don't know. I've made peace with what happened a while ago. So, that was more for him than for me." She reached for my hands and intertwined her fingers with mine. "But what surprised me was what I realized over the last hour while he was there."

"What did you realize?"

"I realized that all I was thinking about was you. Wondering why you were so upset that he was there. Wondering why you'd gone to dinner without me tonight when we've been together every night for weeks. Wondering if you'd grown tired of spending time with me."

"That wasn't it at all," I said, my voice gruff as my hands moved to each side of her face.

"Why, then?" Her voice shook, and I knew what she was asking.

"Because you had the interview today, and it went well. Because you're fucking leaving, and I don't know what that means for us. I know I'm just a stop along the way for you."

"A stop along the way? That's what you think?"

"I'm a realist, Emerson. I have a kid to think about. He's getting attached. I've got to be smart."

She pinned her lips between her teeth and shook her head the slightest bit. "You're worried about Cutler? He's the only one who's getting attached?"

I groaned. "We're both getting fucking attached."

"And that's a bad thing?" she pressed.

"Yeah. It's a bad thing. You just got out of a long relationship, and I'm the fucking rebound guy. I know that. I

255

signed up for that. But things are getting too heavy. I needed to pull back."

"You aren't the rebound guy, Nash. You were never the rebound guy." The tears were falling down her cheeks now.

"What am I, then?"

"You're the man who put me back together and made me realize how good things could be. You're the man I think about every second of the day. It was never like this for me before. That's why I can't even hate Collin anymore. You ruined that for me," she said, and her voice shook with each word.

"Ruined that for you, how?"

"I can't hate someone for doing something that led me to finding what I needed all along. I don't know how it happened, but somewhere along the way of keeping it casual, I fell in love with you, Nash Heart. I didn't know it could feel like this, and it scares the shit out of me. And I don't know what it means for our future or if I should stay or go. I don't even know what I want anymore professionally, because you've changed everything. But I know without a shadow of a doubt that I love you. I love the man that you are. The father that you are. And I love your little boy." Her words were barely audible over her sobs. "And I'm terrified to love again and to trust anyone again. But I can't hold in all these things I'm feeling anymore."

My heart pounded so loud I could hear it in my ears as I watched her lay it all out there. I hadn't expected it. Hell, I hadn't realized how much I'd needed to hear it.

"Emerson," I said, reaching for her hand before resting it against my heart. My large hand over her smaller one. "This right here. It beats every time I look at you. Every time you laugh. Every time you smile. Every time you walk toward me. It's always beat for my son, but I swear to God, my fucking heart beats for you now, too. You brought a part of me back to life. A part that I didn't even realize was gone. I love you, and it scares the shit out of me."

"Beating heart," she whispered, tears streaming down her cheeks.

"I don't want to hold you back, Emerson. I will not be that guy who tells you what to do. If you want to work at that hospital in Boston, I'm going to support you. I want you to chase your dreams and have everything you want. But my life is here. Cutler's life is here. So I don't know how this works."

She was looking up at me through teary eyes, lips turned up in the corners, as she tangled her fingers in my hair. "All I know is that I've never felt like this before. I almost married a man, and it wasn't like this, Nash. And I know that this—what we have—is rare. It's what's most important in life."

"Agreed. So, we'll make it work. But we don't have to have it all figured out right now. All that matters is that we know what this is now. We love each other."

"We love each other," she whispered, smiling up at me. I used my thumbs to swipe away the moisture on her cheeks. "I don't think either of us saw this coming."

"The only thing I see coming right now is you," I said, as I scooped her up in my arms. Her head fell back in a fit of laughter, and I carried her down the hall toward my bedroom. I kissed her hard to keep her quiet before tossing her onto the bed. She reached behind her head and tugged the elastic from her hair and let her long waves fall all around her.

"I need to taste you, baby. Right fucking now," I said.

Her teeth sank into her juicy bottom lip, and she lifted her hips enough for me to tug her denim shorts and lace panties down her legs.

"My girl has the prettiest pussy I've ever seen, and I can't get enough," I said, my voice gruff as I tugged her so that her hips landed at the edge of the bed before I dropped to my knees.

I hooked her legs over my shoulders, and my tongue swiped

along her slit, and I groaned at how wet and ready she was for me. I sucked on her clit as she squirmed beneath me.

Grinding all that sweetness against my lips.

I couldn't get enough.

Couldn't get enough of the way her fingers tangled in my hair. Of the little sounds she made when she was turned on. Of the way the words *I love you* sounded coming from her lips.

Words I never thought I'd need to say to a woman.

Words I never thought I'd need to hear from a woman.

"Nash." She cried out my name as her thighs clamped around my head, and she went right over the edge.

I stayed right there as she ground up against me, riding out every last bit of pleasure.

She tugged my head up, my gaze finding hers.

"I need you inside me right now," she whispered.

"Exactly what I was thinking," I said, before climbing over her and kissing her hard. I was on my feet and hustling over to the nightstand for a condom.

I rolled the latex over my throbbing cock and moved back to the bed. I hovered above her and just stared at her for the longest time.

"I don't know what I did to deserve you, but I'd sure like to keep you, beautiful," I said, my voice all tease, but I meant every single word.

I did want to keep her.

And if there was a way to do that without stifling her dreams, I was damn well going to do it.

Her eyes were wet with emotion, and she intertwined her fingers with mine as I shifted so the tip of my dick teased her entrance. I pinned her arms above her head, holding them there with one hand as I slid inside her, inch by inch.

Taking my time before I buried myself inside her.

I needed her in a way that wasn't familiar.

All of her.

Mind and body.

Her eyes stayed on mine, and I leaned down and kissed her.

Tongues tangled. Breaths came hard and fast as we found our rhythm.

This fucking woman was made for me.

And she was mine in every way.

28

Emerson

Nash disposed of the condom and strode back toward the bed as I propped myself up to watch him. I'd never met a man who was so confident in his own skin. He climbed into bed and pulled me against his chest, wrapping his arms around me and kissing the top of my head.

"What a day," I whispered.

"Yeah, that's an understatement."

I tipped my head back to look at him. "I was pretty freaked out when you didn't ask me to go to your dad's for dinner."

"Well, trust me, I paid for it. My dad gave me a hard time from the minute we walked through the door, wanting to know where you were. If you were coming late. If you were bringing some sort of fairy dust Krispies," he said with a laugh.

"Unicorn Rice Krispies. Come on, Heart, get your pastries straight."

"Yeah, that was it. And then Cutler was relentless." He tightened his hold on me. "I think it hit me today when you texted about the interview."

"What hit you?"

"That I'm so fucking in love with you, I can't see straight.

And then I worried about my boy, because if I'm not able to keep it together, what happens to him? So, my instinct was to pull back. I should have talked to you."

"I get it. It freaks me out, too." My hand found his cheek, and I ran my fingers along his jaw. "I was with Collin for a really long time, and it never felt like this. Like I couldn't breathe when I wasn't with him. Maybe my mom's right and this was supposed to happen."

"What do you mean?" he asked, as his fingers ran soothingly along my collarbone.

"My mom always says that things happen for a reason, and I find the whole saying to be a little annoying. Especially after what happened. Like, there was no real reason for that to happen the way that it did. They could have just told me." I sighed. "But, in hindsight . . . that anger led me to leave the hospital because I sure as hell couldn't work with Farah every day and act professional. And I didn't want to stay in a city where they both lived. I didn't want to go back to Rosewood River, where everyone knew my story. And then I heard about this position in Magnolia Falls, and I jumped at it. So . . . maybe things do happen for a reason."

I could feel him smile against my hair. "I get that. I think things do happen for a reason. I know that everything I went through with Tara was all worth it because it got me Cutler."

"Definitely worth it. That boy . . ." I shook my head. "I miss him when he's not around, you know?"

Nash chuckled. "Yeah. I know."

"He talks to me about things. I hope that's okay with you?"

"I've heard him opening up to you. It's funny, I've asked the guys if he talks to them about Tara or about the kid in his class and their family situations, and they didn't know nearly as much as he shares with you. That's what worried me. And part of why I freaked out earlier is how attached he's grown to you. But at the same time, I like that he talks to you."

"Did you really think I could just leave and walk away from both of you now?"

"I didn't know. We had a plan. I know you like your plans." He chuckled, and I couldn't hide the smile on my face. "I don't know how this will all play out, but I think if we want to make it work, we'll make it work."

"Yeah," I whispered, because the thought of being away from them made me anxious. "What would that look like?"

"This is what I know. I know you're fucking brilliant. I know that you're determined and driven, and I love that about you. So, if you need to go to Boston and I need to be here, then we FaceTime every day, and we visit as often as we can. After a year, if you love it there, then we look at options."

"What kind of options?"

"I sell my company to King, and I'll start over in Boston. Cutler would be fine with an adventure," he said, but I heard the apprehension.

I flipped onto my stomach and gaped at him. "You can't move to Boston. You've got your dad here and your friends and your life."

He stroked the hair away from my face. "I grew up without a mom, and Cutler has, too. And it's worked for all these years, but now that we've had this time with you, I don't want to be away from you. You complete us in a way I didn't know would be possible. That's most important. All the other shit will work itself out. So, we'll do the distance for a year, and if you love it there, then we'll come to you. If you hate it, we'll be waiting for you here. So you just chase your dreams, beautiful, and we'll be right here, cheering you on."

Never in my wildest dreams could I have imagined a man saying those words to me.

And meaning them.

I felt loved and cherished and appreciated when I was with Nash.

I hugged him tighter. "So, we're doing this?"

"Oh, we're doing this. Now that I know you feel the same way I do, it's on, baby." He flipped me onto my back and tickled me as laughter echoed around the room.

And we stayed up for hours talking about our dreams and our future.

And I fell asleep feeling the most content I had in years.

I didn't know what the plan was, but I knew he and Cutler would be right beside me.

That's all I needed to know.

Sleep took me, and I didn't move until the sun had me blinking awake, and I heard a little voice in the room.

"Hey, Pops. Sunny slept over?" Cutler asked.

"She did. Is that all right?" Nash asked, and I squinted to see him coming out of the bathroom before he tried to hustle Cutler out of the room.

I pushed up to sit, chuckling at the oversized tee falling off my shoulder that Nash had given me to sleep in. I'd never spent the night here, but Nash said he'd be up before Cutler, and he'd say that he slept on the couch until he explained everything to him. I patted the bed for Cutler to come sit beside me. "Hey. Good morning, angel face. Don't leave on my account."

"I love waking up and finding you here. It's even better than J.T. being here, but don't tell him I said that."

I pretended to zip my lips and laughed. "I won't say a word."

Winnie came flying around the corner and jumped into the bed, and Cutler fell back into hysterical laughter as Nash informed us that he'd already taken her out and run next door to get her food, so she'd had breakfast, as well.

This man.

"So, we wanted to talk to you this morning," Nash said, moving to sit on the edge of the bed, with Cutler between us and Winnie lying on her back across the bed.

"This is like a family meeting, isn't it, Pops?"

My chest squeezed at his words and the way Nash's gaze softened when he looked at his son. "Yeah, buddy. It is like a family meeting. Do you like having family meetings?"

"Yes. Because Sunny is my girl, and Winnie is my best friend, next to J.T."

"Well, we were thinking about making things more official. You know how Emerson spends a lot of time with us, and we both like it?"

"I know, Pops. And you keep saying she's leaving, and I keep telling you it doesn't matter if she leaves, because I love her no matter where she is." He scooched closer to me, leaning his head against my chest, and my arms wrapped around him. He smelled like coconut and sunshine and sweetness.

I loved this kid so fiercely that it caught me off guard sometimes.

That I could grow this attached in just a few months.

But I had.

"Yeah, you mentioned that a couple of times." Nash chuckled. "And you were right. Me and Sunny talked about it last night, and we don't want to say goodbye. So we thought maybe we'd enjoy this time while she and Winnie live next door, and then when she leaves, we'll talk to her every day and go visit as often as we can."

"We could go with her, couldn't we?"

A lump formed in my throat. They'd both been so willing to just leave their lives to be with me. It made my heart ache, and I kissed the top of his head.

"I don't even know if I have the job yet." Or if I even want the job, if I'm being honest. After the interview and hearing the hours that I'd be working, it didn't sound as appealing as it had when I applied for residency.

Maybe I was different then.

Maybe I hadn't enjoyed life outside of work back then, the way that I did now.

I wouldn't share the apprehension I was feeling at the moment, because I didn't know what I'd do just yet.

"How about this," Nash said, staring at both me and Cutler like we were his whole world. "We take it one day at a time. We know we want to be together, so let's just make it happen, however we need to."

"I like that. I got my pops, my Sunny, and my Winnie. Our family just got bigger, right?"

I chuckled, and Nash shook his head with a big smile on his face. "It did. How about we take the boat out today before it gets too cold to go out on the water? Why don't you go get your suit on."

"Yes!" Cutler hustled out of the bed and ran down the hall, with Winnie chasing after him.

We both pushed to our feet, and Nash pulled me into his arms. "You ready for this? He's all in now."

"I'm all in." I pushed up on my tiptoes. "How about you?"

He took my hand and placed it over his heart, and I could feel the steady beating against my palm. "I've been all in since the day you moved next door."

"You couldn't stand me when you first met me." I laughed as I planted a kiss on his lips.

"I thought you were hot, but you did come barreling through my door pretty early on a Saturday morning."

"I'm glad I rang your bell," I said, my voice teasing.

"Oh, you rang my bell, all right." His mouth crashed into mine, and he kissed me hard.

"Pops, quit kissing my Sunny, and get your bathing suit on!" Cutler shouted from down the hall.

Nash pulled back as he barked out a laugh and turned me toward the bathroom, giving me a little smack on the ass. I'd left a suit here the last time we'd gone out on the boat.

LAURA PAVLOV

"You heard the boy. Let's go, beautiful."

We both changed quickly. I ran next door and packed up some snacks, and the three of us piled onto the boat, with Winnie in tow.

And it was the best day I'd ever had, honestly.

Because it felt different. And in the words of Cutler Heart: It was our first family day out on the boat.

And I wouldn't have it any other way.

* * *

"They are on their way now," Ruby said, as we all gathered near the door of Whiskey Falls, waiting for the newly engaged couple to arrive.

Today was the day that Kingston had proposed to Saylor, and I'd spent the morning with my two boys before we took Cutler over to J.T.'s house for dinner so we could get over here for the surprise engagement party.

"Well, I've got to give him credit," Nash said. "He stuck to the timeline of this ridiculous itinerary. He didn't miss a beat."

River barked out a laugh. "Yeah, I think it helped that he had Katie taking photos and updating us the entire time about what was happening." Katie worked at Saylor's bookstore, and she was also a photographer.

Kingston was a romantic guy, and with Saylor owning a romance bookstore, they complemented one another so well. I was thrilled for her.

"Our girl must be over the moon," Demi said, wrapping an arm around me and hugging me.

"Yeah. Those photos she texted looked pretty swoony."

"Okay, they're parking now," Ruby said. "Get ready. When the doors open, we just start screaming and cheering."

"I'm so ready. Let the fun begin!" Peyton shouted, and Demi started jumping up and down.

Nash moved behind me, my back to his chest. This last week, since we'd been honest about how we felt about one another, had been amazing. The man continued to surprise me. He was always up before me, so he'd been feeding Winnie and taking her out before I was even out of bed.

It was these little things that he didn't think were a big deal that meant so much.

I'd come home from work two days ago, and my car was in the driveway, all clean and shiny. He'd gone to put air in the tires and had my car washed, then just left it in the driveway like it was nothing.

That was Nash.

He was a caretaker by nature, but only for the people that he loved, which were few.

And I was lucky to be one of them.

The door sprung open, and loud cheers filled the air around us. Saylor startled, and King pulled her in front of him as her head fell back in laughter. She held up her hand to show off the ring. "I'm getting hitched!"

Hayes was the first one to wrap his arms around his sister, and he spun her around before turning to Kingston. "Welcome to the family, brother. Hurt her, and I'll kill you."

Kingston barked out a laugh as he pulled Hayes into a hug, and we all took turns congratulating them.

There was food and drinks that Kingston had ordered ahead of time, and we moved to the area that we'd all helped decorate earlier, and listened as Saylor and Kingston retold the events.

"Don't you worry, my friends. I had a professional videographer there, as well, so we'll be watching the video for years to come," Kingston said, his arm around his fiancée as she beamed up at him.

This was how it should be. Watching these two together—a love that was impossible to miss.

I didn't even know it was supposed to be like that.

Yet I'd found a man that I looked at the same way.

And I wanted time to stand still right now because I was truly happy.

I woke up happy. I went to sleep happy. And I was happy in between.

I didn't know life could be this good.

The night was so much fun, as we were eating and laughing, and we'd all been out on the dance floor having a great time.

Nash's phone beeped, and he glanced down at a text before holding it up for me to read the message from J.T.'s father.

JAY

> Can you have Emerson call us? J.T. just fell off the swing set, and I think he might have broken his arm.

I stepped aside to make the call and quickly assessed that he needed to get him to the emergency room right away. I could hear J.T. crying in the background, and I didn't miss the panic in Cutler's voice as he spoke to his best friend.

Nash and I said our quick goodbyes before hurrying out of the bar and driving straight to the hospital to meet them. I knew Cutler would be upset to see his friend in pain, and I wanted to be there for both him and J.T.

Because I may be Cutler's girl . . . but he was definitely my special guy.

And if he needed me, that's exactly where I wanted to be.

29

Nash

J.T. had, in fact, broken his arm, and Cutler was sitting on my lap in the waiting area. Emerson had jumped into action the minute we walked through the doors. The hospital had him sitting there crying in a chair, while Jay and Susannah were trying to fill out paperwork, and they were both notably upset.

My girl took charge and got him back into a room with the on-call doctor, and she stayed right there with him. Cutler and I were waiting for her to come out when Jay strode through the doors and walked our way.

He had a smile on his face, but he looked exhausted. "Man, Emerson got things moving real fast back there."

"I knew Sunny would take care of J.T. Is he okay?" Cutler asked, sitting up and looking exhausted himself.

"Yep. He broke his arm, and they're almost done putting the cast on him now. He can't wait for you to see it," Jay said, rubbing a hand down his face. "Never a dull moment, huh? Sorry to pull you guys away from your night out. But man, that woman of yours sure did make things better for my boy a lot sooner than it would have been if she weren't here. They weren't in any hurry before she took charge."

My chest puffed up with pride. My girl was a fucking rock star.

"Glad to hear it, and don't give it a thought. I would have been pissed if you didn't call and tell us what was going on. This is exactly where we wanted to be."

"My girl, Sunny, is the best doctor around. That's why the best hospital wants her in Boston. But me and Pops will see her all the time and eat all the chowder."

Jay's empathetic gaze moved to mine, and he clapped me on the shoulder. "I get why they want her, but Magnolia Falls wants her, too. I'm sure you guys will all figure it out. It's nice to see you all so happy."

Emerson, Susannah, and J.T. came walking out together, and my son ran to his best friend. "That's a cool cast," Cutler said.

"I want you to be the first one to sign it, Beefcake!"

Cutler signed the cast, and he took his sweet time while we were all looking at one another, because it had been a long night, and we wanted to get these boys home.

We all said our goodbyes, and Emerson said she'd stop by tomorrow to check on him. It surprised me when we got into the truck that Emerson climbed into the back seat with Cutler after strapping him into his booster.

"You going to sit back here with me, Sunny?" Cutler said, his voice sleepy.

"Yep. I know you were upset, and I just want to make sure you're okay, angel face," she said, and when I glanced in the rearview mirror to back out, they had their fingers intertwined.

"I'm okay now," my son said.

Yeah, you and me both, buddy.

There was a feeling of peace that came over me whenever I was with these two.

I drove the short distance home, and when we pulled into the driveway, movement on my front porch caught my attention.

Fuck me.

"Who is that?" Emerson asked, as she unbuckled Cutler, who was staring out the window.

"I guess Tara forgot to call and say she was coming today." I cleared my throat, as I climbed out of the car and opened the back door to help Emerson and Cutler out.

I did my best to remain calm, but I was anything but. It was late, and there was no reason for her to be here on my front porch with a suitcase beside her.

"Hey, I was getting worried about you," she said, as she pushed to her feet.

Tara looked exactly the same. She had dark hair and dark eyes, like Cutler's. She was petite and slim. She knew she was attractive, and she used it to her benefit most of the time. I learned quickly that her exterior beauty did not match who she was on the inside.

"What are you doing here?" I asked, my tone harsh but necessary. When it came to Tara, I needed to keep boundaries in place.

"Well, hello to you, too," she said before she bent down, and her gaze moved to Cutler. "Hey there, sweetheart. It's Mama. Do you remember me?"

He had his hand in Emerson's, and he was standing a bit behind her. I didn't know who positioned them that way. If it had been self-preservation on his part or the need to protect him on her part.

Neither would surprise me.

"Hi, Tara." Those were the only words he said, and for a chatty little dude, it spoke volumes.

Emerson caught it, and she tightened her grip on Cutler and glanced over at me before Tara noticed.

"And who is this? Are we bringing random women around our child?"

"We're not doing this, Tara. You haven't come around for two years, and you think you can call the shots?" I hissed, and

271

Emerson's free hand landed on my back, as if she were trying to calm me.

I shouldn't have this conversation in front of my son. I knew better.

"Sorry, I was just excited to see my boys," Tara said, moving forward and wrapping her arms around Cutler.

His hand dropped from Emerson's, and Tara scooped him up in her arms.

My boys.

She'd never used that term, and it was clear that it was meant to bother Emerson. I reached for her hand, and her posture was stiff, her smile forced.

Cutler looked uncomfortable as he hung in Tara's arms, and his gaze found mine over her shoulder.

Confusion.

Apprehension.

Maybe even a little fear.

That's what I saw when I looked at my boy.

Hell, he barely knew this woman. Why'd she have to come on so strong? This was her shtick. She never stuck around long, so everything was intense and fast and aggressive.

I was fucking tired, and all I wanted was to get my son into his bed and my woman into mine.

Tara set Cutler down and turned to face me. "So, I got here, and I had confused the dates. Turns out, my Airbnb isn't ready until tomorrow, so I figured I could snuggle with my boy tonight."

Cutler's eyes were wide, and he moved to step between me and Emerson.

"Are you serious? Why didn't you just go check into the Magnolia Falls Hotel?" I said, unlocking my door as I tried to figure out how to handle this. "Cutler, go get your pajamas on. No bath tonight. I'll be right in."

Emerson, Tara, and I all stood in the entryway, and the tension was thick.

"Nash, it's really late. Are you seriously not going to allow the mother of your child to stay one night at your house?" She sneered at Emerson, which pissed me the fuck off.

"Okay, this ends here. This is my girlfriend, Emerson. Stop with the looks and the cheap shots, got it?" I narrowed my gaze. "It's confusing to Cutler when you show up like this. I thought you were coming in a few days?"

"Mark and I broke up. I wanted to come see my son. I need him right now."

The fucking balls on this woman. I leaned forward to keep my voice down, unable to hide my anger. "*You* need him right now? Are you for fucking real?"

"Oh, I'm sorry that we're not all like you, Nash. I'm not made of stone. Sometimes I need people," she said. "I missed my family."

I squeezed my eyes closed, trying hard to tamp down this growing anger. "You can't do this, Tara. If you want to come and have lunch with Cutler, I'll allow it. But you're not staying here, and you're not fucking with my son's head. No games. No bullshit. You got it?"

Emerson stiffened beside me, as she obviously didn't know what to do in this situation. This was very on par for Tara. Of course she'd show up now, when our lives were better than ever.

She was the most selfish woman I'd ever met.

"Don't worry, Pops. Tara can read me a story, okay?" Cutler's voice broke through the chaos in my head.

Did he want her here?

Was I the one being selfish?

I scrubbed a hand down my face and glanced at Emerson, who gave me the slightest nod.

"Yeah, sure, buddy. She can read you a story," I said.

Tara smirked and walked right by me, following Cutler down the hall. I moved to the kitchen and pulled a beer from the refrigerator, holding one up for Emerson, but she shook her head no.

273

I tipped my head back and took a long pull.

"Hey, you need to relax. We knew she was coming. She just arrived a little early," Emerson said, her hand running up and down my back.

I turned to face her. "This is bullshit. She planned it. So where the hell should I have her stay? It's almost midnight. Should we let her stay here with us on the couch for one night?"

"I'm going to head home and take Winnie out. I think you should have her stay here on the couch with you and Cutler. This is not something I should be in the middle of, Nash."

"What? Don't leave, baby. That's what she wants you to do." I could feel her pulling away, and it pissed me the fuck off that Tara had shown up and pulled her usual bullshit.

"Remember the other day when Collin showed up, and I told you that I needed to handle it?" she said, wrapping her arms around my middle and resting her cheek on my chest.

"Yep. And I hated every damn second that he was there."

"We both have pasts. That's what led us here, right? And Cutler wanted her to read him a book, and you need to respect that." I looked down, and I swear I saw something flash in her eyes. Maybe it was hurt or doubt. And I hated that my ex had put it there. "He deserves to explore this relationship. It's been missing from his life. And you'll be the bad guy if you don't allow this to play out. I will not take part in denying him anything that he wants, so I'm going to head home."

"Hey." I reached beneath her chin and tipped her head up to look at me. "I love you."

"I know you do." She smiled, but it was forced. And then she pushed up on her tiptoes and gave me a quick kiss. "I love you, too. Goodnight."

She walked out the door as laughter came from down the hallway. I stood out on the porch and watched Emerson walk across the yard.

When I made my way back inside, I walked down the

hallway. I paused in the doorway and watched as Tara made her voice high and low for different characters. Cutler was laughing, but there was still apprehension there. The way his shoulders were stiff and his smile was forced. I could see the discomfort, even if he didn't want to say it aloud.

"Hey, you can stay one night. Cutler, I want you to go get in my bed. You can sleep with me tonight. Tara can sleep in here."

"I love sleeping in Pops' bed." He pumped his fist upward, crawling from beneath the sheets.

I followed him into my room and tucked him in. "Goodnight, buddy. I love you. I'll be in in a little bit."

"Daddy," he said, catching me off guard that he didn't call me Pops.

"Yeah?"

"Do you think Tara came because she knows it's my Star Student Day next week?"

"I don't think she knows about it. Do you want her to be here for that?" I asked.

"Well, Sunny is going to make me unicorn Krispies for my big day. I didn't know Tara would be here, so I don't know what to do."

"Listen, you don't have to do anything tonight, okay?" I leaned down and kissed his forehead. "It's been a long day. I'll be back in a little while. I love you. Get some sleep."

"I love you, Pops. Will you text Sunny and tell her I love her, too? I didn't get to say goodbye."

"Of course I will." I pulled the door closed and walked out to the kitchen, where I heard Tara's muffled voice.

"I don't care, Mark. Two can play that game. I'm going to spend some time with my family." She stood in the corner, sipping a glass of wine and pinching the bridge of her nose. "Yes, as a matter of fact, I'm staying at the house with Nash and Cutler."

I made my presence known and moved around the counter

to empty my half-drank beer in the sink before tossing it into the recycle bin. She turned to look at me and quickly ended the call. "Nash is here, and we want to hang out. I've got to go."

She set her phone down on the table and walked back to the counter to refill her wineglass.

"Don't be using me to make your boyfriend jealous. You weren't invited here. You left me no choice."

"So what is this? Now you have a girlfriend, so I'm the enemy?"

"That's not it, and you know it. You can't just show up and expect to stay here. We have lives of our own. You don't get to come and disrupt everything just because you and your boyfriend are fighting. For once, think about that little boy in the next fucking room. Don't complicate his life just to make your boyfriend jealous."

"Fuck you, Nash. You know nothing." She tipped her head back and downed the whole glass she'd just poured.

"I know enough. What are you here for, Tara?"

"I'm here to spend time with my son. And I don't appreciate you making that hard for me."

"Oh, I'm sorry that I'm not making your unplanned visits easy for you. You haven't seen that boy in two years. I can count on one hand how many times you've called during that time." I moved closer, squaring my shoulders. "It's not about making it easy on you. It's about making it easy on Cutler."

She caught me off guard when she lunged forward and tried to kiss me. I caught her by the wrists and pulled her back. "What the fuck are you doing, Tara?"

Her gaze hardened, and I wasn't sure what the hell she was up to. We'd never once hooked up since the day she walked out that door over six years ago.

"I came here to see if I still had a family worth coming back for."

"You're delusional if you think I've been waiting for you." I took the wineglass from her hand and set it in the sink. "You're upset about your boyfriend, so you came here. Come on, Tara. Do the right fucking thing, and don't be selfish when it comes to Cutler."

"Fuck you, Nash. You think you have all the power?" Her words were slurring a little now as she'd obviously downed the two glasses of wine in a short period of time.

"It's not about power. It's about being a parent to that little kid in there," I hissed, pointing toward the hallway.

"Well, don't be so quick to write me off. You don't have a leg to stand on where our son is concerned. Remember that."

"The fuck did you just say to me?" I moved close, venom leaving my lips.

"You never wanted a paternity test after I gave birth. That's a card that's yet to be played. So watch yourself when you start thinking you're calling the shots."

My head spun as she marched down the hallway toward my son's room, like she didn't just drop a bomb on me.

I picked up my phone and typed into the group text.

> Tara's here. She was just sitting on my porch and insisted on staying the night. She just made a comment, questioning my paternity. I'm trying to remain fucking calm, but I'm ready to lose my shit.

RIVER

> What the fuck? Don't react. Say nothing. I'll be there first thing in the morning. She's signing something this time. She's not going to hold paternity over your head.

HAYES

I never fucking liked that girl.

ROMEO

Who the fuck comes into town after being away all this time and fucks with the dude who has been raising that little boy?

KING

Ride or die, brother. We've got you.

I was shaking as I made my way down to my room and shut and locked the bedroom door. I quickly changed clothes and got into bed, and I lay on my side just staring at my little boy.

The light of my life.

And I'd do whatever I needed to make sure she didn't fuck with either one of us again.

I was done playing games.

30

Emerson

I hadn't slept much at all. This feeling of panic had overwhelmed me and was taking over my body. I had flashbacks of the day I'd taken off of work to surprise Collin. I didn't even tell my best friend I was doing it, because I didn't want anyone at work to find out I was playing hooky.

I'd been working long hours, and Collin had been traveling a ton, and he'd sounded so distant that it had me on edge. So, I'd called in sick, picked up breakfast, and driven the short distance to his apartment. I knew he'd be sleeping in since he'd gotten in late the night before, so I used my spare key and made my way to his bedroom.

The whole thing was still a blur.

The sounds coming from his room.

Her voice. Her laugh. Her moans.

If I hadn't seen it with my own eyes, I wouldn't have believed it.

Farah and Collin were stark naked in his bed, in a compromising position, and I'd just stood there dumbfounded before I'd run out the door.

Unfortunately, I had very clear knowledge that the rug

could be swept out from beneath your feet when you least expected it.

And Tara showing up last night had caught me off guard. Sure, Nash had prepared me that she was coming. But the way that she'd glared at me. The way she'd looked at them—like they were hers.

Like they belonged to her.

She was Cutler's mother. The mother of Nash's child.

That'll get in a girl's head.

So, I'd done what I did best. I'd pulled out the Rice Krispie treats recipe and started making numerous batches of unicorn Krispies for Cutler's big day this week. I'd planned to do that today anyway. Maybe I hadn't planned to start at three o'clock in the morning, but I couldn't sleep, and baking had always been what helped calm me.

I'd bought these clear little baggies to put each one in, with tags that read:

Thanks for making me the star of the day! XO Cutler Heart

So I'd get these bagged and tagged and freeze them so they'd be ready.

And so what if I made three times what I needed? I could give them to the girls. Or bring them to Midge for a treat. Or even Oscar, because he loved my baked goods. And I owed Janelle some treats for bringing me those beautiful flowers.

I opened the back door for Winnie to go outside once the sun came up. I hadn't heard from Nash, but I figured he was busy dealing with all his baby mama drama.

I called Winnie back inside, just as I heard the door open next door. I spotted Tara and hurried back inside. I moved to the window and peeked outside to see Cutler in his jammies, running up the steps to the slide, as Tara waited for him at the bottom.

Why did that hurt so badly? I wanted the best for Cutler.

And if having a relationship with his mama made him happy, I should want that, right?

I leaned against the door and slid down to the floor and cried.

I cried because I didn't know where I fit into this equation.

I cried because I was afraid of getting hurt again.

I cried because just twenty-four hours ago, I was the happiest I'd ever been.

Life had a way of messing with you when you let your guard down.

There was a knock on my door, and I swiped at my cheeks and pulled myself together before pulling it open.

Cutler and Tara stood on my back porch, and he rushed me, wrapping his arms around my legs. "Good morning, Sunny. I just wanted to give you and Winnie a hug since you weren't there when I woke up."

My heart cracked at his words, and all I could do was bend down and hug him. No words came.

"Well, she lives next door, so you can always come say hello to your neighbor." Tara's lips were in a flat line, and her hands were crossed over her chest.

"Winnie!" Cutler called out as he ran toward her near my couch.

I cleared my throat as Tara and I just stood there awkwardly.

"It's a nice morning, huh?" she asked, and I nodded.

"Yes. Is your Airbnb on the water?" I couldn't think of anything else to ask.

She raised a brow. "It's not, but I plan on spending most of my time here with my boys. I'm actually thinking of moving back to Magnolia Falls."

I couldn't speak; I just nodded.

She was coming back? Permanently?

My phone rang, and I startled as I moved toward the counter to see my mother's name light up the screen.

"Cutler, we need to get back. Your dad is making us breakfast. Let's go have some family time, all right?"

"Okay. You want to come eat with us, Sunny?" he asked as he moved toward me, and I silenced my phone.

I shook my head, fighting back the ginormous lump that was lodged in my throat. Would she be here all the time now? Would she try to reconcile with Nash? He seemed to despise her, but she was the mother of his child.

Would she fill that void in Cutler's life? The one I was so eager to fill?

I couldn't resent her for that. She was his mother.

"I'm okay, but thank you." My voice came out shaky, and I saw the gleam of victory in Tara's eyes. She was sending a message, and I was receiving it.

Loud and clear.

"Love you, Sunny," Cutler said, as he hugged me one more time, and I wrapped my arms around him tighter than usual, breathing in all that sweetness.

All that sunshine.

"I love you, too," I said, as I pushed to stand. They walked out the door, and I grabbed my phone and settled on my couch.

There were no texts from Nash.

I couldn't blame him. He'd been as surprised as I was last night when she'd showed up early.

Had they stayed up and talked?

I dialed my mom back.

"Hey, sweetheart. Your text was a little cryptic this morning, and it looked like it was sent in the middle of the night. Is everything okay?"

Her voice always did something to me. Comforted me in a way I could always rely on. Provided a safe place for me to lose it if I needed to.

"Yeah. I'm just a little overwhelmed at the moment." I tried to keep my voice steady when the tears started falling.

"About Boston?"

"Sure. That's weighing on me pretty heavily. And, well, Tara is back in town." I'd filled my mother in on everything going on with Nash and Cutler and me.

"Oh, she arrived early. I know she was supposed to come in a few days, right?"

"Yep. She was there when we came home last night. She couldn't get into her Airbnb until today, so she needed to stay over there."

She was quiet for a long moment. "And I'm sure that has you feeling a little out of sorts?"

"You could say that." My words broke on a sob. "I trust Nash; it's not about that."

"What's it about, sweetheart?"

I sighed as I ran my hand along Winnie's soft fur as she cuddled up beside me on the couch. "I just . . . I don't want to get blindsided again, you know? I don't know where I'm going to live, and I'm not used to not having a plan. But I just can't see it yet."

"See what?"

"Usually, I just know what to do. I've always had this plan, and well, the last one got blown to bits," I said, over a teary laugh. "And it was for the better, so I'm not complaining. But I don't trust myself anymore. So what if I'm walking into heartache again?"

"You just said that you trust Nash, and you don't trust yourself. So is it you that you're doubting?"

"Maybe. I'm just—I see her with Cutler, and it makes me feel like a huge asshole—" My words broke on a sob, and I just let it all out.

"Emmy, talk to me. Why would you be an asshole?"

"Because I'm jealous, Mom. I've never been a jealous person. Even when Farah slept with my fiancé, it wasn't jealousy I felt. It was betrayal. And anger. All followed by

283

relief." I took a few breaths and calmed my breathing. "But this is definitely jealousy. Like she could take them away, and I wouldn't survive that loss."

"Well, you know how I always say that things happen for a reason?"

"Yes," I said, rolling my eyes as I reached over to the coffee table for a tissue to wipe my nose.

"Maybe this needed to happen to help you decide what to do about the future and Boston and all that you've been wrestling with up until now."

"How so? I'm more confused than ever now."

"No, you're not. Because now you know what's most important to you. And that solves the first issue. It sounds like your heart is in Magnolia Falls."

"Yeah, well, so is my boyfriend's ex. And she said she might be moving here. I can't compete with her. She's Cutler's mother. She's Nash's baby mama."

"Emerson," she said, her voice stern.

"Mom," I mimicked back in just as stern a tone.

"I think you should come home for a few days, and we'll sort this out. Let them have this time, and save yourself the misery of watching it, okay?"

"Is that my Emmy?" I heard my father's voice, and my mother told him the short version of what was going on. Before I could get in a word, he was grabbing the phone from her.

"Hey, baby girl," he said.

"Hi, Dad."

"I've already texted Bridger. You tell us when you want to leave, and he'll have the helicopter come grab you so you don't have to make that drive, okay? Come home, sweetie. We miss you."

I nodded. "Okay. I'm going to try to get some sleep, and I'll see how I feel when I wake up."

"All right. Love you, baby girl."

"Love you, too."

My mom shouted the same sentiment, and I ended the call. I led Winnie down the hall and climbed back into bed and let sleep finally take me.

I woke to puppy kisses and rolled over to see it was well past lunchtime, and I'd slept a few hours.

Still no text from Nash. Obviously, there were red flags going off, because the man was always texting or calling, and that's how it had been for weeks.

Something was different.

I decided to pull up my big-girl panties and text him.

> Hey, I just wanted to check in. Are you doing okay?

BEATING HEART

> No. Things are really fucked-up.

> What does that mean? Did something happen?

BEATING HEART

> There's a lot of shit going on. I don't want to pull you into it, but I've got to deal with this right now.

> Can I help?

BEATING HEART

> No. I just need some time, okay?

What did that mean? *He needed time?* Away from me? Time to figure out how he felt about her?
Why does it feel like a slap in the face?

> Got it. No problem.

BEATING HEART

> Thank you.

Thank you? That was it?
No I love you?
Every insecurity I thought I'd buried just reared its ugly head.

I padded through the house and made myself a cup of coffee and looked out the window once again. There was no movement next door, and everything seemed quiet.

They were probably spending the day together.

Reconnecting.

He needed time.

This was the mother of his child.

My phone dinged, and I looked down to see the group text from the girls.

DEMI

> How are you doing, Em? You okay?

They obviously knew what was going on.

> I'm fine. Great party last night, Saylor. Sorry, we had to run out.

RUBY

The party was great. But let's not ignore the elephant in the fucking room.

PEYTON

I'm clearly out of the loop. Is the elephant Nash's penis?

I started to laugh, but the tears fell down my cheeks.

DEMI

The elephant is Tara. She's back in town.

RUBY

And apparently, she's got Nash pretty upset.

DEMI

She knows exactly how to get to him.

What did that mean? Because she was moving back? Because he was confused about his feelings? I was too embarrassed to admit that I'd been kept completely out of the loop. He wasn't confiding in me. He wanted space from me.

PEYTON

Shit. This sucks. How do you feel about everything, Em?

Shitty. Nervous. Scared. Insecure. Angry. Sad.
That about nails it.

> He wants space, so that's what I'm going to give him. I'm heading to Rosewood River for the weekend. I think some time with family will do me good.

DEMI

> I'm so sorry. Do you want us to come over?

> No, I'm okay. Thank you, though. I'm going to leave as soon as I get packed.

RUBY

> Just hang tight, girl. He's just dealing with some shit right now.

And then I typed a message into my sibling group text, which also included my two cousins.

> I want to come home.

EASTON

> What the fuck happened?

BRIDGER

The helicopter is already there and waiting. Sent him after Dad said you might want to come home.

RAFE

Miss you, Emmy. We've got you.

CLARK

Whose ass do I need to beat? I'm still looking for that piece-of-shit ex of yours to show his face.

ARCHER

Just get home. Melody could use some time with her auntie.

AXEL

I'll pick you up from the hangar, and you can let me know who I need to hunt down and beat until they can't walk.

CLARK

I'll happily hide the body.

EASTON

Let's not put that incriminating evidence in a group chat. Save it for Sunday dinner. 😊

I rolled my eyes and laughed because they'd always been this way.

I grabbed my weekender bag and packed up Winnie's food and treats, and we were in the car, heading to the hangar.

Going home usually comforted me.

But for whatever reason, it didn't feel like I was going home. It felt like I was leaving home.

31

Nash

You never wanted a paternity test after I gave birth.

Those ten words had literally flipped my life on its ass. I hadn't slept at all, and I was reeling.

This kid was my world.

Well, he and Emerson.

I couldn't stand the thought of losing either of them. No fucking way. And right now, I needed to fight like hell and make sure there was nothing Tara could do to take him away from me.

She'd woken up and tried to act like she hadn't dropped a bomb on me. Offering to push Cutler out on the swings, like she had a clue how to be a mother at this point. She was here because she and her boyfriend were going through something. She wanted to play house, and I was done with her games.

She'd come back inside, acting like we were one big happy family. We weren't. Not even fucking close.

I'd told her to get in her car and go grab her own breakfast. That hadn't gone over well, and I didn't give a shit. I had River meeting me at his office, and I'd dropped Cutler at my dad's house.

This had been my wake-up call.

She'd showed me her cards. She was going to hang this over my head to get her way, and I needed to establish boundaries with this woman. She couldn't stroll in and out of my son's life whenever her life fell apart.

River was right. We should have done this a long time ago.

I walked inside his office, and he was already behind his desk. Cassie, his receptionist, was off today because it was the weekend.

I dropped into the chair across from him, just as a loud ruckus had us turning, and Kingston, Romeo, and Hayes came strolling through the door. They were holding coffees and bagels.

"You didn't all need to come," I said.

"Ride or die, motherfucker. We always come," Hayes grumped.

Kingston and Romeo passed out the drinks, and Hayes gave us each an individual bag with a bagel.

"Thank you, guys. I'm losing my fucking mind."

"Okay, I've been looking at our options," River said, taking a sip from his coffee before setting the cup back down. "She hasn't paid one dime of child support, nor been involved in his life whatsoever."

"Correct." I let out a long breath.

Motherfucking paternity? I still can't get over the fact that she'd play that card. I was seething.

"So, we bring her in here and we play our own hand." River leaned back in his chair. "Listen to me, brother. She is just trying to get a rise out of you. She doesn't have the determination to follow through with any of it. She strolls into town every one to two years and stays for what . . . two days? Fuck no. She has no leg to stand on."

"What if she demands a paternity test?" I asked, hating the words as I said them.

"Well, how confident are you about taking it?" he asked.

"I mean, we were together for those months, and I don't think she was with anyone else. But who the fuck knows with this woman." I shook my head. "I know that boy is mine. I've never needed a test to prove it. From the minute he was placed in my arms, he was mine." My fucking voice shook, and it pissed me off. "I can't fucking lose him."

"Dude," Kingston said as he moved over to me from where he stood against the wall, yanking me to my feet and pulling me into his arms. "Cutler is your boy. I know it in my gut. He's our family. Has been since the day he came into this world."

"Fucking Tara," Hayes hissed. "She has some fucking nerve coming here and messing with you. With Cutler. How about you let me go talk to her for a little bit?"

"That's a terrible idea." River shook his head. "We can't give her anything to use against us."

Romeo grabbed some chairs from the closet, and he, Kingston, and Hayes all sat down.

"What are our options?" Romeo asked.

"We bring her in here. We tell her we're happy to take a paternity test, because your name is on that birth certificate, and you've been raising that boy. There is no reason to think you aren't the father. So, we offer to take the test, and we also present her with six years of back child support owed, as well as an agreement to future payments."

"She's not going to want to do that."

"Correct. So we get her to sign over full custody to you. You're doing it anyway. It protects you. It protects Cutler. She doesn't get to roll into town whenever she feels like it and call the shots."

I nodded and buried my face in my hands. "I'm so fucking tired, you guys. I'm trying to hold onto Cutler. Trying to hold onto Emerson. To this family that finally feels right. And I could lose both of them in the end."

Kingston and Romeo were on their feet again, squatting down in front of me as a tear rolled down my cheek.

"You aren't losing anyone," Kingston said.

"Listen to me, Nash." Hayes's voice broke through the noise in my head as he moved to stand in front of me. "You are the best fucking father I've ever met. No one is taking that boy from you. And Emerson—that woman loves you *and* that little boy. So, we fight. It's what we do."

He reached for my hand and yanked me to my feet, pulling me against him. His arms came around me as Romeo and Kingston joined right in and wrapped their arms around us.

"Fuck me. You sappy assholes are so damn soft." River came around and slammed into us.

I lifted my head, taking in my brothers. The four dudes who had been beside me the day my kid was born, and every day since. I looked at each of them, one at a time.

"We fight," I said.

"We fucking fight!" Kingston shouted, and we all laughed, and I swiped at my face, embarrassed that I'd come to tears.

River moved back to his desk, and Romeo and Kingston clapped me on the shoulder before taking their seats. Hayes grabbed a tissue and handed it to me.

"Here. Clean yourself up, brother. Those seasonal allergies are a real bitch," he said with a chuckle.

I nodded.

Everything was going to be fine.

River and I spent a few hours drawing up a contract and getting everything figured out.

Tara had called a dozen times because she wanted to see Cutler.

But she was no longer calling the shots.

I told her that Cutler and I would meet her at The Golden Goose for dinner. That was what I had to offer her. And she'd need to be in River's office on Monday after I dropped Cutler at school, because there was going to be a new set of rules put into place. She'd have two options: sign the papers or start paying child support.

I prayed like hell that she signed the papers.

I didn't want her money.

I only wanted my boy.

I was on my way to pick up Cutler but went home first. I wanted to talk to Emerson. I'd been short this morning, and I'm sure I'd freaked her out. My ex showing up was not pleasant for anyone. But Emerson deserved a lot more of an explanation than I'd given her.

I knocked on the back door, and she didn't answer. I used my key and went inside.

No Emerson.

No Winnie.

Fuck.

I checked the garage, and her car was gone.

> Hey, where'd you go? I came to talk to you.

I waited a few minutes, and she didn't respond. The text wasn't showing as read, so maybe she had her phone off. I sent one more text. It's what I should have said this morning.

> There's a lot of shit going on, but it has nothing to do with you. I love you.

> I love you, beautiful.

> I'm saying it twice because it's what I should have said this morning.

I glanced at the time and groaned. I needed to go grab my boy and get to The Golden Goose.

I'd had to give my father the short version of what we'd decided to do. He was nervous; I could see it in his eyes. He'd asked about Emerson, and I'd told him I'd asked her to give me some time to figure my shit out.

"Listen, I thought your taste in women was shit up until you met that girl. Don't mess it up. She's a keeper," he said, as he walked us out to my truck.

"I'm aware. I'm going to do whatever it takes," I said, and he pulled me into a hug, which was not the norm for him. My dad wasn't much of a sentimental guy.

"You deserve to be happy, son. You're a really good man. It'll all work out."

"Thanks," I said, holding up a hand and getting into my truck as Cutler waved goodbye through the window, and I pulled down the driveway.

"Is Emerson coming to dinner?"

"No, not tonight, buddy. It's just Tara. She wants to spend a little time with you."

"I don't think Tara likes Emerson. She wasn't nice to her this morning," he said.

"You saw Emerson this morning?"

"Yep. I wanted to hug her and Winnie. Tara got mad at me after we left."

I gripped the steering wheel tighter. "What does that mean, she got mad at you?"

"I told Emerson that I loved her, and Tara didn't like that."

"What did she say?"

"She said that she's my mama, and Emerson is nobody. And when I said that she wasn't nobody and that me and Pops loved her, she said I was a little brat."

This fucking woman was not going to go anywhere near my kid without me ever again.

"You know that's not true, right?" I asked, as I pulled up to The Golden Goose and turned around to face him. "And you're allowed to love whoever you want. Tara doesn't decide that."

"I know, Pops. You raised the best boy ever, remember?" He chuckled as he unbuckled and leaned forward to high-five me. "I don't think she will stay long, even though she told Emerson she was moving here to be with us. I think she just said those things to my Sunny to bother her."

"She told Emerson she was moving here?"

"Yep. But I don't think she will. She kept calling her boyfriend when we were outside, so I think she wants to go home soon."

Like I said, my boy is an old soul. He is good at reading people.

When we stepped inside the diner, I saw Tara in the distance, and she waved us over. Midge was giving me a look of disapproval, and I met her with the same look. I wasn't happy about Tara being here either.

"Hey, can you keep Cutler with you for five minutes so I can speak to Tara before he joins us for dinner?"

"Of course. I've been trying to hire this kid for years," Midge said with a laugh, and Cutler beamed up at her. "Come on, Beefcake. We've got a seating chart to update."

He fist-pumped his arm, and I made my way over to Tara, who was typing away on her phone.

"What is Cutler doing with grumpy Midge?" she hissed. "I can't stand that woman."

"I needed a minute with you before he joins us."

"I'm not happy that you kept him from me all day, Nash," she said, completely clueless to the fact that I was done with her and her shit.

I leaned forward. "You're not happy? That's fucking rich, Tara. You come to my home, and you drop the paternity card, like it means nothing. And that's because being a mother

297

means nothing to you. But being a father is fucking everything to me. So I'm happy to take your test, because that boy is mine. But let me tell you how this is going to play out," I said, my voice ice-cold as she sat there with her mouth gaping open, eyes wide.

"I was kidding about the test. I don't want it. Of course you're his father, and you're a great dad."

"You're fucking right about that. So don't you ever come here and question that, do you hear me?" I narrowed my gaze. "Monday morning you will meet me at River's office because things are changing moving forward."

"How so?"

"You will either pay back child support for the last six years and agree to paying child support moving forward, or you will sign over full custody to me. You haven't been here for anything. Birthdays, Christmas, the first day of school, or baseball games. None of it. So you don't get to stroll into town and make demands." I pointed my finger at her, doing my best to tamp down my anger. "And if you ever call my kid a brat again or mess with his head any more than you already have, you won't see him again. You got it?"

She just sat there staring at me, processing what I'd just said. "This is because of your girlfriend, isn't it?"

"This is because you're a shitty mom and a shitty human. It's that simple, Tara. I've allowed it because I was scared you'd do something to take him away from me, but you can't. He's mine, and you know it."

"Fine. I'll think it over, and I'll meet you on Monday and let you know what I decide. But Mark will be with me. He doesn't like how you've been treating me, so he's coming to town."

I barked out a laugh. "Of course, he is. Just in time for you to leave."

"Well, we're going on a trip from here, so I won't be staying after all. This hasn't gone the way I'd hoped anyway."

"Hey, Tara," I said, leaning close and keeping my voice low.

"Yeah?"

"I'd bring a lawyer on Monday if you want to fight me, because I will have you served if you don't sign those papers then and there. This ends while you're here. No more games."

She looked away for a few seconds. "Can I still see him while I'm here?"

"That's not happening. We're going on a little trip tomorrow, and we'll be back Monday. So enjoy your time with Mark while you're here."

"Fine. He doesn't like kids anyway. That's what we were fighting about. I'm trying to convince him that it's fun to hang out with a little kid."

Un-fucking-believable.

"We're not girlfriends, Tara. Sing your sad song to someone who gives a fuck. And when that boy walks over here, you better act like you're interested in what he's saying. Just fake it for an hour, and I'll let him sit through this meal. But if you so much as look at him wrong, we're walking out of here."

"This is why we aren't together, Nash. You've never understood me."

I chuckled. "Clearly, I still don't."

I held my hand up and caught Midge's attention. A sense of relief came over me, because I knew this was almost over.

She wasn't going to fight for my boy.

When it came to being the parent, I'd always been the only one to fight for him.

And that would never change.

32

Emerson

My parents' house was the equivalent of Disneyland, by way of being the happiest place in the world. There were always lots of people, lots of chaos, and lots of food and drinks.

My aunt and uncle lived next door, so it was always a big party over here between their two homes. The boys all lived on their own in town, but they'd come over last night to see me, and they'd be here tonight. Sunday dinners were kind of a staple at the Chadwick home, even if a few of them tried to get out of it now and then.

Coming home was exactly what I needed. I'd avoided Rosewood River for months, because of the embarrassment over the wedding being called off and the whole town knowing the dirty details of what went down.

Turns out, I didn't really care anymore. That felt like so long ago now.

It's funny how life worked. Something could feel so big, until the next big thing happened, and then you didn't remember the last thing.

I had fallen in love with Nash. A real, deep, soul-crushing kind of love.

It was different from the love I'd experienced at a young age.

This was real. There was no doubt in my mind that Nash Heart was my future.

And Cutler Heart . . . he was mine, too. Maybe not in the traditional sense, where I'd gotten to start out with him on the day that he was born. But he was mine in the way that mattered.

My mom and I had hashed it all out, and she'd helped remind me what was most important.

"I'm glad you finally found the real deal, sweetheart. Because I always worried that you were settling."

"Why didn't you say anything?"

"Because you were so confident about him being the one. And Collin was fine—well, before he did what he did." She chuckled. "But I never saw that excitement. That deep love that I want each of my kids to experience."

I nodded. "Yeah. I'm happy that I finally understand what you're talking about."

"So don't let a woman who barely plays a role in her child's life take away from something so special. It's rare to find it, and you have to fight for it."

"Yeah, even being away for the weekend has made me realize things."

"Tell me."

"Well, I used to be so determined to work at the best hospital in the country, and I wanted to put in the hours and prove something—I don't even know who I was proving it to." I shrugged. "But now, I realize that I like having a life. I like going to work and helping kids feel better, but I like coming home. I like having dinner with Nash and Cutler. I like swimming in the lake and walking to the diner."

She squeezed my hand. "You're finally living, Emerson. And you like it. You've been living for work, because your personal life wasn't that fulfilling."

I laughed, even though it was true. "I want to have a family. And I want to hang out with friends and throw parties for Cutler and go to baseball games and read him stories at bedtime."

She smiled. "Have you talked to Nash?"

He'd texted me yesterday, and my phone had been dead, and I saw it late last night.

"I texted him back and said I was just giving him some time to figure it out, and I would be there if and when he needed me. I haven't heard back, and that's okay. I know he loves me, and that's all that matters."

"That's the most important thing in life, honey. Surrounding yourself with good people. People you love and who love you back. It's all about family."

"Oh, boy," Bridger groaned as he stepped into the kitchen and kissed my mom and me on the cheek. "Is this the *family is everything* talk?"

My mom swatted him with the dish towel as my father came around the corner and pulled Bridger into a hug. "We've got two of them here, Ellie. It's a start."

"Since when did you get so sappy, old man?" Bridger asked my father, and he rolled his eyes.

"Hey, I'm a man who's crazy about his wife and kids. I have no shame in my game," my father said, twirling my mom around in the kitchen. He hugged her from behind, and her head fell back in laughter.

"Can you two please keep it PG while your children are here?" Bridger grumped.

"Hey, hey, hey . . . I'm not the last one here," Clark said, as he pulled me into a hug, even though I'd seen him last night. He was in the middle of hockey season, but he had a few days off this week, so he'd come home. Clark played for a professional hockey team in LA, but he was in talks to get traded to the local team in San Francisco. He'd always wanted to play for the Lions.

"Is that why you literally slammed the door in our faces? Because you wanted to make sure you weren't last?" my brother, Rafe, grumped as he walked in with my cousin, Axel, who was still laughing as he paused and kissed me on top of the head before wrapping me in a hug.

Aunt Isabelle and Uncle Carlisle came strolling through the door, carrying little Melody in their arms. She was the cutest toddler I'd ever seen, and I scooped her right up, just as her father came in behind them. My cousin Archer was a big guy, all gruff and serious, but he was raising his little girl all on his own and doing a great job. I couldn't wait for him and Nash to meet and bond over the single-parent thing. Although, Archer's story with the mother of his child was a different one and was part of the reason he'd become so closed off.

"Everyone's actually here on time?" my mother said, as she poured a glass of wine for me and my aunt. The guys made their way to the bar to get their drink of choice.

My parents' house was a huge old ranch that they'd completely renovated. I'd grown up here, and the memories inside these walls were endless. We had a stable with a couple of horses and land for days. I loved it here, but it no longer felt like home.

I couldn't wait to get back to Magnolia Falls, and I was flying out tonight after dinner, because I was going to bring Cutler those unicorn Krispies for his Star Student Day tomorrow if it was the last thing I did.

It didn't matter if Tara was there.

Hell, if it made Cutler happy, then I hoped we could all be there.

But her being there didn't mean that I couldn't be there, too. I'd formed my own relationship with that little boy, and he'd wanted those treats, and I wasn't going to disappoint him.

"We're still missing Easton," I said, picking up my phone and

303

seeing the text from him. "Oh, he said he's running late, so we should start eating without him, and he'll get here when he can."

My mother shook her head and chuckled. "Someone is always late. It's just usually Bridger."

"Hey, I heard that. I was the first one here." He came walking into the kitchen with a glass of whiskey in his hand. "But I'm starving, so he better hope we save him some food."

"Please. Mom makes enough to feed a small country," Rafe said, as my mother handed him the platter of grilled chicken breasts and steaks that my father had brought in from the grill. Everyone grabbed a plate of something, from salad to mashed potatoes to rolls, and carried it out to the table.

We always ate family-style at the big farmhouse table in the dining room. Melody wanted to sit between me and her father, and I started cutting up tiny pieces of chicken for her.

"Guess who I saw this morning," Rafe said, as platters were being passed around the table.

"Who?" my father asked.

"Colon Waterstone." The table erupted in laughter, because they loved to pronounce his name the wrong way. Collin never found it humorous, but that never stopped the boys from torturing him. "He was walking through town like he had a stick up his ass."

"I thought I asked you to ease up on him. I don't want to talk about him anymore. We've all moved on." I shrugged. "So let him come home and see his family. You guys terrify him."

"He still has two legs, so that's me easing up on him."

"Well, I never liked him. I didn't want to say it to you, because you were marrying the dude. But let's face it, he was a pretentious ass—" Bridger paused and glanced at our niece. "A pretentious assumption."

More laughter bellowed around the table.

"I agree. You need a man who lights you up, Emmy. That dude was so boring and soft." Archer rolled his eyes.

"Yeah, Collin was not a manly guy, no doubt about it," Clark said. "Remember when Mom grounded me because I took the dude out on the ice to show him some moves, and he barely lasted twenty minutes with me and the guys?"

"Didn't you break his nose?" my father asked, holding up his tumbler as if he wanted to cheer him in celebration.

More laughter.

I rolled my eyes. "You did break his nose. He had to have it reset."

"So it was a win, then." He smirked. "Easton says your new boyfriend is more like us. It's about time you dated a real man."

"Well, in her defense, she only dated the one, and he was a bit of shmuck, but she had nothing to compare him to. Luckily, she's going a different way this time," Rafe said, as if this conversation wasn't insulting at all.

"How about you guys stay out of my business for once?" I sniped, as I placed some salad on my plate.

Loud laughter filled the room.

"That's wishful thinking, my love," Aunt Isabelle said.

"They've always been particularly invested in your business, haven't they?" my mother said with a chuckle.

"I'm here!" Easton shouted from the other side of the house. "And I brought a surprise with me."

"I hope it's a sexy, single woman," Clark said, and my mom swatted him in the chest.

"I hope it's some peace and quiet," Bridger grumped, as he forked a piece of chicken and popped it into his mouth.

"Hi, Sunny." Cutler came into the room, his gaze searching the table for me. I was on my feet, and he ran to me before jumping into my arms.

"What are you doing here?" I asked, as I wrapped my arms around him.

"We took the 'copter here to find you," he said.

305

"Yeah, the big grump was quick to offer it up," Easton said over a laugh, referring to Bridger.

Easton walked into the room with Nash beside him, and all the air left my lungs.

"Hey," Nash said, his gaze locking with mine. "Your brother was nice enough to offer us a ride."

"Well, first I offered to kick his ass, and then he explained the situation, and the ride came next." Bridger pushed to his feet and shook hands with Nash, before offering a hand to Cutler when I set him back on his feet.

"He didn't do anything wrong, so I'm not sure why you were suggesting bodily harm." My mother shook her head before walking over to Nash. "It's really nice to meet you. I'm happy you made it in time for dinner."

She hugged him before doing the same to Cutler, who kept his little hand in mine.

"Bridger likes to lead with anger first, then he softens," Easton said with a laugh.

Everyone made introductions, but I was still standing there, stunned. "What are you guys doing here?"

"Your mom invited us for Sunday dinner." Nash smirked. "And I needed to talk to you, and I didn't want to wait until tomorrow."

"This is so romantic," Aunt Isabelle whisper-shouted, rubbing her hands together.

"Well, son, you're going to learn quickly that this family has no secrets. So, you may as well get it all out there right now, and then we can eat," my father said, raising a brow.

"You don't need to talk here. We can go outside." I reached for his hand as a wide grin spread across his face.

"Easton said this is kind of my christening into the family, so I'm going to say what I have to say right here." Nash cleared his throat.

"Go Pops!" Cutler waggled his brows.

"I'm here because I missed you. I love you. Tara showing up definitely caused some stress, and I'll fill you in on all of that later," he said, glancing at Cutler and making it clear he didn't want to share the details in front of his son. But then Nash glanced around the table as if he were asking for permission to skip that part.

"We can live with that," Clark said, and everyone laughed some more.

"Proceed." Bridger raised a brow, arms crossed over his chest.

"Damn, this is a tough crowd." Nash smirked. "You know how your mom says that everything happens for a reason?"

"Yeah." I moved closer to him because I couldn't stand that there was any distance between us.

"Well, Tara's coming back forced me to take a hard look at how I wanted my life to look moving forward. The two most important people in my life are standing right in front of me."

Easton moved to stand beside me, which caused more laughter to erupt around the table before he winked and moved to take a seat.

"I will walk through fire for you and Cutler. You've filled a void that I didn't even know existed. And as corny as it sounds, you complete me, Emerson. You complete us. You are the missing piece that made us a family," he said, moving closer and reaching for my free hand, as Cutler stood beside us.

"I love you," I whispered.

"I know you do, beautiful. Never doubted it for a minute." He kissed my forehead. "So, I've put things in place to make sure no one can do anything to hurt us moving forward. And it made me realize that the most important thing to me is that we're together. So I don't want to spend a year away from you." His gaze held mine. "If Boston makes you happy, Cutler and I have agreed to make that move with you. King will run the business, and we'll figure out the rest once we decide if we want to stay."

I shook my head, tears falling from my eyes now.

"Don't cry, baby. This is a good thing. I'm proud as hell of you, and I want you to have all the things you want."

"Damn. This guy is good," Rafe said, and my mom shushed him, clearly not wanting anything to interrupt this moment.

"Pops. You shouldn't say hell with that little girl sitting at the table," Cutler whispered, and everyone chuckled.

"Oh, shit. Sorry. Shit, I did it again."

"Trust me, she's being raised by a pack of wolves. This isn't the first time someone has slipped," Archer said. "Go on. I'm enjoying hearing you fawn all over my cousin. She deserves it."

"Damn straight," Easton said, and Cutler raised a brow at him, as well.

I couldn't hold it in any longer. "I don't want to move to Boston."

"What? Why? It's your dream hospital."

"It *was* my dream, when my life was unfulfilled. I was living for work because I didn't have anything exciting to come home to." I shrugged, the tears streaming down my face. "But they offered me the job yesterday, and when they went over the schedule and the hours—I don't want to live in a hospital. I want to live on the water, with my boys. I want to have my own practice in Magnolia Falls, with patients that I know personally. I want to be home for dinner every night and eat out by the lake and go to Cutler's Star Student Day, and barbecue with our friends on the weekends. I want a life, Nash. I want a life with you."

His eyes welled, and he shook his head. "I don't know what I did to deserve you, but I'm not questioning it. But know this: if you change your mind, we are on board. Right, Cutler?"

"Yep. Sunny's our girl. We go where she goes."

"We go where she goes," he whispered. "Always."

"Well, hopefully, right now, she'll go to the table and start eating because I'm starving," Easton said.

My mom moved everyone around and led Cutler to the chair beside me, making a place for Nash on the other side of me.

"You all start eating. We'll be right back," I said, kissing Cutler on the cheek and leading his father out of the dining room and into the kitchen.

I backed up against the wall and looked up at him. "I love you. Thank you for coming here."

He took my hand in his and placed it over his heart. *Beating heart.*

"This beats for you. I love you."

I smiled up at him. "I didn't want an audience, but I need you to kiss me right now. I missed you."

He leaned down and covered my mouth with his, just as my father stepped into the kitchen and cleared his throat.

"Welcome to the family, Nash." He clapped him on the shoulder.

"Way to ruin the kiss, Dad," I groaned.

"Sounds like you two have a lifetime for that." He chuckled.

And he was right.

This was just the beginning.

33

Nash

The weekend had been a blur and ended in the best way. After I'd reached out to Emerson's brother, Easton, he'd arranged for me and Cutler to come to Rosewood River.

We had become friends since that first day we met, and we'd texted a few times. He was a cool dude, and as it turns out, her whole family was amazing.

It didn't surprise me. My girl was the best, and of course, she'd have a family that adored her.

Today was a big day because it was Cutler's Star Student Day at school, and then we had the meeting with Tara at River's office to deal with after we dropped him off.

Emerson was in the bathroom with Cutler, helping him style his hair for his Star Student Day. This kid lived for these special moments, and he'd found a woman who wanted to celebrate them with him.

"What do you think, Pops?" He strolled out of the bathroom looking like a damn mob boss. He wore a white button-up, a black leather coat, and dark jeans with black dress shoes, and his hair was gelled and slicked into place.

Emerson was just staring at him like he was the most perfect thing she'd ever seen.

"You look cool, buddy."

"Look at my Sunny's shirt," he said.

Emerson puffed her chest out, and her tee read: *Beefcake's Girl*.

She had a basket full of these Rice Krispie treats that my boy was obsessed with. And damn if it didn't make me proud that she knew what to do and how to make it special for him.

"I like it," I said, waggling my brows because, damn, my girl was gorgeous.

"Good. You have a matching shirt that you need to go put on." She moved to the counter and tossed me the tee she had sitting on the barstool.

Beefcake's Pops.

These weren't written in Sharpie. She'd had them made in advance.

And I fucking loved it.

I went to change into the ridiculous tee, and the three of us made our way to school. Normally, I'd just hand the teacher the store-bought treats and head to work, but today, we took photos together in front of the classroom, and all the kids came running over to see what he'd brought.

Cutler beamed up at Emerson as his classmates came over to say hello to their pediatrician. She was basically a celebrity here.

Apparently, she'd called Doc Dolby while she was home to tell him that she'd had a change of heart, and she wanted to stay in Magnolia Falls. I'd laughed my ass off when she'd told me that he'd never really interviewed anyone else because he felt confident that she'd change her mind. He'd just figured if she left, he'd step back in and start over with the hiring process.

LAURA PAVLOV

He'd found the person he wanted to take over his practice, and he'd been determined to keep her.

Just like I was.

"Thanks for making my Star Student Day the best. Sorry, Pops. But Emerson makes the best treats," Cutler said, and she bent down to hug him goodbye.

"I know. Unicorn Krispies are not in my wheelhouse." I chuckled.

"Have the best day. We'll pick you up after school, okay?" Emerson said, leaning down to kiss his cheek.

I noticed that her eyes were wet with emotion as I took her hand in mine, and we walked out of the school.

"You okay?" I asked.

"Yeah." She turned to face me as I opened the passenger door. "That was just really special. I loved getting to be there for him."

"He loved it, too. Thank you for being there for my boy."

"Of course," she said, as I drove toward her office.

"Oh, I'm not going in until later. Doc is covering. I want to be there with you today, if you're all right with that."

I paused at the stop sign to look at her. "You sure about that? Tara's a lot to handle, and she'll have her boyfriend there, so things may get ugly."

"We're in this together. That's how this works. The good and the bad. I want to be there beside you."

And that's exactly where I wanted her to be.

"Thank you." I cleared my throat.

"Are you okay?" she asked, as I pulled into the parking spot near River's law office.

"Yeah, I'm good. I'm not used to counting on anyone but the guys. So you keep catching me off guard by showing up every time I need you."

"Get used to it. I'm not going anywhere." She smirked, and I jumped out of the car and came around to get her door.

312

"Easiest thing I've ever needed to get used to." I pressed her up against the car and kissed her, before pulling back and leading her inside.

Cassie, River's assistant, was just handing him a cup of coffee when we walked in, and he was pinching the bridge of his nose and calmly trying to tell her that she'd made it wrong. *Again.* It took everything I had in me not to laugh as she repeated the order three times and left with the mug.

"Hey," he said, coming around to clamp me on the shoulder before pulling Emerson in for a hug. "If you two order coffee, it might be best to just order it black."

We chuckled as Cassie returned with his coffee and took our orders.

Two black coffees.

We made our way to the conference room and took our seats, just as Cassie brought Tara, with the guy I assumed was her boyfriend right behind her, sans legal representation.

Shocker.

She didn't care enough to find someone to help her understand what today was about. She could have hired someone or reached out to postpone the date until she found someone to represent her. But she'd never take the time to do that.

It shouldn't surprise me.

She'd never cared, had she?

"Hey," Tara said, her eyes landing on Emerson, before glaring in her direction.

I found my girl's hand beneath the table and intertwined our fingers. "This is my husband, Mark."

River and I shared a look of surprise as he turned back toward Tara. "I hadn't realized you were married. So this will affect both of you, then."

"We've been married for over a year. So I won't tolerate my wife being mistreated by anyone," Mark said, and I covered my mouth with my hand to stifle a laugh, and he definitely noticed.

She was not the victim.

"And you are choosing not to have council present?" River asked, as he opened his file.

"Mark and I can speak for ourselves." Tara leaned forward, her smile forced. "There is no need to take a paternity test; I know that Cutler is your son. I shouldn't have said that."

"You don't need to apologize, baby. You were upset," Mark said, reaching for her hand.

"Well, it was a shitty thing to say to a man who loves his son, and it's a dangerous game to play, Tara. But it's for the better because it was time for this to come to a head," I said.

"Meaning?"

"This is how things are going to play out." River took charge, sliding over a packet to each one of them. "These are the numbers for back child support, should you pursue custody. You would also be expected to pay child support moving forward, as well. You have never paid a dime for your son, and all the financial and emotional responsibility has fallen on the shoulders of my client, who does it happily. He would like to continue to do it."

"Well, then why would I pay him if he wants to continue with the arrangement that we have?" she asked, as her husband gaped at the numbers on the pages that were set in front of him.

No shit, jackass. Raising kids is expensive.

"We're not paying this. She sees that kid once every couple of years, so there's no need to pay. You can keep the arrangement you have, as we don't want children," the scrawny asshole hissed, and Tara shrugged.

Emerson squeezed my hand beneath the table.

"Great. Then you will need to sign over full custody to Nash. This means that you don't get to come to town and decide when or how often you see Cutler. You are giving up that right, but you gave it up years ago anyway. This is just a formality to protect my client and his son."

"*Our* son," Tara said, and Mark shot her what looked like some sort of warning look.

"Your name is on the birth certificate, but you haven't been a mother to that little boy, and you know it," I said. My voice was even and calm, and I reserved judgment because I wanted to try to talk some sense into her. "Come on, Tara. Do the right thing here. You don't want to be part of his life, so you can't just come around whenever things go wrong in your relationship and mess with his head."

The room fell silent, and she looked away, staring out the window for a long moment.

"He's right," Mark said, keeping his voice low. "We've got our own lives, and it doesn't include this town or the people in it. You've said it yourself."

"That doesn't mean I don't care about him." She looked back over at me, chin high.

"No one's saying that you don't care about him. I was sort of hoping that you did care about him enough to do the right thing," I said.

"Listen, we're not here to judge you or debate whether or not you care. This is a legal matter at this point. You either take responsibility, which includes financial responsibility, or you sign the papers and let the man who's been raising him continue to do so," River said, as he pushed the custody agreement across the table.

"And what if I want to come to town once in a while and say hello?" she asked.

"Then you call Nash, and you schedule a visit. But you won't make demands or play head games with either one of them. The truth is, you should be thanking this man for stepping up for your son. Cutler is the best kid I've ever known. He has a massive heart, he's smart, he's kind, he's everything you want your child to be. And that's due to the job that Nash has done. Day in and day out. He's shown up for that little boy, and if you really look at your son, you'd see that," River said, as he stared right at her.

My chest squeezed at his words.

All I wanted was to do a good job raising my little boy. If it was the one thing I accomplished in life, it would be a win.

So hearing him speak this way about my son, it hit me hard.

Because Cutler was the best kid in the world. He was all the things River had just said, and then some.

Tara's eyes watered the slightest bit, and she nodded. "He's a really good boy, Nash."

"He is," I said, and Emerson's grip on my hand beneath the table tightened again.

"Then just sign the papers. Nothing changes. He's not saying you can't come visit every couple of years. But at least we won't have to pay for the kid." Mark wrapped an arm around her shoulder.

I was equal parts relieved and offended by his words.

There was no price that I could put on the happiness my son had brought into my life. If you said I'd have to give away everything I owned and every penny I'd made until the day I died just to keep him with me, it would be a no-brainer.

I would give it all.

But not everyone felt that way, and Tara had never had that maternal bond with him. Sometimes I felt guilty that a part of me was relieved I didn't have to share him. I loved having my boy with me full-time.

I didn't know what I'd do if it hadn't worked out that way.

Tara picked up the pen and signed her name. "I never wanted to be a mama, you know?"

I nodded. "I do."

"But it doesn't mean that I don't want the best for him."

"Understood," River said, reaching across the table and picking up the piece of paper. I didn't miss the look of relief in his gaze when it met mine.

"So, we're going to leave town later tonight." Tara shrugged. "Can I say goodbye to him?"

There was Emerson, squeezing my hand beneath the table again, urging me to do the right thing. The kind thing.

"How about Emerson and I pick him up early from school and meet you two at The Golden Goose for a milkshake before you get on the road?" I said, looking over to see the corner of my girl's lips turn up the slightest bit.

Tara turned to Mark. "I'd like to do that so I can say goodbye."

"As long as we aren't buying for everyone," her husband grumped, and it took all I had in me not to rip his head off. I had no desire to go sit with these two assholes at the diner. But I was doing it for Cutler so he wouldn't wonder why she didn't say goodbye.

"I'm happy to spring for the shakes," I said, and River barked out a laugh.

"Sorry. It's just—" River shook his head. "Some people have a whole lot of nerve."

The comment went straight over their heads, as they were already discussing what kind of ice cream they'd get.

There was no love there between the four of us, but what mattered most was the love that I had for my son.

That's the reason I pushed to do the right thing, even when I didn't want to.

We agreed to meet at the diner in an hour, and Emerson and I made our way to the school to pick up our superstar student early.

He was thrilled when he saw us.

I didn't tell him why we were going, just that we wanted to celebrate him.

We parked two blocks away from the diner, and Cutler walked between Emerson and me, one hand in each of ours as he filled us in on his day.

"All the kids said my parents sent the coolest snacks ever," Cutler said, and my fucking chest felt like it would cave in from the way it tightened at his words.

Emerson beamed as she smiled at him. "We'll have to come up with cool new snacks every year now, because we'll just have to keep getting better and better."

I pulled the door open and followed my family inside.

These two are my entire world.

And I was going to hold on tight and enjoy the ride.

I glanced around the diner and didn't see Tara and Mark, but I just asked for the large booth in the back.

They never showed up that day, and my ex sent a text saying that they needed to get on the road so they wouldn't hit traffic.

But none of that mattered, because my son actually never inquired about where she went.

Because he had everything he needed right here.

And so did I.

Epilogue

Emerson

A winter wedding in Magnolia Falls was as good as it got. Saylor wanted to be married on their property, and Kingston wanted his wife to have whatever she wanted. There was snow covering the ground, and they had several tents with industrial heaters to keep the space warm, and everything was winter white and holiday-themed. Hayes had given Saylor away, and there hadn't been a dry eye in the room when Kingston and Saylor read their vows.

You could feel the love that surrounded those two. Their reception was the largest I'd ever attended. Everyone in town had come out, and they were all fawning over Lincoln Hendrix, the star QB whom everyone knew well. I'd really enjoyed getting to know Romeo's brother and his wife, Brinkley, but Nash and I found ourselves at a table with Cage Reynolds and his wife, Presley, gaping over the fact that our kids couldn't seem to stay away from one another.

Little Gracie Reynolds had met Cutler in the fall, when Cage and Presley had come to town with Brinkley and Lincoln. Lincoln was interested in purchasing a ranch so he could have a home near Romeo and their sister Tia, who'd come home from school to attend Kingston and Saylor's wedding.

Nash and Kingston would be renovating the place, and they'd become good friends, as we'd gone to Cottonwood Cove a couple weeks ago so Saylor and I could try out the Tranquility Day Spa that Presley co-owned with her best friend, Lola.

"Look at the way he's twirling her," Presley said, as her son slept in her lap. The little angel was just a few months old, and Gracie adored her little brother.

"He never stops talking about her. I think J.T. is getting sick of hearing about his new bestie." Nash barked out a laugh.

"He's about the only kid on the planet that I'd let twirl my little girl around on the dance floor," Cage grumped. "But I'm a big Beefcake fan."

I smiled. "They're pretty adorable. He was so excited you guys were coming to the wedding. He wanted her to see him carrying the rings down the aisle."

"We wouldn't miss it for the world," Presley said. "We were thrilled to be included in their special day."

"It was a nice wedding, huh?" Nash said, his hand finding mine, as our fingers intertwined.

"It was beautiful." I stared out at the dance floor, watching Gracie try to twirl Cutler, and he clearly didn't love the idea of being spun around, but he went along with it.

I loved him as if he were my own, and in a way, he was.

Things happen for a reason.

I knew that I belonged here in Magnolia Falls with Nash and Cutler.

We visited with everyone as the party just kept on going. River, Ruby, Demi, and Romeo came to join us at the table.

Demi gave me a look, and I followed her gaze to the dance floor, where her brother, Slade, was slow dancing with Peyton.

"I think something is going on there," she whispered to me.

She was definitely right. Peyton always found an excuse to hang out with Slade.

"I think you're right. Is that okay with you?" I asked.

"Yeah. He's been doing really well with his sobriety. He loves working at the gym with Romeo, and he seems crazy about her. I don't know why they don't just tell me they're dating at this point."

"It's okay. I like watching her squirm when she's with him, and she's always glancing over to see if you notice," Ruby said over her laughter. "It's hilarious."

Just then, Peyton marched in our direction, her hand in Slade's. "Demi. We have something to tell you."

"Really?" Demi said, feigning surprise.

"Tell her, Slade." Peyton raised a brow at the man beside her.

"I don't know why it's a big deal, but Peyt and I are dating. I don't really need your blessing, but she sure seems to need it. And I'm done sneaking around."

"Baby, that was not as well done as it could have been." Peyton raised a brow, and he tugged her forward, planting a kiss on her lips. We were all smiling, watching them.

"You have my blessing, but maybe let's not make out in front of me just yet." Demi was laughing hysterically, which had Romeo on his feet, hurrying over and bending down in front of her. He placed his hands on her cute round belly with this look of concern that was almost comical.

"Our boy loves when his mama laughs," Romeo said.

We'd had a gender-reveal party not that long ago, and they were having a boy. We were all thrilled for them, but Cutler seemed to be the most excited about having a new brother, as he called him.

"Are you going to grab her stomach every time she laughs, hiccups, or coughs?" Hayes grumped as he joined us at the table, pulling up a chair beside me.

LAURA PAVLOV

"Yeah. This little dude is active. He's always kicking around in there, and I fucking love it."

"I want to make fun of you real bad right now, but I get it," Nash said as he rubbed the back of my neck. "Hey, I heard John Cook announced that he was finally retiring."

Hayes nodded slowly. "Yep. He'll be retiring in a few months. Lenny and I are both up for the position, but that fucker is practically campaigning for it now. He keeps mentioning how his wife loves to host potlucks and fundraisers, and I can't compete with that. I sure as shit don't want to."

"Play the game, brother. You're damn good at your job. You deserve the promotion. Maybe you could marry Trish Windsor real quick," River said over his laughter. Nash had filled me in that she was a woman who'd pursued Hayes hard, and he avoided her any time she came around.

"I'd rather get demoted than be alone with that woman. She tried to tie me up, remember? I'm not into that shit."

"Unless you're the one doing the tying, right?" Romeo teased, and Hayes balled up a napkin and tossed it at him.

"Something like that." Hayes shrugged.

"Sad news about Abe Wilson," River said, taking a long pull from his beer. "I wonder if Savannah will come home for his funeral."

"Who's Savannah?" I asked.

"Savannah Abbott lived next door to Hayes when we were growing up. She and Hayes were—what do you call that, baby? When they're inseparable?" Romeo was now sitting with Demi on his lap as he rubbed her belly.

"Besties, baby."

"Pfft." Hayes shook his head with disgust. "I don't use the word *besties* in my vocabulary. We were neighbors, and we looked out for one another. And then all that shit went down with her family, and she went radio silent."

"Ahhh . . . she ghosted you," Ruby said with a laugh.

"Whatever. Call it what you want." Hayes stared out at the dance floor, but he looked a million miles away.

"You two were tight. I remember you and Kate having some brutal fights about how jealous she was over that friendship," Nash said. He'd filled me in on Hayes's ex-fiancée who'd slept with his coworker at the firehouse. She sounded like a real piece of work.

"Yeah, Kate liked to go off about anything and everything. I should have run for the hills long before I caught her riding Lenny like it was her fucking day job."

Laughter bellowed around us.

"That's called red flags," Demi said with a brow raised. "Well, I hope Savi comes home for the funeral. She was always so sweet and kind to everyone. I hated that she left town so abruptly. But she and the Wilsons were really close. The last time she came home was over a decade ago—for Lily's funeral, right?"

Hayes nodded, and something crossed his gaze that I couldn't read. Sadness, maybe? "Yep," was all he said.

"I wonder who he left his millions to," Romeo said. "That man owned the largest piece of property in Magnolia Falls. He's got no kids, so it'll be interesting to see what happens with his estate and land."

"He married that crazy-ass woman, Sheana, for a short time. If she gets that land, I'd guess we'll have a strip mall in town within a few months." Hayes took another pull from his bottle.

I gave Nash a questioning look, and he leaned down close to my ear. "Abe was a sweet old man who lost the love of his life, and then a few years later, he got worked over by this young gold digger whom everyone in town despised. Thankfully, he figured it out quickly and filed for divorce."

"And she just left?" I asked, my mind blown that someone would be so cold.

"Yep. She got a large settlement and moved out of town."

"Money brings out the crazy in people," Hayes said, shaking his head with disgust.

"She got what she wanted," Romeo said, as Kingston sauntered our way.

"Hey now, why aren't we out on the dance floor?" Kingston asked, as he dropped into a chair across from me.

"Because we've been here for seven hours. This is the longest wedding known to man," Hayes grumped. "And I don't dance."

"Yeah, I think this party is wrapping up." River pushed to his feet. "It was a great wedding. You sure know how to throw a party, brother."

All the guys were hugging goodbye, and Ruby, Demi, and I were walking over to say goodbye to Saylor.

"What's the story with Hayes and Savannah? He looked pretty distraught over the mention of her name," I asked.

"Yeah. They were really close back in the day, and a bunch of stuff went down with her family right around the time that Hayes and Saylor were going through a bunch of stuff, and River and Romeo got sent to Fresh Start. So I think it was a rough time for everyone."

Fresh Start was the juvenile detention center that Ruby worked at now.

"When it rains in Magnolia Falls, it sure does pour." Demi shook her head, eyes heavy with emotion. "I hope she comes back for Abe's funeral. She was always so happy and nice."

"Yeah, she was funny as hell. Even my blackened heart couldn't help but smile around the girl," Ruby said with a chuckle.

"Who are we talking about?" Peyton popped her head into the little circle we'd formed, appearing out of nowhere.

"Savannah Abbott. We're wondering if she'll come back for Abe's funeral."

"Oh, I always loved her. She was one big glass of sunshine, if memory serves. But that family scandal of hers was all everyone in town was talking about. I don't blame her for moving and staying away." Peyton shook her head and shrugged at the same time.

"It wasn't her fault, and, speaking of scandal . . . How about the fact that you've been secretly dating my brother?" Laughter echoed around us, just as Nash came up behind me and wrapped an arm around my waist.

"You ready to head home, beautiful?"

I turned to see Cutler on his hip, with his head resting in the crook of his father's neck.

We said our goodbyes and made our way out to the truck. Cutler slept all the way home, and Nash carried him inside, and then I got him undressed and ready for bed. We had our routine, and tucking this little boy in at the end of the night was the highlight of my day.

Well, aside from what happened every night in the room across the hall after he was long asleep.

"Hey, I have something for you," I said, leading Nash down the hallway. He had his tuxedo coat slung over the barstool, his dress shirt unbuttoned low, exposing his muscled chest.

"Oh, yeah? I have something for you, too," he said as he pulled me into his arms and kissed me.

I knew the day that Tara had threatened that Nash might not be Cutler's biological father had really messed with his head. So we'd agreed to have him do a paternity test that we'd keep between the two of us, because he needed to know just in case she ever tried to pull anything legally with Cutler. I'd already seen the test results, because I didn't even know how I'd tell him if the outcome had been different than it was.

I handed him the envelope, and he opened it. His eyes welled with emotion as he read the words that he'd known in his gut were true.

Cutler was his son in every way. Nash had never cared if Cutler was his son by blood. Hell, his best friends were his family. They were brothers not by blood but by history.

But knowing that Tara could never come back and claim Cutler wasn't his, brought him peace of mind.

She'd signed the papers, and we hadn't heard from her since, which he told me was pretty normal for her.

And it didn't matter if she came back around, because he had all the paperwork in place to protect his little boy.

Our little boy.

At least he felt like ours.

He was thriving, and that was all that mattered. His asthma was under control now, and the new meds were working wonders. He hadn't had an attack since that day out on the lake, but we were prepared and ready if he did.

"So, what do you have for me?" I asked, waggling my brows as he wrapped a hand around my neck and kissed me.

"Come on, and I'll show you." In the next breath, I was flung over his shoulder as he carried me to the bedroom where I slept every night, even though all of my things were still next door in my rental house, as my lease had a few more weeks before it was up.

And tonight was just about enjoying the moment. And that's exactly what we did. He dropped me onto the bed and buried his head between my thighs as I writhed beneath him.

I loved this man so fiercely that it was hard to wrap my head around sometimes.

He took me right over the edge like he always did, before he undressed me and pulled me on top of him so I could ride him into oblivion.

Which is exactly what I did.

I fell asleep in the warmth of his arms, and he held me there until the sun flooded our room.

I felt him slip out of bed, but I wasn't ready to get up just yet.

"I'll get your coffee, okay?" he whispered against my ear.

I heard the sound of Cutler's laughter come from out in the hallway before he climbed into bed with me, and Winnie jumped up and started licking my cheek. I propped my back against the headboard and opened my arms for Cutler to come on over for his morning cuddles.

This was our routine.

Nash brought in a cup of coffee and set it on the nightstand beside me.

"So, we have a little present for you," Nash said.

"A present? For what?"

"Pops and I want you to live with us!" Cutler shouted.

"Beefcake! That wasn't what we practiced." Nash shook his head at his son.

"Sorry about that. But I got excited. And it's true, we do want her to live with us."

Nash handed me the little box he was holding, and my teeth sank into my bottom lip.

"What is it?" I asked.

"It's a key to the house. To our house." Cutler covered his mouth with his hand when Nash shot him a warning look.

"For God's sake, buddy, let her open it first."

"But it is a key to the house." Cutler bounced on the bed beside me.

"Yes. Your lease is up, and we want you to move in here with us," Nash said.

I pulled the lid off the black box and stared down at the key sitting on the cotton inside, but it was the ring it was attached to that had me gasping. The platinum band held a breathtaking round diamond. It was classic and gorgeous.

"Why is she looking like that, Pops? Does she not want to live with us?"

"There's something else in that box that I didn't tell you about because, well, you're not good with secrets." Nash moved to the side of the bed and dropped down on one knee. "I want to spend every day of the rest of my life with you, baby. I love you in a way I never knew possible. I want to live with you. I want to laugh with you. I want to fight with you. I want to grow old with you."

My chest was beating so hard I could hear it in my ears as the tears sprung from my eyes. "Are you serious?"

"Will you marry me, beautiful?"

I nodded and sprung forward, dropping to my knees in front of him and wrapping my arms around his neck and kissing him hard.

"Sunny?" Cutler's voice had me pulling back and turning to see him down on one knee, too.

"Yes, angel face."

"I want to spend all my days with you, too. I want you to run my bath because you make the tub hotter than Pops."

"Hey," Nash said over his laughter, but Cutler smirked and continued.

"I still think you have the best balls in town, Pops, but I like the way Sunny runs my bath. I like the way you read me every night and the way you teach me new things to bake every Saturday. I love riding horses with you and going out to the lake to swim with you. You're my forever girl, Sunny. Will you marry me, too?"

If it were possible to have your heart explode in your chest, mine would be doing just that right now. I was overwhelmed and overcome with emotion—in the best way.

"I would be honored to spend my life with my two favorite boys. I love you so much it hurts sometimes," I said, but my words were barely audible.

But they heard me.

The three of us—we didn't need words to know how much we loved one another.

It was the way we looked at each other. The way we cared for one another.

The way we fit together like a family.

They wrapped their arms around me, and I breathed them in.

All that joy.

All that happiness.

All that love.

Acknowledgments

Greg, my heart always beats for you! Love you so much!

Hannah, thank you for giving me the inspiration to write a pediatrician. I am BEYOND proud of you and the difference you are making in the lives of so many children! Love you!

Chase, thank you for letting me steal all your funny sayings and bringing the text messages to life! Love you!

Willow, endlessly grateful for your friendship! Thank you for always supporting me and encouraging me and making me laugh! Love you so much!

Catherine, thank you for celebrating all the things with me, for listening, for making me laugh and for being such an amazing friend! Love you!

Kandi, when this book releases, Baby Hamm will be out in the world, and Auntie Laura can't wait for daily pics to join our voice messages! Thank you for always believing in me and celebrating the good days and listening on the tough days! My world is such a better place with you in it. Love you!

Elizabeth O'Roark, thank you for ALWAYS making me laugh, and for letting me pressure you into giving me all of your books early! I am so thankful for your friendship! Love you!

Pathi, I would not be doing what I love every single day if it wasn't for YOU! I am so thankful for your friendship, and for all the support and encouragement! I'd be lost without you! Thank you for believing in me! I love you so much!

Nat, I am SO INCREDIBLY thankful for you! Thank you for taking on so much, and never hesitating to jump in where you are needed. Thank you for the daily encouragement, taking so much off of my plate and going to signings with me so that everything runs smoothly. I am forever grateful for you! Love you!

Nina, I'm just going to call you the DREAM MAKER from here on out. Thank you for believing in me and for making my wildest dreams come true. Your friendship means the world to me! I love you forever!

Kim Cermak, thank you for being YOU! There is just no other way to say it. You are one in a million. I am endlessly grateful to have you in my corner, but most importantly, to call you my friend. Love you!

Christine Miller, Kelley Beckham, Tiffany Bullard, Sarah Norris, Valentine Grinstead, Amy Dindia, Josette Ochoa, Kate Kelly and Ratula Roy, I am endlessly thankful for YOU!

Meagan Reynoso, thank you for reading all my words early, giving fabulous feedback, and working so hard creating the PR packages with me. I love you!

Paige, remember that one time you came to find mother at the Gaylord because she was lost? LOL! I love you so much and I'm so grateful for your friendship!

Logan Chisolm, I absolutely adore you and am so grateful for your support and encouragement! Love you!

Kayla Compton, I am so happy to be working with you and so thankful for YOU! Love you! Xo

Doo, Abi, Meagan, Diana, Annette, Jennifer, Pathi, Natalie, and Caroline, thank you for being the BEST beta readers EVER! Your feedback means the world to me. I am so thankful for you!!

To all the talented, amazing people who turn my words into a polished final book, I am endlessly grateful for you! Sue Grimshaw (Edits by Sue), Hang Le Design, Sarah Sentz

(Enchanted Romance Designs), Emily Wittig Designs, Christine Estevez, Ellie McLove (My Brother's Editor), Jaime Ryter (The Ryter's Proof), Julie Deaton (Deaton Author Services), Kim and Katie at Lyric Audio Books, and the amazingly talented Madison Maltby, thank you for being so encouraging and supportive!

Crystal Eacker, thank you for your audio beta listening/reading skills! I absolutely adore you!

Ashley Townsend and Erika Plum, I love the incredible swag that you create and I am so thankful for you both!!

Jennifer, thank you for being an endless support system. For running the Facebook group, posting, reviewing and doing whatever is needed for each release. Your friendship means the world to me! Love you!

Rachel Parker, so incredibly thankful for you and so happy to be on this journey with you! Love you so much!

Megan Galt, thank you for always coming through with the most beautiful designs! I'm so grateful for YOU!

Natasha, Corinne and Lauren, thank you for pushing me every day and being the best support system! Love you!

Amy, I love sprinting with you so much! So grateful for your friendship! Love you!

Gianna Rose, Stephanie Hubenak, Rachel Baldwin, Kelly Yates, Sarah Sentz, Ashley Anastasio, Kayla Compton, Tiara Cobillas, Tori Ann Harris and Erin O'Donnell, thank you for your friendship and your support. It means the world to me!

Mom, thank you for being my biggest cheerleader and reading everything that I write! Love you!

Dad, you really are the reason that I keep chasing my dreams!! Thank you for teaching me to never give up. Love you!

Sandy, thank you for reading and supporting me throughout this journey! Love you!

To the JKL WILLOWS . . . I am forever grateful to you

for your support and encouragement, my sweet friends!! Love you!

To all the bloggers, bookstagrammers and ARC readers who have posted, shared, and supported me—I can't begin to tell you how much it means to me. I love seeing the graphics that you make and the gorgeous posts that you share. I am forever grateful for your support!

To all the readers who take the time to pick up my books and take a chance on my words . . . THANK YOU for helping to make my dreams come true!!

Obsessed with Magnolia Falls?
Continue your journey with the rest of the series . . .

Hating her was my end game, loving her was just the beginning . . .

Demi Crawford is Magnolia Falls royalty. I'm the boxer from the wrong side of the tracks. We couldn't be more different.

Her family is enemy number one, and it made her guilty by association. *I despised her before I even knew her.* It was easier that way.

But now she's moved in next door to me, and she's everywhere I turn. She is beautiful and honest and sweet. Everything I know I shouldn't want.

They say there's a fine line between love and hate, and I don't know when I crossed over. She is the right hook I never saw coming. But the secrets between us will threaten to tear us apart.

Lucky for her I'm a born fighter.
And she is definitely worth the fight . . .

I may be the lawyer, but she's the one judging me . . .

Ruby Rose declared me the enemy before I had a
chance to defend myself. I may be an attorney,
but this girl had appointed herself judge and jury.
And I'd never minded a good verbal sparring.

But the more we fought – the more I craved her.
Until our arguing turned into a bit of a wager.
One I was determined to win.

One time. Sixty seconds. A secret only we would share.

But from the minute we crossed the line, there was
no turning back. Ruby Rose may have given me
more than sixty seconds, but she wasn't offering forever.
And now my world doesn't work without her in it.

But how do I convince her to stay,
when she already has one foot out the door?

She's the one girl I can't have, and the only one I want . . .

Saylor Woodson is my best friend's little sister,
and she's completely off limits.

We have a history, a connection – one that no one
else knows about. I've kept my distance for years,
it was easy when she was away at school.
But now she's home, and she's everywhere I turn.
And the way that I want her is inexplicable.

I want to keep her and make her mine.

Once we cross that line in the sand, I'm drowning
in this girl and can't find my way up for air.
Guilt hangs over me like a dark cloud, but I can't
seem to walk away, no matter how hard I try.

*And now that I've had a taste of forever,
I'm willing to risk everything to keep it.*

ONE PLACE. MANY STORIES

Bold, innovative and
empowering publishing.

FOLLOW US ON:

@HQStories